Me! Me! Me!

& Other Stories

Helene Simkin Jara

*This book is dedicated to all the people who
still enjoy holding a book in their hands,
listening to audiobooks,
and love going to live theatre.*

Contents

Alternate Realities
sci-fi & fantasy

SECTION 3
Days in the Life
creative nonfiction & true stories

1

Here and There

quirks & childhood stories

The Navy Hat

She was a trained speech therapist, a good Lutheran, and felt it was the right thing to do to help people who were less fortunate than she. She always remembered birthdays, sent cards and flowers, and invited people into her home for special celebrations. It always annoyed her when people who were in her social class were less generous than she. If they spoke poorly about a certain class of people, she was too polite and well-brought-up to question them. She would just sit with her hands folded in her lap and nod without making eye contact. When other members of the country club were in the hospital, she would visit them when it was permissible.

And then she was diagnosed with a serious form of cancer. She told few people. When she was missing at meetings where people were asked to give donations to those in need, there was talk. Where was she? Luckily, she was given the opportunity to try an experimental drug. It was a chance at survival. She told no one but her husband.

The treatment worked. After a year of quiet suffering, she began to feel almost human again, albeit with less energy. Her gratitude for being alive doubled her normal inclination towards kindheartedness. The first time she saw him, he was sitting on the sidewalk in front of Safeway. He looked to be about 60 or so, with disheveled salt and pepper hair under a Navy hat. His clothes looked unwashed; his body broken. The color of his skin was mottled, yellow and gray. He wasn't smiling, but she imagined he may have had a few teeth missing, and more than likely it was painful. He wasn't asking for money exactly. He just looked up at her and squinted into the punishing sun.

The Navy hat reminded her of her late father. She foraged around in her bag for some money to give him.

"Here you go," she said cheerfully, handing him a 20-dollar bill.

He looked startled. Grabbing the money, he mumbled something fairly unintelligible to her. Being a speech pathologist, she noticed the manner in which he spoke, quickly diagnosing it as dysarthria, a neurological injury resulting in poor articulation. She made a mental note to talk to him about it if she ever saw him again. At home she decided not to talk about the man to her husband, who, although he was a neurologist and inclined to philanthropy, still had a distinct disdain for the less fortunate.

The following Wednesday, she had to slip out to go to Safeway to quickly grab a card and some flowers for an older couple in an assisted living situation, when she saw the man again. He looked distinctly more downtrodden. As she got closer, the odor of his clothes almost made her walk around him and enter the supermarket from another door; but then again, there was the Navy hat. The image of her father was vivid in her mind. She decided to approach the man.

"Here you go," she said, handing him seven dollars. "Maybe you can buy yourself a burger. You look like you may be hungry." She felt badly that she had so little money to give him, but at least it was something.

He looked up at her, his eyebrows furrowed. "A burger? A burger? Where can I get a burger?"

The way he articulated the words would have been difficult for most people to understand, but she did. She hesitated, but then said, "You know, there is help for people with speech difficulties." She smiled kindly at him.

"There's nothing wrong with my speech!" he garbled. "Where can I get a burger?" he repeated.

She was chagrined that she may have inadvertently insulted him. She pointed to Burger King. "It's right across the street."

He turned his head towards the street and looked back at her annoyed. "Are you gonna go and get it for me?"

She stopped short. "No. I'm sorry. I don't have the time. I want you to know, though, that I gave you the money in honor of my father, who was also in the Navy. I saw your hat."

He looked up at her, amused and irritated. "I was never in the fucking Navy!"

She just stood there, unable to think of anything to say. She took a deep breath, turned and walked into the supermarket. She stopped at the greeting cards, unable to concentrate on them. Finally, she picked out one that was blank inside. No words. She smirked to herself at the irony. Then, walking over to the flowers, she selected some orange tulips. The cashier smiled at her and said, "Oh, how pretty! Are these for someone special?"

"Yes, yes. They're for… for my father."

The cashier tried to hide her surprise, as she couldn't help but notice that the woman buying the card and flowers must have been at least 70 years old. Perhaps she was going to put them on his gravestone.

She came home, holding the flowers and the card. Her husband was sitting at the kitchen table.

"For the Millers?" he smiled at his wife's generosity.

"Yes, dear. For the Millers." She walked into her bedroom, put the flowers and the card on the dresser, looking at the photo of her father smiling in his Navy uniform.

"And for you, too, Daddy. These are for you, too."

The Promise

I need you to listen to me. Really listen. You need to know that I never knew what Dad did. I didn't. I know you think I did. But I didn't. I thought he was an honest man. I thought he was trustworthy.

When you sent me away to boarding school, I know you both were well-intentioned. And yes, I was jealous that Jennifer got to stay home. I was angry for a very long time. I had many evil thoughts about her. From my young point of view, she always got way more attention than I did. Yes, I know she had epilepsy. But, to me, it didn't seem like such a big deal. To me, it meant that she got everything she wanted, including to stay home with you.

I don't know if you realize how horrible they were to me at that school. The kids hated me because Dad was so famous. I had no friends. The teachers expected me to be a genius like Dad. It was impossible to measure up to him. And the kids would say stuff like, "We heard your sister is a freak. How does it feel to have a freak sister?" I never knew what to say. When you came to visit, why did you have to bring her? And dress her like that? She looked like she was from another century. I mean, Dad could have afforded to at least buy her cool clothes.

And then, yeah, I needed to escape mentally from that place and from feeling abandoned by you two. So, when the opportunity arose to take whatever, to not be in the present, I took it. I took the money Dad was sending me for who knows what and spent it on drugs. Lots of drugs. And of course, I failed my classes. Half the time, I didn't even show up. I couldn't have. I would wake up in the gutter somewhere, or in someone's bed. So, Jennifer wasn't the freak. I was. I hoped you would get a call from a hospital or a jail to come and get me. As you know, that never happened.

I fantasized that the three of you were sitting out on the verandah, eating Belgian waffles with fresh strawberries and whipped cream every morning for breakfast, staring out at the sea.

Then taking walks together on the beach, laughing, and maybe singing together. I imagined you never thought of me at all.

I only found out what Dad had been doing because I read about it in the newspaper. It was even on TV.

I want you to know that I'm so sorry. When that happened, I was only thinking about myself. I felt sorry for myself because I knew I'd be teased non-stop. I even thought about running away from that school and going incognito somehow. Not sure how or what I was thinking.

The next day at school, instead of giving me shit, the kids just shunned me. No one would talk to me at all. The teachers didn't look at me directly either, or if they did, it was with pity. I can't even imagine what you went through.

And Jenny? How did you explain to her what happened with Dad? I mean, I know she has seizures 20 times a day. It must affect her brain somehow. And you had to deal with this alone, really, with your sisters clear across the country. And I know they never liked Dad.

So, I mean, they gave him 10 years. Jesus! He cheated people. Old people. Vulnerable people. He took their money shamelessly. And, according to the news, he had been doing this for over 15 years! Since before I was born, even.

I'm sure you had no idea what kind of man you married. He must have seemed so…I don't know, such a good catch, as people in your generation must have said. And then, boom! You lost everything. We lost everything: the house, the cars, everything. I guess the worst thing for you, and I guess for me too, and probably Jenny, was losing who we thought our dad was. And the shame of it all.

Did you ever visit him? I didn't. I feel kinda bad about that. I guess I feel like I owed him something. But I couldn't bring myself to go. I mean, what would I even say? I couldn't say what I was thinking, like, Dad, did you ever hear of karma?

I must admit, when that happened, I shaped up immediately. I went cold turkey, as they say. I suppose I should be grateful for that, at least.

But, Mom, when they offed him in prison, did you feel relief? That's a weird question, but I somehow feel the need to know. I'm guessing you were shocked, sad, and maybe even a little relieved. That's how I felt, anyway.

Did he write to you? Did you write to him? What about Jenny?

I know I never made as much money as Dad did. Of course not. We won't go there. But I want you to know that I will support you emotionally and financially forever. Jenny too. I never told you I loved you. I'm sorry about that. Very sorry. I hope you know that I do love you. You were my rock. And Jenny's rock.

They tell me that you aren't well. That you can't remember lots of stuff. Maybe that's your way of dealing with all of this. I get it.

I understand now you did what you thought was right. You married him in good faith. If he wanted to send me away, even if you weren't sure, you did what any woman in the '50s would do. You supported your husband's decisions. I'm sure you suffered along with every seizure Jenny had. I can see it in your eyes.

So, I hope it's not too late for me to say these things to you, and that you can hear and understand what I'm saying. And I hope it's not too late for you to forgive me for all I put you through. I hope you can maybe be proud of me. Of whom I've become. I learned how not to be, because of Dad. I promise you I'm a man of my word and that's because I had a mom like you.

I've been offered a really good job. And yes, they knew about Dad, but offered me the job anyway. I'll be making enough to buy us a house. We won't have to rent anymore. I can hire someone to help you and Jenny. And if you want to have a yard and a garden like we had before, with the maple trees, rose bushes, lilacs, and mulberry bushes, we can, and we will. I promise.

The Tank

Clarise is sitting in the leather chair of her therapist's office, looking at the fish tank. As usual, she is picking at her cuticles and biting her lower lip.

The therapist clears her throat.

"Clarise?"

"What?"

Clarise knows she hasn't been forthcoming. Her mother is paying a lot of money for her to go to this therapist, as she has paid a lot of money for her to get orthodonture, a personal trainer, massages once a week, and a credit card with unlimited funds. Ever since Clarise got out of rehab, her mother, who was mostly absent before, has been hovering over her to prove to who knows whom that she is a good mother.

Clarise is now staring at the plaque on the wall near the fish tank which says, *Shit or Get Off the Pot.*

The therapist, noticing this, remarks, "Do you like what it says?"

Clarise's shoulders shrug. Even if she could figure it out, she isn't about to tell the therapist.

The therapist clears her throat again. "Clarise? You might want to know that your father contacted me today."

This gets Clarise's attention.

"My father?"

"Yes. He asked for a Zoom conference. He's in Brazil."

"What did he want?"

"He said it would be okay if I discussed this with you. He wanted to know how you were doing, if you seemed happy, if you were still not using."

Clarise smirked. What does he care?

"He appeared to be quite concerned," the therapist continued.

"Oh, really? If he's so concerned, why doesn't he just come back?"

"Would you like that, Clarise? Would you like your father to come back?"

Duh.

"What would you do if he came back? I understand he doesn't live with your mother."

Clarise watches as one of the tetras in the fish tank swims in circles.

The therapist watches her for a while. "Do you like the fish?"

"Don't they get bored? I mean, they just swim around endlessly."

"I never thought about that." The therapist begins to squirm in her chair. "I thought that they were happy. They have food, a clean place to live, other fish to be with." Feeling a headache coming on, she looks at the clock. 15 more minutes.

Clarise looks directly at her. "You must feel so good about providing everything you think those fish need, don't you? Did you ever imagine they might be miserable?"

The therapist rubs her temples. Now we're getting somewhere.

"Are you miserable, Clarise?"

Clarise doesn't answer, but keeps staring at the fish in the tank. "I bet you buy them only the highest quality food, and get someone to come and clean the tank for you."

The therapist finds herself wanting to stand up, walk over and slap her. Instead, she says, in her most professional voice, "You are very observant, Clarise. Yes, you're right. I get them the best food available, and pay someone to clean the tank every month. Do you feel that is wrong?"

The therapist knows she has gone too far. She is getting defensive.

"I think those fucking fish hate your guts," Clarise spits out.

The therapist laughs out loud, quickly covering her mouth with her manicured hand.

"Why is that so funny?" Clarise's cheeks are red.

"Because, because..." The therapist tries to compose herself. "Because I never thought of those fish as having any opinions."

Clarise smirks. Right. Of course, you didn't.

The therapist, now composed, folds her hands onto her lap and looks directly at Clarise. "If the fish could talk, what would they say?"

Clarise walks up to the tank, looks at the fish, and turns towards the therapist.

"They would say, 'Fuck you and your fucking high-end food. Fuck you and your perfect fish tank.'"

"And then what?"

"We want out of here. We don't even like each other."

Clarise and the therapist both go silent. The therapist glances at the clock.

"Where would you go, Clarise? Where exactly would you go if you could escape?"

Clarise eyes the open window, walks over to it, and looks down to the sidewalk below. The office is on the third floor. The therapist feels her stomach clench.

Clarise turns toward the therapist with a wicked grin plastered on her face. "Oh, don't you worry. I'm not going to jump."

The therapist swallows hard. "I never thought that."

Clarise lets out a bark of a laugh and walks over to the fish tank. Within seconds, Clarise shoves her arm into the fish tank, grabs a fish, goes back to the window, and tosses it out.

Sputtering in anger and fear, the therapist walks up to Clarise and grabs her wet arm.

"You…you shouldn't have done that! You killed that fish!"

"Did I? Did I? Or did I give it its freedom?"

The therapist lets go of Clarise's arm.

"This session is terminated. Actually, I am calling your mother and father and telling them I no longer am willing to see you."

"No need," Clarise says, still grinning. She goes back to the fish tank, sticking her arm inside, and flings water at the stunned therapist's face. Clarise grabs her backpack and happily skips out the door.

The therapist immediately grabs her phone and looks out of the window. She watches as Clarise bends down, gently picks up the dead fish, kisses it, and puts it in her pocket. Clarise looks up, smiling broadly in the direction of the therapist's office, then disappears down the street.

We Will Miss You

The signs were everywhere. *Bob's Retirement Party 5:00 p.m. Boardroom #5.* There was a sign on both the men's and women's bathrooms. There was a sign in the staff lounge. There was a sign on the front door of the building. There was a sign on the utility room. There was a sign on the supplies room. There were even signs at the entrances to both parking lots.

Babs leaned over towards Charlie's cubicle and whispered, "Do you think they want to make sure he really leaves?" Charlie had just taken a large sip of his morning coffee with cream and two sugars. His eyes grew wide as he looked over at Babs. The coffee went up his nose, setting off a rather long series of coughing.

Two cubicles down from Babs and Charlie, Randolph sent an email to Jonathan. "Yo. I wonder what they're going to get the old geezer with all that money they soaked out of us." The reply was, "A one-way ticket to Mars?"

At the water cooler, Susan looked over at Dolores who was filling up her water bottle. "Do you think his wife is coming?" Dolores bit her lip. "Oh my God, I hope so! Remember the last time she came?" Susan put her finger to her lips and said in a hushed voice, "Was that color, like, directly out of the bottle, or what? You think she slept in curlers?"

Mr. Petersen, the VP of Happiness Unlimited, was about to become the president. He looked particularly dapper in his lilac Armani suit and thin red tie. He had been waiting for this moment for the past 20 years. The shit-eating grin seemingly permanently plastered on his rather squarish face.

The door to Bob Stanisich's office was closed. It always was, even though he professed to having an open-door policy. Would he clean out his desk? Had he already? Would he take that bottle of Chivas Regal with him? What about the Aqua Net hair spray, and the Listerine?

At 4:50 p.m., the door swung open to reveal Mrs. Stanisich in all her glory. Was that a muumuu? Oh, yes it was! Did it have plumeria on it? Were the colors really bright red, orange, royal blue, and purple? Oh, yes. Was she also wearing yellow sandals? Yes. And was her toenail polish turquoise? Yes.

Mr. Petersen rushed over to greet her.

"Welcome, Mrs. Stanisich! Welcome! So glad you could make it! You must be so excited to finally have your husband home with you all the time!"

Mrs. Stanisich raised an eyebrow and snorted. "That remains to be seen," she said grimly. She swiveled her head left and right looking at all the gaping employees. They managed to smile back at her, as best they could.

Mr. Petersen cleared his throat. "Well, this is the moment we've all been waiting for," he announced. Then, he tried desperately to reword what he'd just said. "What I mean by that is, this is the moment we are going to show your husband just how much he's meant to this company and to us all for so many years." He strode over to boardroom #5 and gallantly opened the door. "Shall we?" he said, motioning for all to follow Mrs. Stanisich and sit in the folding chairs that were plastered against the walls. Susan had decorated the room earlier in the day. There were seven mylar balloons floating up to the ceiling with messages like, "Happy Retirement" and "We Will Miss You." There was also a big present tastefully wrapped, sitting on the mahogany table at the center of the room. Everyone wondered what was inside, except for Mr. Petersen…and Susan, of course, who had taken everyone's twenty-dollar bills and bought it.

Each of the employees dutifully walked in, nodded to Mrs. Stanisich, and sat in a folding chair. Then, they waited. And waited. And waited some more. Babs looked over at Susan. Randolph looked over at Jonathan. Charlie looked over at Dolores.

Mr. Petersen ventured, "Well, I wonder what's keeping him?" He was looking directly at Mrs. Stanisich, who shrugged her shoulders. No one else said a thing. Moments passed. Finally, Mr. Petersen rose and announced, "I'll just go check on your husband, and make sure he knows we're all waiting to bid him farewell."

Susan looked over at Mrs. Stanisich after Mr. Petersen left the room. "I hope he's okay, Mrs. Stanisich." A murmur of consent traveled around the room.

The door opened, and Mr. Petersen walked in, looking ashen. The employees all looked up expectantly.

"I'm afraid something is amiss."

They waited. Mr. Petersen held onto the mahogany table.

"I don't know how to tell you this," he said, blinking furiously. "But Mr. Stanisich seems to have vacated the premises."

"Vacated?" everyone said in unison, including Mrs. Stanisich.

Mr. Petersen nodded, looking unhappy. He then reached into the pocket of his lilac Armani suit and pulled out a piece of paper.

"He left a note."

"What? He's nowhere to be found?" Jonathan asked, as always, stating the obvious.

Dolores looked around the room at the stunned faces. Mrs. Stanisich must be in shock, she surmised as she didn't look particularly worried.

"Will you read us the note, Mr. Petersen?"

Mr. Petersen seemed to like having someone else give him orders. He reached into his pocket, and pulled out his reading glasses, smoothing out the folded paper.

"It's been a great 20 years. Sorry to spring this on you all. But I'm taking this opportunity to basically disappear from the world I've been so accustomed to. No, I'm not suicidal. I'm just getting the hell out of Dodge, as it were. Pardon my French. Don't look for me. Just go on with your lives."

Everyone turned to Mrs. Stanisich. She grabbed the note from Mr. Petersen's hands and appeared to reread it several times. Then, she got up from her folding chair, smoothed out her muumuu, looked at everyone, and unsuccessfully suppressing a smile, she said, "Well, toodle-oo! I'm off to go on with my life!"

Mr. Petersen sputtered, "Don't you even want the present?"

Mrs. Stanisch looked at him incredulously. "What is it? A plaque?"

Mr. Peterssen demurred, "Well, yes, it is!"

"Toss it in the circular file!" Mrs. Stanisich replied. "Toodle-loo!"

They heard her footsteps going down the stairs and ran to the window to look at her skipping down Third Avenue as her colorful muumuu flapped gaily in the breeze.

Jonathan piped up. "I don't think she's going to look for him."

Triple

She stood at the corner of 5th and Main under the streetlight, in her London Fog raincoat, smoking a Gauloises. It was coming down in buckets. It was late; 1:00 in the morning. The neon sign of Shelly's bar was flashing. No one seemed to be coming out. That man had hired her to check up on his wife. He told her money was no object.

"Meet me across the street from Shelly's," she had told him. "I'll be there at 1:00 a.m. I'll only wait 15 minutes. If you're late, it's your funeral. And give me $250 cold, hard cash as a retainer. Once I find out who she's been whoring with and where they live, you'll owe me the other $250. Capiche?"

He had agreed without hesitation. He said he'd be wearing a purple fedora with a red feather on the side.

Now it was 1:10. He had five more minutes. The rain was still coming down hard. Then she saw the figure of a man in a black raincoat walking toward her. And yes, he had on a purple fedora with a red feather. He walked briskly up to her and stood close… too close. She could smell his cologne, and she liked it. She took a step back and studied his chiseled face. His high cheekbones were prominent. But what took her breath away were his turquoise eyes. Turquoise. She reached into her black leather bag for another Gauloises. As she was shaking it out of the box, he grabbed her hand with one of his, flipped open a lighter with the other. He didn't let go until he saw her take a drag off her cigarette. Then he helped himself to one from her pack as well. She watched his generous lips. She was mesmerized as he tilted his head back and deeply inhaled.

"I suppose you want the money," he said looking deeply into her startled brown eyes.

She nodded, watching him reach into a hidden pocket in his raincoat. He had the bills folded neatly in his hand. As she reached down to open her bag, he stopped her with his other hand, drew her close, and deftly stuffed the money into her bra, as if he had known exactly where he wanted to put it.

"I want you to find out everything, please," he said, his turquoise eyes pleading.

She couldn't find her voice at first, but when she did, she said, "Yes. Yes. I assure you, I will."

He grabbed her wrist and pulled her closer to him. Lifting her chin and looking into her eyes yet again, he whispered, "I'm counting on you."

They heard noises coming out of Shelly's and turned to look. There were couples, tipsy couples opening their umbrellas, stepping gingerly into the puddles in the street.

"That's her!" he said, the muscles in his jaw flexing.

"Where?"

"The one in pink."

She watched as a stunning woman in a pink trench coat clung to another equally stunning woman in black. They both stared as the two women stood under another lamppost, locked in an embrace, passionately groping each other, giggling. She continued to stare as the two women pressed up even more closely against each other.

"I guess you have your answer then. Shall I find out who that woman is?"

He flicked his Galoises into the street, crushing it with his black patent leather boot.

"I want you to find out everything about her. I'll pay you triple if you can take her away from my wife."

"Triple?"

"Triple. I'll wait here. She won't notice me, apparently."

What kind of assignment was this? she thought to herself as she sauntered toward the two women. When she got within two feet of them, she slipped on the wet pavement. She thrust her arms out to brace herself from the fall but landed with a thud on her side. The man and the two women rushed over to her.

"Are you okay?" they said in unison.

And then the woman in pink recognized her husband.

"Oh my God!"

His attention was no longer on the detective. Her husband grabbed her arm and pulled her to him.

"Who is this woman?" he demanded.

"I… I'll explain later."

The detective slowly got up, with the woman in black helping her. Their eyes met. The couple was now halfway down the block as the detective and the other woman watched them.

"Can I buy you a drink?" the woman in black offered.

"Yes. Oh, yes. Please do. Buy me a drink and I'll return the favor."

They walked arm in arm back into Shelly's. After all, Shelly's was open until 2:00 a.m., and he had offered her triple.

Through the Window

Johnny,

You never knew this, any of this, but now that I'm gone, I feel free to tell you why I was never in your life much. The bottom line is that I'm an evil person. A son of a bitch. I'm sure your mother has used that expression if she ever talked to you about me. She's not the only one. I'm not sure why I've done such harm in my lifetime, but one thing I want you to know is that I hope I didn't pass that gene onto you. And yes, you are my son, in case you ever wondered, or hoped you weren't.

Hopefully when I tell you certain things now, you won't freak out. You may say to yourself, I wasn't imagining things.

You see, when your mother kicked me out, and she had every right to do that, I couldn't bear not to at least see you. So, I did. Even though she had a restraining order against me, I did see you. I had to.

How, you might ask? I watched you through your bedroom window. I could crouch down in the bushes and wait patiently until I saw your light go on. I watched you looking at yourself in the mirror, doing your homework at your desk, talking secretly to your girlfriends on your cellphone. No, I couldn't really hear what you were saying, the double-paned windows took care of that, but I could see you, my only son, my handsome boy as he grew up.

Sometimes I would watch through the living room window and see you eating dinner, sometimes secretly sneaking food to Benji under the table. It's a good thing Benji can't hear too well or he may have given me away.

Other times I would park my car across the street from your school and crouch down, barely being able to see you through my window. By then, you had no idea what kind of car I had. Thankfully, neither did your mother. I did, by the way, see you hit that homer! Way to go! I was so proud of you. It was all I could do to keep myself from running out to the field and giving you a high five.

I want you to know that my heart broke every Christmas and every birthday for you because if I could have, I would have given you anything you wanted. Of course, I couldn't give you what you may have needed, a dad, a dad who was present in your life. I regret that so much.

I'm not excusing myself. I was too self-centered to suddenly reappear in your life. I was also afraid, terribly afraid that you'd reject me. That would have been too much to bear. So, I just watched my son grow up through the window.

I hope you'll forgive me some day. I hope you believe me when I say I love you. You were the world to me.

The Understanding

Sandra wasn't sure when it all began. Probably in the sixth grade. It was when her mother moved to Farmington. She wasn't sure why she had no friends, or why none of the kids even wanted to talk to her. Was it because she was new, or maybe she didn't know what was cool as far as clothes or certain words that were popular? For instance, she heard the girl who always sat in front of her say, "Hot dog!" Hot dog? What did that mean? Was it a good thing? A bad thing? It seemed like a good thing, but what if she used it and they all laughed at her?

At least it wasn't as hard as when her family first came to the United States and she didn't speak any English. That was really awful. She didn't know what anyone was saying, ever; neither the teachers nor the kids. Her parents had to work in the fields, so they came home tired. And, of course, they didn't speak English either, so they couldn't help her. Since she was the oldest, she had to try and assist her four siblings with their homework; mostly, she could only help with math. And then there was the problem with their clothes. Her sisters and her brother each had only one outfit to wear. Their shoes were threadbare, and either too tight or too big.

Sandra also had to cook for the family. She would make a big pot of beans, and some rice with tomatoes and onions every night. On Sundays, her mom didn't have to work, so she made tortillas. They were so yummy.

After the first year, Sandra started to pick up the English language. She felt as if a whole world had opened up, only now she understood what it meant when the kids would call her or her siblings "beaner" or "wetback." And then, when her father got really sick, she had to be the one to translate at the doctor's office. The doctor told her father he had a bad heart and needed to take medication and not work so much. Her father just nodded respectfully, but Sandra knew he could do neither. Six months later, her dad had a heart attack and died while picking Brussels sprouts. All the other campesinos donated money they didn't have to help fly his body to Mexico for his burial. Of course, the whole family had to go, so again, they pooled their money for Sandra, her siblings and her mother to take the three-day Greyhound bus trip. The kids missed a month of school, and the boss of the fieldworkers wouldn't rehire her mother.

Sandra's mother was desperate. She found a very distant relative who lived in Farmington. This relative was wheelchair-bound and needed help around the house. Sandra's mother agreed to clean and cook for her in exchange for living with her four children in one of the two bedrooms of the house, where they all slept on the floor. Sandra had to take her sisters and brother with her to the new school to get them enrolled. Her mother couldn't leave Tia Elena alone for more than an hour.

Sandra dreaded meeting the principal, Mrs. Martin, and explaining why their mother couldn't come. She and her siblings sat in the five folding chairs facing the principal's desk. She seemed like a nice lady. Sandra kept staring at a pin Mrs. Martin wore on her navy-blue suit. It looked like a chile pepper. Why would she want to wear a chile pepper? She also couldn't help but notice the principal looking at the children's clothes and shoes.

The following Monday, Sandra and her siblings were summoned to the nurse's office. The nurse, Ms. Baker, examined each of their scalps very carefully. She then brought out three big bags. One had a special shampoo, soap, toothbrushes, toothpaste and combs. Another had four sets of clothes for girls, and one for her brother. The last bag had new shoes for each of them. Sandra didn't know what to say. "Thank you, Ms. Baker," she whispered, and nudged her siblings to follow suit.

While Sandra's sisters and brother were very happy to have new clothes, Sandra felt both grateful and sad. She had begun to keep a diary every night. The school had given each of the children a backpack with pens, notebooks, and paper. When they opened the backpacks, there were also three protein bars each, and three pair of socks. It was almost too good to be true.

Sandra took out one of her notebooks to use as a diary. That night, she wrote, "Well, hot dog! If this isn't great! We have been so *afortunados. Son muy amables*, but why do I feel so sad? Even Mama looked both happy and sad. I think she felt like I did. Happy we were given so much, but sad we had to accept this because we are so *pobres*. And everyone knows it. They call us wetbacks. I just smile. And those girls yesterday who surrounded me and asked me if I had my period yet. I didn't know what that meant. Period? It seemed like it was a good thing and that I should say I had it, so I did. They just laughed and walked away. And then, Ms. Baker, the nurse, called me into her office and offered me some what they call Sanitary Napkins. I didn't know what to say. I didn't know what they were for. When she explained it to me, I just turned red. And then she said, "You know, for when you get your period." My eyes grew wide. So that's what that meant. I felt so stupid, I almost cried. Ms. Baker patted me on the shoulder and said she understood. It was kind of her, but I don't think she really understood.

Sandra wrote in her diary that night: "They probably are mad because I get the highest scores in class, even in English! And I hate to feel too proud like Papa, but if they don't want to talk to me, I don't want to talk to them either. Someday, I'm going to be a lawyer and be rich. Maybe some of those *pinche gabachas* will need me. Hot dog!"

The Suggestion

She walked into the room and knew it was a mistake. For one thing, she had been planning to surprise her husband with the new sexy lingerie she had bought from Victoria's Secret. Their marriage had been dead for quite some time, and her therapist suggested she try something totally unexpected.

Normally when she came home from work, he was already sitting in the Barcalounger watching TV, a can of beer on the rug beside him, and a bowl of either peanuts or popcorn balanced upon his generous stomach. She would say, "Hi hon," as she opened the door, and he would grunt, reacting with vague acknowledgement of her presence. She knew better than to hope he'd made dinner or even ordered takeout, so she'd kick off her shoes and stomp around barefoot in the kitchen, opening cupboards and the refrigerator to see what she could put together. Usually, it was a half-assed salad of some sort and whatever protein was available: chicken, hamburger meat, tuna. Then, a hunk of French bread and some wine for herself. She'd putter around trying to ignore the TV blaring in the next room while she chopped, stirred, and poured. Most often during the next commercial he'd yell out from his chair, "Is it ready yet?" Because he never turned around to look at her, she would stretch her arm out towards him, her middle finger extended. That was always momentarily satisfying. When his show was over, he'd sit down, inhale the dinner, leave his dishes on the table, throw his napkin down, and shuffle back into the living room to watch another show. If the occasion arose when they were actually seated at the table at the same time, there was no conversation to speak of; not even, "Pass the salt."

She'd clean up and go off into their bedroom. After changing into her long woolen pajamas, she would grab a book and hunker down under the covers. She kept dimming the lights until her eyes got tired. This technique worked well for years. She never had to take sleeping pills. She only became vaguely aware of when he may have joined her in bed because of the warmth of his big body and her needing to pull the covers back over to her side.

It wouldn't have bothered her at all, really, until she joined a book club, and one of the women began talking about her husband and their exciting sex life. "Really? He does? Oh my God!" commented the other wide-eyed women. She was too embarrassed to ask anyone else if they too had rambunctious husbands, although from the looks on their faces when this woman talked, it didn't seem so.

She decided a month later to see a therapist. She'd never been to one, but three of the five women in her book club went religiously and swore by it. They said it not only improved their outlooks on life, but their sex lives as well. She figured it was worth a try.

She wondered if she should tell her husband she was in therapy but decided not to. At least, not right away.

She didn't know quite what to expect from meeting the therapist. She sure didn't expect her to be so attractive. Normally, she didn't pay much attention to other women's looks per se, but this therapist was different. She found herself staring at her luscious brown skin, her long, flowing white pants, her perfectly shaped, perky breasts. What was happening to her? She had never had these kinds of thoughts before. The therapist just sat there in all her magnificence and listened to her intently, looking at her with her deep green eyes.

On Thursdays, her therapy day, she started to pay attention to what she was wearing to her appointments. When the therapist suggested she buy some sexy lingerie and surprise her husband, she went right out to shop at Victoria's Secret. She even modeled the lingerie for her therapist at her next appointment, blushing the whole time.

She told the women at the book club that her birthday was that Wednesday, so she wasn't coming. She decided she would put on that see-through pink teddy with the pom poms and a pair of black fuck-me heels and surprise her husband during his show. What she didn't know was that the women had decided to surprise her and come to her house with a cake. Of course, they had to tell her husband about it. When they did, he was surprised because he hadn't remembered it was her birthday. He swore to keep it a secret.

While she was in her bedroom, changing into her sexy outfit, the doorbell rang.

"Honey? Will you get it? Whoever could that be at this hour? Probably some poor teenager trying to sell something," she chortled to herself.

Her husband dutifully opened the door and let the women in with the cake, champagne and balloons. They motioned with their fingers on their mouths for him to be quiet.

He sighed and obeyed, reluctantly turning off his program.

After admiring herself in the mirror, she called out, "Honey? Who was it?" Getting no answer, she opened the bedroom door and sauntered into the living room.

"Surprise!!!" the women in her book club sang out, with their champagne glasses in their hands… but then stood there with their mouths agape when they saw her.

Her husband was mortified. The women quickly left after drinking one obligatory glass of champagne, leaving the cake and balloons.

Two weeks later, she filed for divorce.

The Spree

Elizabeth Farnsby loved all animals. She always had, ever since she was a child. Her husband unfortunately was allergic to cats and dogs. He refused to let her even have a hamster. They never had children either. She had had five miscarriages in the early years of their marriage, and they had given up trying after that.

She took to visiting parks where people brought their dogs so she could pet them. As she walked to the park, she saw and was able to pet orange tabbies, Persians, gray tabbies, and tuxedo cats. Animals just seemed to gravitate towards her. When she went to the dog park, she always brought a baggie full of dog treats, soft and crunchy ones. All the dogs would run to Elizabeth and obediently sit when asked, mouths open, tails wagging. This satisfied her desire for animal love for many years.

Then came the day when her husband left her for his secretary. She remembered pinching herself, trying not to smile when he told her. She was finally alone and could have however many damn animals as she wanted.

The first morning her husband was gone, Elizabeth sat in her kitchen with a cup of chamomile tea and opened her laptop to the SPCA page. *Oh my God!* The puppies, the older dogs, the kittens, the cats! She wanted all of them.

That day, she brought home two older cats whose owner had passed away. The poor things. They came with the names Binky and Boots. So sweet. She had already gone to the pet store, of course, and bought kitty litter, two different kinds of canned food, two kinds of kibble, and three cat toys for each of them.

After a week of being in pure cat heaven, she went back to the SPCA and brought home two adorable kittens: one pure white, who she named Snowy, and the other black, who she named Ebony. For them, she just had to buy a cat tree. It cost close to $90, but they needed it.

Then came time for their vet visit. She had to complete it in two different trips, because she only had two cat carriers. It was expensive but they were worth every penny.

The older cats slept with her. The kittens seemed to like the beds she had bought for them. Those were the most expensive in the store, but Snowy and Ebony were so deserving.

Elizabeth was happy every day now. Her husband felt quite guilty for leaving her, and sent a her a nice, fat check every month. Of course, she put it all towards cat food and vet bills. She could live happily on macaroni and cheese.

One day, with two cats at her feet, one on her lap, and one right behind her on the back of the chair where she sat, Elizabeth opened her laptop to the SPCA site. Oh, oh, oh! The poor black lab! He was eight years old. She was sure no one else would adopt him. And look at his sweet, grey muzzle and his sad, cloudy eyes. It said he was used to cats. That did it. She brought him home three hours later.

The dog had such a funny name: Bartholomew. When she got into bed with Binky and Boots, he jumped up there too. Oh, well, there's room. Binky and Boots objected vehemently, but Bartholomew either pretended he couldn't hear them, or he really didn't. They got used to each other within a week. Elizabeth had to sleep in a small section of the bed and not move, but that was the least she could do.

She had to walk Bartholomew of course, so she took him to the closest park. She usually left very early in the morning because poor old Bartholomew had a hard time seeing, hearing, and walking, and she was afraid the younger dogs would overwhelm him. He was so good. He just dutifully did his business once they got to the park and sat by her side while she rested on the bench.

She did see a rooster on their walk early one morning, so she started bringing him treats. Who did he belong to? She saw him every day on the same street, but she never saw where he really lived. He recognized her now, so would always come out of the bushes and run to her. One morning, she saw a bobcat who looked like it was going to attack the rooster. Elizabeth was beside herself. What could she do? Bartholomew didn't even seem to notice the bobcat. So, she stood up and waved her arms around. She even tried to roar like a lion. It felt ridiculous but she was alone, and besides, she'd never forgive herself if the bobcat killed the rooster. The bobcat ran away after Elizabeth's performance. Shortly thereafter, if they were looking, the neighbors would have seen a middle-aged woman walking with an elderly dog, and a rooster tucked under her arm.

When she came home with Cluck Norris (the name she gave the rooster), she put him in the pantry with a box of straw, food and water. The next morning, she looked at Cluck and thought, *Poor thing. He's all alone. He needs a companion.* So, off she went to the pet store and came home with a hen, a big cage, some more straw, and some more chicken feed.

Eight months later, there was both a litter of kittens and four baby chicks. That made Elizabeth ecstatically happy. She was running out of money both for food for the animals and for herself, and for the inevitable vet bills that would keep coming the in the foreseeable future. She had lost 20 lbs., which was good, but she needed to get more clothes. Well, I could always go to Goodwill. She did feel a little weak, not quite herself. Maybe it was because she was now only eating rice. She would have to ask her husband, who by now had filed for divorce, for more money. She didn't want him to know why, though.

Elizabeth asked to meet him in a coffee shop in town. She couldn't bear to have him see the four cats, five newborn kittens, one old dog, Cluck Norris, his hen, and their brood. He wouldn't understand.

When her husband saw her, he was stunned. He said, "Look, I'm sorry to have caused you so much anguish. You are very thin. Here's a check for $5,000.00. Will that be okay? Please take care of yourself. Maybe you should get a dog?" He signed the check, stood up and left abruptly.

Elizabeth Farnsby had a big smile on her face. She got in her car and drove straight to the SPCA.

The Quilt

What lies behind us and what lies before us are nothing compared to what lies within us.
—Anonymous

"Oh my, Gladys! Look at this!"

Beatrice took Gladys' hand, the hand that she had held for the past 40 years. Together they walked over to a chest of drawers and opened the first one. In it were hundreds of swaths of fabric in a variety of patterns and colors.

Beatrice squealed with delight. They looked around the room: the soft couch covered with an afghan of many colors, the fireplace with logs burning so brightly, the Wedgewood stove with a tea kettle, the sweet teapot with a crocheted purple cozy over it, the china teacups replete with bachelor buttons as a design, the Persian rug with reds, greens, blues and purples, the window with white lace curtains adorning it, the view outside of the field of poppies and the clear, blue lake with swans.

"Gladys! Let's get to work! Imagine the quilt we can make! Oh, love, it's going to be delicious fun!"

Gladys went over to the round table, noticing the tablecloth. "Look, Bea! It has pansies on it! Your favorite!"

Beatrice clasped her pudgy hands together. "Oh my! Oh my! Aren't we blessed!" She began taking out yards of fabric squares from the chest of drawers and placing them on the couch.

The smell of freshly baked goods coming from the kitchen found Gladys perusing the kitchen. The three cinnamon buns were warm to the touch. Not questioning how they got there, she placed them on a silver tray, found two cloth napkins, and proceeded to bring it all into the room that the two lifelong partners had just discovered.

Just then, the door flung open. A young man of about 30 years old, looking very distressed, was standing there staring at the cellphone in his hand.

"Damn it to hell! It's fucking not working! There's no fucking WIFI here!"

He started pacing the room, looking frantically around and not finding what he was looking for. He saw the two contented women sitting on the couch who were looking up at him.

"Is there a password here?" Gladys looked over at Beatrice and back again after she shrugged her shoulders.

"A password! I asked if you know the password. Isn't it written somewhere on one of these walls?"

Gladys cleared her throat. "I'm afraid I don't know what you mean by a password."

"A PASSWORD! FOR THE WIFI! A PASSWORD!"

Beatrice looked over at Gladys. They both were at a loss. Wanting to help the frantic young man, Beatrice said, "We don't know about any password, but would you like a spot of tea? It's quite good."

"NO, I DO NOT WANT ANY TEA! I NEED TO CHECK MY EMAIL AND I CAN'T GET INTO THE INTERNET!"

The two women—who were holding hands, he noticed—said nothing.

"THIS IS HELL! THIS IS FUCKING HELL!"

A booming voice was then heard from above. They couldn't tell where it was coming from, except that it seemed to be coming from the sky.

"YES, IT *IS* HELL," the voice from above boomed. "YOU ARE ABSOLUTELY RIGHT."

The young man got quiet. Gladys spoke up. "To us, it seems like heaven." Beatrice nodded and smiled at her sweetheart.

"YES, IT *IS* HEAVEN. FOR YOU TWO, IT IS DEFINITELY HEAVEN," the voice echoed throughout the room. Beatrice, Gladys, and the young man paused and looked at one another.

"What the hell was that?" the man asked with a look of abject fear on his face.

Gladys and Beatrice exchanged glances. "We're not quite sure."

Beatrice then got up and poured some tea. She walked over to the chest of drawers and picked up four different swaths of material. "Young man, we are making a quilt and would be very interested in your opinion about which of these would look good next to each other."

They watched as his face changed from shock to resignation to a reluctant interest. "Well," he offered, "I did take design in college. In fact, I was quite good at it." He strode over to the couch, first putting his cellphone and laptop down on the table. Looking a bit sheepish, he remarked, "I guess I won't be needing these for a while now, will I?

Gladys took the swaths and moved them closer to where the young man could see them. His brows furrowed, deep in thought. He picked up each square and placed them one by one against one another, changing the pattern over and over until he seemed satisfied.

"This is the best design. The colors complement each other."

He looked quite satisfied with himself as both Beatrice and Gladys nodded and smiled. "A quilt, you were saying?"

"Yes, we are making a quilt! We would be honored if you'd help us with it. It seems like you have an eye for patterns."

The young man grinned, walked over to the chest of drawers, and started pulling out yards and yards of fabric. Beatrice patted the couch and motioned for him to join them.

He hesitated, but then relaxed. "Well, thank you. I believe I will. You two will teach me how to make a quilt, then!"

"Do help yourself to a cinnamon bun first though, dear. And pour yourself a cup of tea, too, if you'd like."

The young man looked over at the table which now seemed not only to have warm cinnamon buns, but chocolate chip cookies as well. He looked around and shook his head.

"Hmm. I guess this is heaven after all," he said as he took a bite of cookie, walked back in, and joined his two new friends. The three of them soon got down on the floor happily arranging the squares of material.

The Perfect Stick

Linda and Tina sat side by side on the curb in front of Linda's house, their backs facing the lawns leading up to their front porches.

"How can we do it?" Linda looked straight ahead into the street.

Tina shrugged and tried to sound confident. "I guess we just take bologna sandwiches and a couple of cookies?"

Linda nodded. After a couple of minutes she said, "How long before you think they'd notice?"

Tina shrugged. "Oh, I don't know. Maybe an hour?"

Linda nodded again. Then she said, "Are you going to make the bologna sandwiches?"

Tina hadn't thought that far. "Oh, I don't know. I guess so."

Linda said, "Well, if we're going to run away, we really need to have food, don't you think?"

Tina screwed up her 10-year-old face. "Yeah, I guess so. But why do I have to make the sandwiches? I never made one before."

Linda crossed her arms over her flat chest. "Well, it was your stupid idea."

Tina pouted. "My idea was not stupid! You said you were mad at your parents bossing you around, and I said I was too."

Linda stood up and stared down at her friend, who lived two houses down from her. "You know what? I think it was a really stupid idea, and I'm going to get all my friends to fight you. I have tons of friends and you don't have any."

Tina stood up. "Oh yeah? Well, I don't care. Just because I'm new here, doesn't mean I don't have any friends. I'm coming over to fight you before dinner with all my friends, and we're going to win."

Linda smiled as evilly as a 10-year-old can smile, and said, "Fine! I'll see you on my front lawn!"

Tina walked up the block to Janie's house, the only other girl she really knew. She really liked going to Janie's, because she had a ton of board games, and Tina loved board games. Tina's mother had yelled at her when she heard that Tina had told Janie that she was only happy to be invited to her house because she had board games. Her mother said that wasn't a gracious thing to say. Tina didn't understand that at all. There were lots of things Tina's mother said that she didn't understand.

Tina knocked on Janie's front door. Janie's mother came to the door and greeted Tina—if not warmly, at least politely. "Oh, Tina. It's you. Well, I'm sorry to say that Janie isn't here right now. She is at a ballet class."

"A ballet class?" Tina couldn't imagine Janie, who was at least three inches taller than her and kind of a tomboy, wearing a tutu. Janie had three older brothers with whom she played basketball and baseball all the time.

"Yes, dear. A ballet class." Janie's mother began slowly closing the door. "Why don't you come by tomorrow? She'll be home then."

Tina looked downtrodden. "It'll be too late."

Janie's mother frowned. "Too late for what, dear?"

Tina knew it would be a bad idea to tell Janie's mother why, so she said, "Oh, never mind. It's okay." Janie's mother shook her head and shut the door.

On the way back to Linda's house, Tina saw a perfect stick. It was about two feet long and two inches wide. She picked it up. *This is a perfect fighting stick. Linda will be so jealous.*

As she approached Linda's vast lawn, she saw, to her dismay, about ten kids, boys and girls, spread apart on the grass, each with sticks in their hands. Linda looked triumphant. *Who are all these kids? They aren't all in our grade. Who are they, and how does she know them, and how did she find them that fast? Well, their sticks aren't as big as mine.*

Linda was afraid to get too close. *Ten kids?* She didn't stand a chance. She stayed where she was on the sidewalk, holding her stick, and watched them. Then, Linda's front door opened. Her father, the local doctor, was standing there. He was, in fact, Tina's doctor. When the pond had frozen over last winter, and Tina had slammed her mittened hand in the car door of her parent's Plymouth Plaza, she had walked right up to Linda's front door, crying. Dr. Feldman gently took off the glove, examined her hand, and iced it. The worst part of that day was him saying, "Well, young lady, I'm afraid it's no ice skating for you today!"

And now here he was, arms crossed, with an angry look on his usually kind face. "You better not hurt Sheila. She's only seven!" He pointed to Sheila, a kid of about seven years old from the neighborhood, standing there with her buck teeth and saddle shoes, holding a really stupid looking stick. Tina looked at Linda's father in disbelief. How could he think she could hurt Sheila? Or that she even would? And, anyway, there were 10 of them and only one of her, even though she had the best stick.

Tina just hung her head and walked back to her house. She didn't see Linda for three whole days. On the third day, Linda came by on her bicycle. Tina was timid about talking to her, but she approached her slowly.

"Hi." Linda looked over at Tina with a soft smile.

"Hi."

"Wanna play?" Linda said, looking down at the ground.

"Sure!" Tina felt her heart beating. "Wait a minute. I'll be right back."

Tina walked back into her house, went upstairs an dinto the back of her closet, where she had hidden the stick. She held it behind her back and walked down the stairs, and back outside to where Linda was waiting.

As she got closer to Linda, Tina thrust the stick out towards Linda. "Want my stick? It's a really good one."

Tina watched as Linda's eyes lit up. She took the stick, smiling, and said, "Sure! Thanks!"

Tina looked over at Linda. "So, what should we play?"

"Dinosaurs!" Linda said resolutely. "You be the boy, and I'll be the girl, and you will save me from the scary dinosaurs."
Tina's eyes lit up. "OK!" She really didn't like always having to be the boy, but it was okay for today. And anyway, she had just seen her little sister Barbara and Linda's little sister, Judy, playing in the yard.

"Okay! Barbara and Judy are the dinosaurs, and we'll hide behind the bushes. The two girls ran hand-in-hand and hid behind the mulberry bushes, giggling. Tina looked over at Linda and put her fingers to her lips.

Although playing dinosaurs was entertaining, it wasn't quite exciting enough to continue for weeks at a time. The following weekend, Linda came by with a serious look on her face.

"I'm going to show you a secret, but you can't tell anybody. Especially your parents, okay?"

They walked over to Linda's house together hand in hand. Then Linda took Tina over to the side of the house where there was a door. It looked like it was a door to the basement. Linda motioned for Tina to be quiet as she gently opened the door. The two girls quietly went inside, stepping down into the dank room. It was hard to see in there. There were no windows. Linda reached into the back pocket of her dungarees and took out a candle. Then, she reached into the front pocket and took out a book of matches. She lit the match and then the candle. Now they could see. The floor was dirt. There were cobwebs everywhere. Tina was scared.

Linda whispered, "I'm not ever supposed to go down here. And, of course, I'm not supposed to have matches."

Tina whispered, "Where did you get the candle?"

"I found it in the kitchen in one of the drawers with all kinds of stuff in it."

Linda looked over at Tina. "This is a very secret place. No one else knows about it. Well, maybe my parents do. But no one else."

Tina liked the idea of having a secret place. They could hide from their sisters or even their parents. "Let's name it. It'll be our club."

A sly smile crept across Linda's face. "Yes! And I came down here yesterday and guess what I brought?"

Tina shrugged. "What?"

Linda went behind a few wooden boxes and drew out the stick that Tina had given her. "The perfect stick! I put this down there in case something scary happens and we need to defend ourselves."

Tina started to tremble. "Defend ourselves? From what?"

Linda whispered, "Oh, I don't know. It's just in case. So, what are we going to name our secret club?"

Tina furrowed her brows. She wanted to give it a special name. A mysterious name. She thought of "The Perfect Stick club", but then thought maybe that was too stupid. And anyway, if Dr. Feldman ever found the stick, he'd blame it on her. He'd remember the day of the fight. "How about the X-59 club?" She had no idea where she came up with that name, but she blurted it out.

Linda's eyes lit up. "Yes! Yes! The X-59 club!"

Tina looked over at her best friend. "Should we invite anyone else?"

Linda was deep in thought about this proposal. "Well, how about Glenda from across the street? She's big and strong and I'm pretty sure she can keep a secret."

Tina smiled. "Yes, Shirley! Let's invite Glenda tomorrow!"

A week later, the three of them crept into the room. Linda lit the match and then the candle. As she held it in her palm and moved it around, Tina and Linda gasped. Shirley looked at them. "What's wrong?"

Linda looked at Tina and then at Glenda. "Someone's been in here."

Shirley looked very scared. "How can you tell?"

Tina gravely said, "the perfect stick has been moved."

"The perfect stick?"

Linda blew out the candle and grabbed the hands of both Glenda and Tina. "Let's get out of here."

The three girls sat on the curb together to discuss what to do next.

Linda said, "If we tell my parents that someone has been in there, I'm going to get into big trouble."

Tina blurted out, "But, if you don't, whoever that person is, might do something bad to your house."

Glenda looked at the two of them. "Like what?"

Tina said, "Like set the house on fire!"

Linda bolted up. "Oh no! I left the candle and the matches down there!"

Linda ran home. Tina went to her house and couldn't eat dinner. Glenda bolted across the street, holding her stomach.

Tina didn't see Linda for a whole week. When they caught up walking home from school, Linda told her that her parents had grounded her for a whole week. She also said that Glenda told her parents everything, including about the X-59 club. They had consequently forbidden her to play with Linda and Tina.

Tina didn't quite know what to say, other than, "Well, we did have the perfect stick."

The Other Side

Sharon, Robert, and Patricia were cleaning out their recently deceased father's room. Patricia wanted to wait for at least a week or two, but Sharon insisted on getting it over with. Robert seemed indifferent. He wanted to hire someone to clean it, but his sisters refused. Their father had been dying for the past three years, but he'd stubbornly lingered on, much to the dismay of close family members.

Sharon lived in the same town as their father, and had consistently visited him way beyond the time when he still knew who she was. Being the middle child and mostly ignored, Sharon felt that it was her duty to attend to him. The hospice nurses had told her that even if it seemed like he didn't recognize him, it was still possible that he did, and that she should whisper very close to his ear when she spoke to him. She didn't particularly care for the odor of his earwax, but she wasn't about to say something to the kind nurses, or clean his ear canals herself.

Patricia, who lived about two hours away, came to visit their father about every other weekend. She was the eldest, and used to deciding how things would go if necessary. She had already made sure he'd be cremated. His ashes would be planted in a forest along the coast.

Their mother had run off to an ashram 10 years before, and would occasionally send them letters bathed in patchouli oil. She always signed them, "Namaste." When the siblings wrote back to inform her of how ill her husband was, she had responded, "This is his path. May he find enlightenment."

Robert lived in a palatial mansion in Pacific Palisades with his boy-toy Sal from Ecuador. He wrote scripts for TV.

"Look, let's just get this over with," he said while looking at his iPhone. "I need to get back as soon as possible. Torty is sick and we don't know what's wrong with her."

Patricia looked over at Robert. "Torty? Who the hell is that?"

Robert shoved a photo from his phone into her face. It was a long-haired cat of some kind.

"Isn't she the sweetest little pussy?"

Sharon and Patricia exchanged looks, while Sharon vacuumed furiosly around the hospital bed that had been moved into the dining room in the downstairs of their father's house. The vacuum cleaner began to suddenly make a groaning noise. They all turned to look at it.

"Something's caught," Sharon announced.

"No shit, Sherlock," Robert said, without looking up from his phone.

Sharon bent down to examine the vacuum cleaner. She extracted a long hook.

"What the...?"

Patricia looked at the hook and back again at Sharon.

"Why was there a hook embedded into the shag rug?"

Robert, who occasionally wrote murder mysteries, piped up. "Maybe there's a secret room under the shag rug, with dead bodies in it."

Soon all three of them were on their hands and knees, ripping up the green shag rug. There was a square cut into the wood floor that had the eye for the hook on the top. The three siblings looked at one another, not sure who was going to be brave enough to open it.

"Whatsa matter, girls?" Robert taunted. "You think Dad had a dead body in there?"

"Shut up, asshole." Patricia grabbed the eye and yanked open the latch. There was a small square space about five inches deep, with a red silk box in it. The red silk had golden leaves decorating it. Patricia took the box out and placed it on the rug.

Sharon looked ashen. "What's inside?"

Robert giggled. "Hmmm. Now what could dad have been hiding from us for all these years?" He reached over, held onto the top, and looked over at his sisters. "Shall I do the honors?"

"Go for it, Mr. Big Guy." Patricia was trying to keep her normal bossy demeanor in check, but not succeeding entirely.

Robert reached down with his manicured fingers and opened the box. Inside was a crinkled brown piece of paper with writing on it. He smoothed out the paper, reached into his pocket, and put on his reading glasses.

He squinted. "It's kind of hard to read. It's in cursive and very ornate."

Patricia grabbed it from him. "It says, 'When you read this, make a spoke with salt on the floor, write down a question on a piece of paper, burn it, and rub the ashes on your forearm while asking a question for a person on the other side to answer."

Patricia guffawed. "Oh, right. Yep, that's exactly what we're going to do, Dad. You freak."

Sharon looked over at her. "Yeah, but what if he really meant it? What if we really can ask him a question?"

Robert looked over at her. "Oh, this is too good. Way too good. Let's do it! Where's the salt?" He walked over to the kitchen, grabbed the salt, and made a line on the hardwood floor. He was giggling again. "Who has paper?" He looked around. Sharon jumped up running to the desk drawer and pulled out a notepad and three pens.

Patricia said, "No fucking way am I going to do this. It's ridiculous. Dad must be laughing."

Sharon looked greyer. "From where, Patty? From where?"

Robert said, "Okay, Sharon, why don't you do the honors?"

Sharon dutifully wrote down a question—no one knew what it was—and folded up the paper into her shaking hand.

"Okay," Robert went on. "Now we gotta burn it." He looked around for a candle. Of course, Sharon knew exactly where one was, as well as the matches.

"Do it! Do it! Do it!" Robert commanded Sharon who readily complied. They watched as she lit the paper on fire, holding it away from her as it burned to ashes. Then she rubbed them on her forearm.

She looked over at Robert. "Do you think I'm supposed to ask the question out loud, or will he know what it said anyway?"

Robert shrugged. "I dunno. Try it both ways."

Sharon concentrated very hard. They heard nothing. She waited. Nothing.

Robert said, "OK. Now ask it out loud."

Sharon said, "Are you sure you want me to say it out loud?"

Robert nodded. Patricia merely rolled her eyes.

"Okay." Sharon took a deep breath. "Did you really ever love us, Dad?"

They looked at her, startled.

"That was your question?" Robert grimaced.

Sharon looked down sheepishly. "Yes," she whispered.

They waited 10 more minutes and heard nothing.

Patricia snorted. "Well, I guess you have your answer from the other side. Good one, Dad!"

The New Doctor

"Hey, did you hear who's taking over for Dr. Matthews?" Matilda was gripping her cellphone and pacing in the kitchen.

Her neighbor Beatrice lowered her voice to a hushed whisper. "I heard it's a new young doctor from the city. And I also heard he's very, very handsome."

Matilda tittered. "Really? Who did you hear that from?"

Beatrice hesitated for a few seconds. It sounded like she was walking around outside or something. "Eleanor said she saw a man with a suitcase get off the train."

"So? How did she know it was the doctor?" Matilda was now looking out her kitchen window at the neighbor's front lawn. It was always so perfectly manicured. Of course it was; she could afford a gardener.

"She said he just looked like a doctor. Anyway, he wasn't from around here, that's for sure. He looked like he was from the city. She said he looked a bit lost."

"Aw. Poor dear," Matilda cooed. "Maybe we should bring him a cake, or some cookies or something. You know, to make him feel welcome."

Beatrice snorted. "You just want to get a good look at him!"

"Well, that could very well be true. I heard he's staying at the Baldwin's until he can find a place."

Beatrice lowered her voice even more. "That could get very convenient. We all know Jack travels a lot."

After a moment of silence, Matilda said, "Well, I'm going to make him some pecan pie and bring it over to the Baldwins tomorrow."

Beatrice couldn't help but laugh out loud. "What are you going to say? 'Wanna trade this for a Pap smear?'"

"Stop! You're killing me."

The next morning, Matilda was humming in her kitchen as she put whipped cream on top of the pie. The Baldwin's house was only a block away. She was trying to decide whether to drive over there or not. She decided to take her car, because of the pie. What if she dropped it while walking over? That would be a disaster. Besides, everyone would see her going there with that pie.

The Baldwins had one of those stately homes made of stone. Apparently, it wasn't Jack who had the money; it was Elizabeth. Her family had lived here for three generations, and her father had been a banker. Why they never had children, no one knew. But they were generous. They donated to the schools, the library, the hospital, the church, even the orphanage. Best of all, they had lavish parties three times a year: Halloween, Christmas, and New Year's. Even though the whole town was envious of their wealth, they couldn't be unduly judgmental.

Matilda parked her Honda Civic right in front. It was a long sidewalk, and she had to be careful while she walked to the front door with the pie. She was only 42, but sometimes, she found herself feeling dizzy. She decided she'd ask the handsome new doctor about that. Matilda's kids, Hazel and Jonathan, were both away at college. Her husband George, although he tried to be attentive, basically just worked at the insurance office, came home, expected dinner which he inhaled with his two glasses of Merlot and plopped himself down on the sofa in front of the TV. So, if she was dizzy or, God forbid, fell, she wasn't sure he'd even notice or know what to do.

Matilda, pie in the crook of her left arm, lifted the brass knocker with her right hand. She knocked three times. After a minute or two, Matilda began to wonder if anyone was home. Then Elizabeth opened the door. She ushered in Matilda with a startled look.

Matilda put on her most charitable smile. "Hello! I hope I didn't disturb you. I wanted to welcome the new doctor to our town with a pie."

Elizabeth quickly looked over her shoulder and back again. "Oh! That's very kind of you. I'm sure he'll be thankful." She did not open the door any wider, just stood there gaping at Matilda.

Matilda understood she was not going to be invited in. Did she notice smeared lipstick on Elizabeth Baldwin's face? Was the top button of her blouse undone? Matilda quickly put that thought out of her mind. With a gesture of generosity, she thrust the pie into

Elizabeth's hands, which Elizabeth accepted with a smile while firmly shutting the door.

Hmmm! The minute she got back home, Matilda dialed Bernice.

"Well? Was he handsome?"

"I didn't even get to see him! I think she was hiding him! It was very weird."

"Was Jack there?"

"Didn't seem like it."

"Hmmm."

"Well, I'm going to make an appointment as soon as possible."

"Me too. You first."

The following Wednesday, Matilda sat in the waiting room. The office had the familiar odor antiseptic and room deodorant. There were fresh red carnations in a vase near the front desk. That was a new touch. Dr. Matthews had never had those. I bet Elizabeth bought those flowers for him.

The receptionist, Shelly, with her too tight-fitting white uniform, clicked away on the computer with her purple press-on nails. She seemed the same to Matilda. Maybe he wasn't her type?

And then Olivia, the medical assistant, called Matilda's name, opened the door to the hallway, and motioned for her to go into Room 6. Matilda felt her heart beating erratically. Uh oh. What if I…? She felt the need to hold onto the chair in the exam room, which was spinning. The next thing she knew, she was looking into the face of Olivia and… and… who is this? The new doctor? She realized then she must have fallen down, perhaps even passed out. But this doctor? He wasn't handsome at all. Not really. His teeth were remarkedly crooked, his lips thin, his hair balding, his nose didn't fit his face. He held out his arm and with Olivia's assistance, they lifted Matilda upright and sat her up on the exam table. Olivia put a blood pressure cuff on Matilda and gave her a reassuring smile.

"Did I… did I?"

The doctor spoke then. Even his voice was annoying: nasal and whiny.

"Yes, Mrs. Thompson. You took a tumble. How are you feeling?"

Matilda looked over at him. "Disappointed."

The doctor furrowed his brows and glanced over at Olivia. "Disappointed?"

Matilda found herself blushing. "Oh, never mind."

"We'll need to do some blood work."

Matilda sighed. "Right. Whatever."

The doctor and his medical assistant exchanged glances. "I'm sure you'll feel better in no time. We'll have you wait here until you feel you can walk."

"Oh, I'm fine. I'm just fine."

"Oh, Mrs. Thompson? Thank you for the pecan pie. It was so kind of you."

Matilda nodded. "Just being hospitable."

The Mail

Edith Sweeny had lived in Jasper all her life. Her parents had lived there as well as her grandparents. She was the youngest of five and, as was the custom, it fell to her to care for her parents as they aged.

Her older brother Jake had joined the army when he was 18, not to be heard of since. They didn't even know if he was alive.

Susan, Gladys, and Germaine, her older sisters, had each run off with the first boy who had looked twice at them. They lived in separate counties, just far away enough so they had good excuses not to visit, except for Christmas.

Edith's father was very strict, and after he had downed a few whiskeys, often became physically violent and verbally abusive. In a typical rage, he had thrown one of the kitchen chairs. It had one broken leg and was left like that, as a reminder never to cross him.

Her mother, Clara, was quiet and obedient. If she had any concerns, she kept them to herself.

Edith didn't really know what her father did to make money. Even now, once a week, men in fancy cars would pull up into their driveway with bottles of wine for her father and on occasion, bouquets of flowers for her mother. When the men came, she watched her mother visibly shaking and wringing her hands. The men would sit in the kitchen, smoking cigars, drinking wine, and playing cards. Edith's mother would serve them peach pie with whipped cream and gingerbread cookies. She would shoo Edith off into her room, giving her a stern warning to stay away until the men had left.

Edith had a job in town at the library. She would shelve books and recommend some when asked. She assumed that, unlike her sisters, she would never marry, as she was considered plain. That was fine with her. Her brother, when he was still in the house, would twist her arm until she cried, then laugh at her and call her a big ugly baby. When she looked in the mirror, she frowned. Her washed-out hair was neither blonde nor brown. She wore it pulled tightly back into a bun. Her lips were thin and her chin receding. The rest of her was rather box shaped. When her brother ran off, she was relieved.

Her long-suffering mother died suddenly of heart failure. That left Edith to care for her volatile father by herself. She took to working long hours at the library and taking circuitous walks home. She hoped by the time she arrived, her father would be passed out on the couch, a lit cigar in a nearby ashtray and a half-empty bottle of whiskey on the floor. That wish was granted almost every night.

Sundays, the library was closed, so Edith took to going to the nursing home and reading to the elderly. As long as she left her father something to eat on the table, he seemed satisfied, if somewhat put out. But Sunday was usually the day the men would come in their big, fancy cars, so he was occupied.

Edith almost never checked her parents' mailbox because they never received any mail. This past Sunday, however, as she walked past it, something caused her to stop and look inside. There was one letter pushed way far to the back. It was addressed to her mother.

Edith had to open it. Who didn't know her mother had died? The return address had initials: J.S. Well, her brother was Jake. But Jake? They hadn't heard from him in over ten years. She thought about dutifully showing the letter to her father first, but she knew he'd be drunk and more than likely, passed out. She opened it.

Dear Ma... she quickly skimmed to the bottom. *Love, your son, Jake.*

Oh my God! It was from him! Jake! Her right arm began to recoil from memory.

Dear Ma,

I hope you and dad are well. I heard that Gladys, Susan, and Germaine got married and got the hell out. Does Edith still live with you? As you know, I joined the Army. I guess that was a good move. Well, not entirely. I learned a lot of lessons, I guess. I've had some good times and some bad. I'm not sure why I was the way I was but, I must have caused you a lot of pain. Sorry about that. I hope you can forgive me. I'm not going to ask after Dad. I guess I'll find out soon enough.

I got into some trouble and got a dishonorable discharge, and then I got in more trouble and spent the last five years in prison. Sorry I never wrote you. Prison is not cool; I can tell you that.

I really do miss your peach pie, Ma. When I come home, and I will be coming soon, I hope you can make me some. I'm planning to hitchhike home in the next few weeks, if anyone will pick up a felon off the side of the road. And Ma, I learned some pretty good martial arts in the Army and in prison. So, if Dad gets violent with you like he used to…well, let's just put it this way: I'll take care of it. I should have done that long ago. Oh, and not to surprise you, I have a pretty big scar on my face from a bad fight. I kicked that sucker's ass though. You'd be proud of your son.

See you soon,

Love,

Jake

Edith folded up the letter, put it in her pocket, walked back to the house, her heart beating like crazy. Getting out a suitcase, she packed what she could, took her savings from beneath her mattress and some money out of her father's wallet. She walked to the Greyhound station and bought a ticket to Philadelphia: 3,000 miles away.

She sat on the bench, wishing for the clock to speed up. When the bus finally arrived, Edith saw a car pull up and her brother—at least she thought it looked like him—got out.

She turned her head away, clutched her suitcase resolutely, walked up the steps, found a seat near the front and stared out the window in the opposite direction.

The Lump

"Mom, I want to be a nurse."

Barbara looked over at her 16-year-old daughter as she washed up the last of the crusty dishes from dinner.

"Honey. I know it sounds like a cool job, but believe me, it's not that great. There are a lot of disgusting parts to it."

Her daughter, Lydia, scrunched up her face.

"Why? I like disgusting stuff."

Barbara sighed and started drying the plates. "I mean, there's lot of blood and guts, and gross smells."

Lydia stared at her mother. "You mean like the kind of gross stuff Fluffy drags in, half-eaten? I like that!"

Barbara turned to face her daughter. "Yes, sweetheart, but these are people. Human beings. Not mice, or gophers, or opossums."

Lydia rolled her eyes, gathered up her homework and went into her room. Over her shoulder, she called, "Okay, Mom. Whatever you say."

When she got into her room, the first thing she did was take out her cellphone to see if Sam had texted her. Of course, he had. Seventeen times.

—*This class is too hard. I hate it,* was the first text.

—*What was I thinking?* The second.

—*Jesus, I'm only in high school.* Third.

—*My dad expects me to get an A.* Fourth.

—*They shouldn't let high school kids take Community College classes.* Fifth.

—*They brought in a cadaver today.* Sixth.

—*It stank. Gross! I think it was formaldehyde.* Seventh.

—*I couldn't even get a good look. Everyone was in my way.* Eighth.

—*We're going to be tested on everything that I couldn't see.* Ninth.

—*What am I going to do?* Tenth.

—*Jesus, how am I going to identify muscles?* Eleventh.

—*Lydia, does your mom have an anatomy book?* Twelfth.
—*Why aren't you answering me?* Thirteenth.
—*I'm freaking out!* Fourteenth.
—*Meet me tonight. I'll leave the window open.* Fifteenth.
—*Maybe you can quiz me?* Sixteenth.
—*Be quiet going through the window.* Seventeenth.

Lydia waited until she heard her mother go into the bedroom after her bath. Her mother always did the same thing. Took a bath, grabbed her book, went into her room, and was asleep within an hour. She never came out.

Walking to Sam's house was easy. He was only four blocks away. She liked to go by the big elm on 7th Street. There was something peaceful about that tree. She and Sam had kissed under that tree after their first date. The tree had a big hole in the trunk and they used to leave each other secret messages in it. *Poor Sam,* she thought. *I wonder how hard Anatomy is? I know I'll have to pass that class too if I want to be a nurse.*

Just as she was passing by the tree, she saw a blanket with a big lump under it. *That's weird.*

She noticed that the powder blue blanket was dirty and it looked like it had blood stains on it. *Like period stains. Weird.*

Lydia kicked at the lump under the blanket. It felt like a body. Creepy. Yep. It's a body all right.

And then she thought, *Maybe I should call Sam? He could come out here and meet me. If it is a real body and no one sees us, maybe he could study the muscles or whatever he needs to do for his class. Then we could call the police or whatever.*

She texted him:
—*Sam? Yo. I might be a little late.*
He texted back:
—*Why? What's up?*
—*A body.*
—*What?*
—*A body.*
—*What are you talking about?*

—There's a body right here under the elm tree.
—You're shittin' me.
—Nope.
—A body?
—Yep.
—Like a human body?
—Yep.
—Is it dead?
—Duh. It's a body.
—Um.
—You wanna come look at it? You could study it.
—That's weird, Lydia.
—I know. I just want to help you pass your test.
—I can't believe you just said that.
—I know. I can't either.
—Does it smell?
Lydia leaned closer to the body and took a sniff.
—Gross! Yeah! Super gross! I think I'm going to puke.
—Listen, go home and call the police.
—But, my mom will find out I've been outside and not in my room.
—You're right.
—Just go home then. I'll talk to you tomorrow. I've got to study.
—OK.
—Just go home.
—OK.
Lydia ran to her house, her heart beating fast. She put her hand up to her mouth to keep from puking on the way.

The next morning, she just played with her Rice Krispies.

"What's wrong, dear? You're not sick, are you?"

"No."

"Well, why aren't you eating your cereal? You always eat your cereal."

Lydia stirred the spoon in the bowl a few times.

"Mom?"

"Yes?"

"I don't want to be a nurse after all."

"Oh really? That was a quick change of mind."

Lydia looked down at her bowl.

"Why the big change?"

"Oh, I don't know. I just thought about how gross you said it can be."

Barbara smiled. "Smart. So, have you thought about something else?"

"No, not really. I just don't want to have a job that's gross."

Barbara laughed. "Well, I'm sure there are plenty of jobs that aren't gross."

Lydia took her bowl to the sink, dumped it out and went to her room. There was a text from Sam.

—*Is it still there?*

—*I don't know."*

—*Did you tell your mom?*

—*Of course not.*

—*I thought about going to look at it, but I just couldn't.*

—*Smart.*

—*So weird.*

—*Yeah. How are you going to do on your test?*

—*Oh, I don't know. I think today, I'll just elbow my way to the front of the cadaver and hold my nose.*

—*Is it a female or male?*

—*I'm not sure. I couldn't get that close. One person who did, passed out.*

—*They did?*

—*Yeah. She just keeled over right there.*

—*Sam? I don't want to have that be our special tree anymore, OK?*

—*OK.*

—*I told my mom I don't want to be a nurse.*

—*What did she say?*

—*She seemed relieved.*

—*It's not for everybody, I guess.*

—*That's for sure.*

—*See you later?*

—*I think I need a few days just to think if that's okay with you.*

—*Sure.*

—*Good luck on your test.*

—Thanks. Oh shit!

—What?

—Look at the morning paper! It's all about the body you saw.

—Oh my God! I feel sick.

—Yeah, well.

—I'm not going to tell anyone.

—No, I don't think you should.

—Let me know how you did on your test.

Lydia walked into the kitchen. Her mother was sitting at the table, the newspaper open to the front page. BODY FOUND NEAR TREE ON SECOND STREET. Lydia blanched. Her mother looked up.

"It's awful, isn't it?"

Lydia nodded, biting her lip.

"And it was only two blocks from here. Near that elm tree!" Lydia nodded again.

Her mother closed the newspaper, stood up and took her coffee cup to the sink. Over her shoulder, she said, "Well, I guess they'll find out more soon. Maybe it's someone we know."

Lydia grabbed onto the table. She felt weak. Her mother turned towards her and said, "Lydia! You look like you've seen a ghost!"

"Mom! You seem so nonchalant about this! How can you not be freaked out?"

"I'm sorry dear. I told you, being a nurse, well, you do see a lot of gruesome things. I guess after the first few years, you just kind of get used to it. I mean, it's awful, but you train yourself not to take it home. If you did, you'd have nightmares all the time."

"Even if you know the person?" Lydia looked over at her mother. Who was this woman? Lydia had never really thought about what her mom really did. It had seemed so vaguely interesting to her, and her mother often seemed rather chipper.

"No, of course not, dear. If you know the person, then it really is very hard. Lots of thoughts go through your head. But I guess, as a nurse, seeing so much, you begin to appreciate what you do have."

Barbara went to her daughter and put her arms around her. As Lydia softly cried onto her shoulder, Barbara caressed her hair. Lydia broke the embrace and looked up at her mother.

"Mom, I hope it's not someone we know."

"Yes, dear. I do too."

The news that night gave the name of the deceased. It wasn't anyone they knew. Still, it took Lydia three years before she could walk in the direction of that tree.

The Interview

Baxter Struthers, the VP of Wanderlust Incorporated, opened the door to the board room, adjusted his navy-blue tie, and sat down at the head of the large table in Room six, where they interviewed candidates.

"So, a good friend of mine, Eric Falconer, is applying for the position of PR Manager. He's got excellent references and I would normally recuse myself in that I've known him for so long, but I really haven't been in touch with him for the last five years. I figure it'd be okay. What do you think?"

Baxter tried not to look over at Charlotte, with whom he was having an affair. Just an hour before, they were pawing at each other in the hotel room three blocks down the street.

Charlotte, not looking directly at Baxter either, adjusted the twinkle in her eye and smiled at the other four people on the committee one by one. She was good at this technique. It was said she could disarm a rabid puma with that smile.

"I'm sure that if Baxter feels that he could be fair during this interview, we can all trust his judgement, can't we?"

Jane Beachwood, the CFO, tapped her perfectly manicured, fire-engine red, press-on nails on the table. She despised Charlotte, and had suspicions about her relationship with Baxter, but she wanted to get home to her novel and get this interview over with. They needed someone to do publicity as soon as possible. The last employee had been a disaster. He had spent most of his so-called "business lunches" at the beach, the telltale grains of sand falling onto the floor everywhere he walked.

"Yes, yes, yes." (Tap, tap, tap.) "Let's get on with it, shall we? What did you say his name was?"

Baxter knew that Jane would approve of anything he asked. He had seen her staring at him over the water cooler on several occasions, and couldn't help but notice that she must have gone to a real hair salon instead of cutting her own hair like she seemed to have done when she first started working there. *And those nails! God, they're awful.* Listening to the tap, tap, tap was akin to listening to a faucet drip.

"Eric Falconer."

Peter Jensen, the president of the company, wiped his brow. He was always wiping his brow. No one was sure why he was always sweating, but it could have been all the hard candies he had in the bottom drawer of his desk that he constantly chomped on. He was diabetic and wasn't supposed to be eating candy. No one dared say a word about it. He crunched a few times before he said, "Yes, yes. Let's interview this man. If Baxter says he's exceptional, then he probably is." He grinned, his triple chin jiggling, as he looked from employee to employee.

And then there was Avis. Avis in her perfectly coiffed French twist, her voluminous breasts poured into her Pepto Bismol-colored angora sweater that matched her form fitting angora skirt and two-inch hot pink heels. She was poised over her laptop, at the ready to take notes during the interview. As she handed each person a series of interview questions, her cloisonné bracelets clinked. She didn't get a vote, being the secretary, but she was invaluable, nonetheless.

Baxter looked over at Avis. "10:15 is it?"

Avis checked her notes. "Yes, he's coming at 10:15. I've put each of your initials next to the questions you are to ask him."

Baxter smiled. He loved efficiency. Especially efficiency in an angora sweater.

At exactly 10:15, the door swung open. All eyes were on Eric Falconer. And then they weren't. They were all trying to not look at him. It wasn't that his hair looked as if it had leaves or twigs in it, although it did, and it was pulled back into a man bun. Perhaps it was the open black leather jacket he was wearing, with apparently no shirt underneath it, that made them look down at the table. Or maybe it was the silver ankh that was dangling from a chain on his curly grey chest hairs. It could very well have been the half-moon earring in his left ear. Or, it could have been his tight, black leather pants. But most of all, it must have been the cowboy boots, cut away at the bottom to reveal sandals and crusty toenails badly in need of a pedicure.

Eric smiled widely as he skimmed the startled faces of his possible new colleagues. In a booming voice that could address a room full of 500 people but not five, he bellowed, "Shall I sit down?" He motioned grandly to the empty chair: the hot seat, as it were.

Baxter sputtered as he looked at his old friend, trying to make sense of this new and improved Eric. "Um, sure. Yes. Ahem. Sit down. I must say… well, I really don't know what to say, Eric, but you've changed—shall we say, quite a bit—since the last time I saw you."

Eric unceremoniously peeled off his leather jacket and hung it on the back of his chair. The ankh on his naked chest caught the light from the florescent light on the ceiling.

Baxter cleared his throat a few times, grabbed the paper with the questions, and shoved one towards Eric. "We, uh, have a few questions to ask you. You can look at them now if you'd like." He looked over at his fellow employees, including the president, who sat unmoving, as if anesthetized.

Eric grabbed the paper, quickly looked over at the questions and snorted. He bellowed yet again. "You really expect me to answer these inane questions? Really? I've just come from a human potential workshop at Esalen Institute in Big Sur, and I will not subject myself to corporate bullshit."

All eyes were on Baxter. Not Eric. Baxter.

Baxter stood up, walked back behind Eric's chair, grabbed his leather jacket, and put it back on Eric's bare shoulders.

"You're so very right, Eric. You do not have to answer any inane corporate bullshit questions. All you must do is kindly get your ass out of here. Now!"

Baxter was aware that his voice sounded desperate. At first, Eric seemed taken aback. Then, he smiled. Standing up, he walked briskly towards the door, opened it wide, turned around, and said, "Adios suckers! Good luck with your robotic lives!"

When the door closed, Peter quietly asked Avis to look out the window to make sure Eric was gone. Avis gathered up the questions and practically whispered, "I'll post an advertisement."

The Heir

Lawrence sat in his new-ish Barcalounger. "New-ish" because he had hauled it into his apartment from a block away, where he had seen it on the sidewalk with a "free" sign on it. It was pretty grubby looking, several holes with stuffing coming out, cigarette and who knows what else stains on it, but hey, he had never had a Barcalounger before. He got up and went to the refrigerator, opened it, and pulled out a PBR. Standing in front of the refrigerator, he guzzled down one can, burped, and grabbed another.

He gathered up all the shitty junk mail ads and political stuff and was about to toss it all into the trash, when he saw a letter with his name on it. *What?* The handwriting looked constipated. The return address was from someone named Maybelle Murphy in North Carolina. *Who the hell is that? Maybelle Murphy? North Carolina? Give me a fucking break!*

He sat back down, beer in hand, and opened the letter, scratching his undershirt over his belly.

Dearest Lawrence,

This may come as a shock to you, but your father and I were rather, shall we say close, some 50 years ago. When he married your mother, I was devastated. I had hoped that we could have reignited our friendship over the years, but alas, that never was to be. I knew that he had one son and that his wife passed exactly one year to the day after he did. May they rest in peace. I couldn't bear to live in the same town, for fear I would run into them both, so I moved to Sedgewick, North Carolina and have lived a quiet, if lonely life for over 50 years. I never married, have no children, and, having been an only child, have no close relatives.

I'm writing to you because I have terminal cancer and am not expected to live beyond the next few days. I am dictating this to one of the hospice nurses who is kind enough not only to write without judgement, but to find you on the internet and mail this letter to you.

I have led a frugal life and have a lovely three-bedroom home and a 2010 Subaru that I am leaving to you in my will. I had the house repainted two years ago and a new roof put on. I've kept my car in good shape.

There is a sweet woman named Betsy Miller who has been my caregiver for the past 10 years. I'm indebted to her. She would be very grateful if you would be willing to keep her employed. I don't give her a huge salary, but she has room and board. She is an excellent cook and cleans the house. This, of course, is entirely up to you.

Just know that (I think I can safely say this now) my deep love for your father is the reason it would give me great joy to know his son may be living here.

Sincerely,

Maybelle Murphy

P.S. Enclosed is the deed to the house, the pink slip to the car, and a little extra something.

Lawrence reread the letter three times. He got up, looked at himself in the mirror, and laughed until he found himself almost weeping. Why was that? His dad was a piece of shit. He had made his life miserable. Lawrence had seen him smack his mother around on one too many occasions, and he had felt the sting of his father's belt steadily until Lawrence grew taller and belted him back one Sunday after church. The next day, his father threw him out, calling him a good-for-nothing loser, which Lawrence believed. He could never hold down a job, never keep a girlfriend. His father was right; he was a loser.

He read the letter again. *Sedgewick? How the hell am I ever going to get there?* And then he saw the folded-up check in the envelope. It was for $500. He had almost tossed the envelope out. What a dumbass! $500? Jesus! This is a fortune!

The next day, Lawrence went to the bank, cashed the check, paid his rent in full, emptied the $200 he had left in his account, went to Goodwill, and bought shirt, pants, shoes, and a suitcase. Then he went to the Greyhound terminal and bought a ticket to Charlottesville, North

Carolina. He figured he was so rich now, he could hire a cab to take him to Sedgewick, no matter how far away it was.

The bus ride was long; after three days and nights, finally Lawrence arrived at the destination. He had sat next to a kind, elderly woman who had seemingly bathed herself in Lilies of the Valley perfume, and continuously prayed using her rosary beads. She clutched a Bible and never once said a word to him. That was okay. He was used to people ignoring him. He hadn't brought any food, but the old lady kept handing him baloney sandwiches and grape soda. She must have had ten of those in her bright orange bag. Lawrence didn't understand why she didn't talk. Maybe she didn't speak English? She didn't look foreign to him. But he accepted the food and drink gratefully.

At Charlottesville, the passengers all spilled out of the bus. Lawrence helped the old woman with her overhead suitcase, took down his own, and stepped outside in a torrential downpour. Of course, he hadn't thought to bring an umbrella—not that he had one—but after a quick wave to the old lady, whom he now noticed had a bluish tinge to her hair, he hailed a cab.

The driver stopped in front of a house with a perfectly manicured lawn, with two stone lions out front. Lawrence's breath caught in his throat. *Is this it? Oh, my God. This is mine now?* He tipped the driver generously (he was rich now, wasn't he?), and noticed a light was on inside the house. Walking up to the front door with his suitcase, he ran his hand through his hair, made sure his "new" Goodwill shirt was tucked in, and rang the bell. No answer. He waited and rang again. What would happen if he couldn't get in? Maybelle hadn't sent him a key. *Maybe this is all a hoax?* But it couldn't have been. There had been a $500 check, which he had cashed, and was using.

Then the door opened. Lawrence stood there looking at a buxom, middle-aged woman with a heart-shaped face, big green eyes behind large black glasses, a white blouse with pearl buttons, a big gold cross hanging on her ample bosom, a long, navy-blue skirt, and sturdy black shoes. She smelled like lemons.

"Oh, you must be Lawrence! Do come in, you poor thing. You must be so very tired. I hope you're hungry. I've made lamb stew and peach cobbler." She took his drenched coat, hung it up on a coat rack, and motioned for him to sit in an overstuffed burgundy chair while she warmed the food.

Lawrence, stupefied, put his suitcase down, sat in the chair, looked up towards the heavens and silently said, "Thanks, Dad. Thanks."

The Guest

The hostess, Marty, put out a chair and a table setting for her, just in case she actually showed up. She snickered as she placed a tiara from the Dollar Store on her plate. Oh, and even better, she put a special gold rimmed plate from Annie Glass at her setting.

The doorbell rang. Marty grabbed her wine glass and opened the door. It was Steve.

"Greetings!" He was carrying a bouquet of yellow roses as he bent down to peck Marty, French style, on either cheek.

"Well, these are lovely!"

"Of course, they are, my dear. But just to be perfectly clear, these are for June. Our precious June… in case she decides to bless us with her presence."

Marty tittered as she rushed off to get a vase from the kitchen. She called out, "How good of you to remember her favorite flower!"

"Yes, well…" Steve had entered the kitchen and was watching Marty arrange the roses after she snipped off the bottoms. "We always did enjoy pleasing her, didn't we? It's not as if she didn't tell me pointedly how much she adored yellow roses, every chance she got."

Marty looked over at Steve and in her best deadpan tone said, "She did encourage showering her with gifts, didn't she?"

The doorbell rang again. Steve pranced over to get it. He looked at Marty. "Allow me, my dear. You've got your hands full."

He opened it to Josh, who barely fit in the doorway and was covered in snow. "Steve! My man!"

Josh stomped in, snowflakes melting onto the floor in the hallway as he took off his enormous dark green trench coat and shook it. "Damn! It just started coming down hard." He pulled out a bottle of Chardonnay from inside his coat. "In case her highness deigns to pay us a visit, I brought her favorite wine."

Steve rolled his eyes. "She's way too fucking famous now, really. Isn't she?"

They both made their way to the kitchen. "Mmm. Something smells good in here!"

Marty grinned. "Thank you, hon. I made *Daube de boeuf provençale*. Her favorite."

Josh walked up to the stove and grabbed it with both of his enormous hands. He leaned over, taking in the aroma. "Why don't you just hump it, while you're at it? Maybe you'll make tiny toaster ovens," Steve mused aloud.

The doorbell rang. Steve ran to the door, saying over his shoulder, "I'll give you and your oven some privacy."

Meanwhile, Marty was arranging three different French cheeses, Italian salami, and Greek olives on a heart-shaped platter. "Who's at the door?" she called out.

Steve opened it to Violet, who was also covered in snow. As he gallantly took her coat and hat, shaking off the snow and hanging the items on the coat rack, Violet murmured, "Do you really think she'll come?" She reached into her enormous orange bag and brought out of tray of brownies covered in tin foil.

"No, not really," Marty, Josh, and Steve said in unison.

Violet looked at them one by one. "Then why are we doing this?"

Marty grabbed the tray of brownies, sniffed it to detect weed, and whisked it off to the kitchen. Over her shoulder, she said, "Because she might come."

"I think we should just eat," Josh said, looking forlorn as he sat down at the table. "I'm famished. If she comes, she comes. Isn't she always fashionably late?"

"Did you see her on Oprah last Tuesday?" Steve asked as he lifted his spoon.

"Yes," they all said in unison.

"I thought she handled herself pretty well."

Marty snorted. "Of course she did! If it was me, I would've peed myself."

Violet nodded. "She looked really, really good. I wonder if all the guests have a makeup person. I mean, she always looked good to me, but she looked even better on TV."

Josh had already helped himself to the appetizers and was now digging into the *Daube de Boeuf*. "She's probably forgotten her friends, now that she's so hoity toity." Steve agreed, raising one of his bushy grey eyebrows.

"I mean, we gave her the idea for the book, didn't we?"

Marty stabbed her cheese a bit forcefully. "I guess we did. You're absolutely right!"

"And now," Josh continued, "We're… we're what? Chopped liver?"

A group giggle ensued as more wine was poured. The others tried to ignore that Josh was talking with his mouth full.

Violet said, "I'm surprised she still has the same phone number."

Marty looked pointedly at her. "Doesn't she? Or, I mean, does she?" She used her napkin to politely wipe the juice off her chin.

Steve said, "You did call her, Marty, didn't you?"

Marty stopped eating. "Um, no. I thought you had."

"Who me? No."

Josh smothered a slice of French bread with Brie. "You mean, no one remembered to even call her?"

Violet started to laugh so hard she got the hiccups.

Steve said, "Didn't Oprah say she'd be back as a guest again?"

Violet stopped hiccupping. "Turn it on, Marty! What if she's on right now?"

Marty said, "Alexa, turn on the Oprah show." And there she was. June. Their former friend, June. She was wearing an electric blue pantsuit and fire engine red heels. She had on a bright red scarf and was dangling several gold-colored bracelets.

"Hey! I gave her those bracelets last year after she hinted big-time!" Steve said.

"Yeah, and I gave her that scarf! She practically twisted my arm to buy her that scarf," said Violet.

They watched as Oprah took June's hand, looked directly into her eyes and said, "What's the most surprising thing that has happened to you with the popularity of your book? Be honest, June. You can tell us."

June let go of Oprah's hand, rearranged her scarf and said, "Well, what's most surprising, and frankly disappointing, is that my group of friends have deserted me. We used to be so close. Now, they don't even talk to me."

Oprah grabbed her hand again and said, "Oh, June. That must be so hard. So very hard."

Marty, mouth agape, looked over at her two friends. "What the fuck? We deserted her? Deserted?" Steve put down his wine glass. "Oh, you poor dear. You poor fucking famous dear." Josh nodded as he helped himself to another portion of stew. Their eyes were glued to the TV as they watched June continue.

"Yes, Oprah. It is. It really is very hard."

The Crashers

Samantha Burberry put on her bathrobe, the one with cherries on it, and her blue fuzzy slippers that had yellow smiley faces all over them. Then she took out the big hand-held mirror and her makeup case from her bathroom. As she looked at her wrinkled face, the dark circles under eyes, her dyed red hair with the grey roots showing, she said to herself, *sotto voce*, "I'm going to make you into a fucking movie star. It may be Thanksgiving, but I will not allow you to wallow in self-pity."

First, she got out her lipstick, twisting the bottom so the very last bit of the brilliant, deep red color was visible. Her ropy hands weren't very steady holding the tube, especially after having downed three scotches, but she smeared on the lipstick, missing some parts of her thinning lips and getting some of it onto her teeth. *So fucking what?*

Then Samantha grabbed the glittery, powder blue eye shadow and rolled it onto her drooping eyelids. "Lookin' good, gal," she said aloud, smacking her lips and winking. She walked away from the bathroom and into the kitchen. Steadying herself with one arm on the table, she held onto the back of the dinette chair, eyeing the dog door. *Why haven't I just called someone to seal this off?* Melton, her yellow lab of 15 years, had passed three years before.

She wobbled over to the cupboard, opened it, and took out two of her favorite green china dishes, shaped like avocado leaves. *Should I light a candle? Why the hell not?* Smiling to herself, she held onto the chair closest to the refrigerator and grabbed the turkey leg she had bought from Safeway at lunchtime. Then she took out the little containers of mashed potatoes and green beans and popped it all into the microwave. Pleased with herself, she put her arm around her waist, pretending she was dancing with a very handsome man who was smiling down at her with a lustful look. Swaying to a song inside her head (*Some Enchanted Evening*), she poured herself another Scotch.

The microwave dinged. The aromas of Thanksgiving wafted through her kitchen. Samantha was most pleased. Putting the servings of turkey, mashed potatoes and green beans on the table, she sat down carefully into her wooden kitchen chair. *Oh, I should've taken the linen table napkins out.* She pretended to be talking to the prince whom she decided was seated right next to her, holding her hand and looking deeply into her powdery blue shadowed eyes. "Allow me," she tittered while cutting a slice of turkey for the prince.

With her unsteady hand, the turkey dropped to the kitchen floor. "Oops!" Samantha batted her eyelashes at the prince. "How clumsy of me! Well, never mind. I'll just get it in the morning." She knew she was a tad too tipsy to bend over and get the turkey off the floor without landing there herself and possibly having a difficult time getting up again. "Silly me," she said to the imaginary prince.

And then she heard an unmistakable sound. The familiar sound she had heard for 15 years. The dog door.

"Is that you Melton? Have you come back from the dead?"

Samantha swiveled her head towards the dog door. No, it was not Melton. Not Melton at all. She found herself staring into the eyes of not one, but three full-grown racoons. They were scrambling towards the turkey that had dropped, their claws scratching on her hardwood floor.

"Stop! Stop!" she cried, unsuccessfully trying to shoo them out. All three just looked up at her with their beady eyes and continued skittering around the kitchen floor looking for scraps. Then she remembered the saying of the month. Samantha had a wall calendar with daily pearls of wisdom at the top of each new month. This month's read, "One has no control over what happens in life, but one has control over how one reacts to it."

Hmmm, okay. Time for an attitude adjustment. She reached over and dumped her avocado leaf shaped plate full of mashed potatoes, turkey and green beans onto the floor. The racoon family dove at it, their nails clicking on the floorboards. After devouring this feast in about two minutes, they reared up on their hind legs and looked at Samantha expectantly.

She looked over at her prince and exclaimed, "Aren't they just the most darling creatures?" She then took her cue from the racoons. Unsteadily, but resolutely, she opened the refrigerator door, humming and smiling. Grabbing cheeses, bread, butter, and eggs, she threw it all to the floor.

Watching the animals devour it all greedily, she sat back down and clapped her hands. "Bravo! Bravo!" she cooed at them. When the food was all gone, every last little morsel, the racoon family waddled out the dog door *en masse*.

"Come back again tomorrow, you little darlings!" she cooed after them, holding onto doorways and chairs as she made her way back to the bathroom. She grasped the top of the vanity and looked at herself in the mirror. Winking once more at her reflection, she said, "You do have a lot to be grateful for after all, don't you?"

Strut Your Stuff

"Shhh. I won't tell anyone you're here. Just be very, very quiet. I have a special key to the makeup room. They're all onstage now, so they won't be back for an hour. We have plenty of time. I promise you, this will be your moment. You will never be forgotten."

"You sure about this, Ron?"

Ron had found his big brother, James, the week before in a halfway house. He believed he would never see James again; he had gotten 25 years to life. He had heard that James was out, but no one knew exactly where he had gone or even how he had been released.

Throughout their childhood, Ron had adored James. As far as Ron was concerned, James was better than God. Their dad had overdosed on heroin when the boys were five and eight. Their mom was left to work two jobs to put food on the table and a roof over their heads, so James was both a father and a mother to Ron. James knew which restaurants would give out free food at the end of the night, and which neighborhoods in which to ferret around in the garbage cans to get the really good stuff.

One thing Ron really loved was going to Goodwill and trying on different kinds of clothes, especially around Halloween. He just loved the masks, the glittery shirts, the hula skirts, the fake blood, all of it. Since the Goodwill store was next to a theater company, Ron would hang out and watch the actors in their costumes and makeup. He didn't think he wanted to be an actor, really. But he definitely wanted to make himself look different. Try on different skin, so to speak. And anyway, James had confided in him that what he wanted more than anything in the world was to be famous, and to be on a stage someday. He wanted people to notice him. Maybe even be shocked by him. Ron never forgot this. He swore to himself that one day he would help James get his wish.

By the time Ron was in high school, James was off doing his own thing. Most nights he didn't come back home at all. Their mom was kind of a mess. She was down to just one job, cleaning the house of

Julia Fessina, the famous opera star. She would come home exhausted, plop down onto the sofa, turn on the tube, and smoke a joint.

Ron was now involved in the high school drama club. He loved the backstage stuff the most, like doing makeup for the actors and fitting them into their costumes.

One night, Ron asked his mother if the opera star ever threw out old costumes. She looked over at him and smiled. "All the time!"

Ron begged her to bring them home. "Whatever rocks your boat, sweetheart. I'll bring you whatever she says she doesn't want anymore."

And then they got the call from the police that James had been at the wrong place at the wrong time and had been arrested for attempted murder. Their mother was inconsolable. She blamed herself for not being home enough, for leaving James in charge of his little brother.

"Ma, listen. It's not your fault. We can go and visit James every week. I'll go with you. I promise. And before you know it, he'll be out, and I'll help him like he helped me."

Ron's mother kissed him, but her face was ashen. She never seemed the same after that phone call. In fact, she wasn't. Ron got a phone call from Julia Fessina one afternoon, frantic, telling him his mother had fallen and wasn't responsive, that she had called an ambulance and that he needed to come over to her house right away.

When he got there, the opera star flung open the front door and led him into the living room where his mother was sprawled onto the floor. Ron ran to her, bent down and shook her. He knew she was gone.

The singer came barreling into the room with a suitcase full of costumes, crying. "Here! Take these! Take them all! Your mother said you loved costumes. There are even skulls in there. Four of them! It's not my fault she died! I swear, it's not my fault!"

Ron looked up at the crazed opera star, trying not to focus on the poorly applied lipstick on her lips. "I'm not blaming you" he repeated like a mantra as the ambulance arrived and took his mother away. He left with the suitcase.

Five years later, after searching for what seemed like forever, he found his brother in the halfway house on 3rd Street. "James! James!

Come with me!" he pulled at his brother's shirt.

"Ronnie…I'm no good. You don't want to know me. That's why I didn't contact you. I'm a piece of shit now. I have nothing. Nothing."

"No, listen! Come with me. I've got this cool backstage job at the theater by Goodwill. I'll show you. I'll make you into a new man. A different man. You'll get your wish. Remember your wish?"

"No." James looked at his little brother with cloudy eyes.

"You wanted people to notice you! To be shocked by you. I can make that happen! I can!" He tugged at his brother's sleeve again and pulled him into the street and over to the backstage of the theatre. It was there that he began to strip off his brother's soiled shirt, pants and shoes.

"What the hell are you doing, man?" James looked at his little brother like he had just stepped off a spaceship.

Ron deftly put pancake makeup all over James' face, torso, arms, and legs. He covered up James' genitals with a loincloth. Then he lifted his most prized possession of human skulls on a rope and tied it around James' waist. Ron spun his brother around towards the mirror.

"Look at you! Just look at you! Oh, people will notice you now. For sure, they will. Try strutting around. The skulls make a terrific clinking noise."

James stared at himself in the mirror. There was no denying he was spectacular. Bizarre, yes. And, spectacular. James grinned for the first time in years. He saluted himself in the mirror.

"Okay, now strut!" Ron commanded. James looked at his little brother. They could hear the music coming from the stage. It was loud and obscene. But not as loud and obscene as James in his getup.

"Okay. Now's the moment you've been waiting your whole life for. Go out there and show them who's boss, big brother."

Ron opened the door and walked James to the wings. Then, he deftly shoved James onto the stage. A gasp was heard throughout the audience, the singers, and the orchestra. A stunned silence followed. Then James strutted across the stage, the skulls clinking. He walked from one side to the other and back again. Then he did what he had always wanted to do: he bowed deeply. The audience burst into applause, thinking that perhaps this was an addition to the otherwise rather dull opera they had been witnessing.

James strutted offstage and high-fived his little brother. After a happy, tearful moment, Ron suddenly came to his senses, and threw some clothes over James.

"Okay, now, get the hell out of here as fast as you can."

James hugged his little brother, skulls clinking, opened the backstage door and fled back to the halfway house.

The following day, the two of them could be seen standing over their mother's grave. "Mom, you're not going to believe this…"

Shortest Day of the Year

Moon, the bliss ninny, waltzed down Pacific Avenue in downtown Santa Cruz, her dreads flopping onto her shoulders, long flowery skirt grazing the sidewalk spattered in pigeon shit, seven silver bracelets tingling on her right wrist, ample bosom erupting from her red velour form-fitting blouse. The scent of patchouli oil wafted from her person with every step she took. She looked up to the sky, beaming with appreciation, clasped her hands together and sang out, "Happy Solstice! Thank you!"

Other people walking down Pacific Avenue ignored her, as they ignored most everyone else. There were millennial tech workers, university students, harried tourists, local retirees, people with dogs on leashes, at the ready to pick up their dog's feces in one of those little green plastic bags, and/or keep them from lunging at the other dogs and various unhoused panhandlers.

Moon, clunking along in her Dr. Martens, decided to bring good cheer to one and all. As she passed the Pacific Roasting company, she happily espied a group of senior men sitting together at the outside table, drinking coffee and reading the paper. "Happy Solstice!" she sang as she pranced past their table. They raised their pumpkin spice lattes and double espressos to her in unison. "Yes! Yes! Happy Solstice!" Robert, a regular there, turned to his buddy, John, and said, "I'm just happy to be still alive!" John nodded in agreement, "Yeah, old man. I hear ya."

Moon skipped down a couple of blocks to the sketchier end of the mall. There she encountered a makeshift cardboard lean-to with a homeless man emerging from it. She beamed at him, "Happy Solstice!" The man grunted and turned away. She watched as he walked over to some shrubbery near the sidewalk and urinated.

Determined not to let this behavior upset her, Moon merely turned away as if she hadn't seen that. The man turned to her and snarled, "Got any spare change?" She felt around in her embroidered Guatemalan purse, found $1.50, and handed it over.

"Thank you, young lady. Very kind. Very kind." He took the money and went directly back into his lean-to.

Moon stood there, thinking about what she could do to truly make a difference to this poor man. She decided on a boba drink. The big round balls of tapioca reminded her of the moon. This, in her mind, would be the perfect drink to celebrate the winter solstice. She would buy one for herself (after all, her name was Moon), and one for this man.

Moon lifted the flap of his cardboard and said, "I'll be right back!" The stench hit her right away, but she squelched any reaction. Walking back towards Pacific Thai, she greeted passersby with "Happy Solstice!" Some smiled, some looked at her as if she were speaking a foreign language. She ordered two matcha green tea boba drinks. She figured the matcha would be healthy and might help her and her newfound unhoused friend avoid the flu this winter.

Moon didn't think she could knock on the cardboard with two teas in her hands, so she kicked it. The man jumped out immediately, yelling, "I'm going! I'm going! Can't you leave me the fuck alone!"

And then he saw that it was her. She looked startled and sad, like a puppy that had been whipped for bad behavior. "What the fuck is that shit?" he grumbled, looking at the cups.

"It's boba tea. I thought you might want one." She extended her bejeweled hand towards him.

"Tea? Tea? What the hell do I want tea for?"

"Well, I thought... I thought that the bobas looked like the moon and well, my name is Moon, and I thought, since it's the winter solstice, we should celebrate the shortest day of the year with some heathy tea." Moon looked beseechingly at him. "It's matcha tea."

He scratched his head and squinted at her. "You're out of your fucking mind, lady. I don't want no tea. I need a place to live, and I need for the po-po not to hassle me."

Moon hung her head. "Oh, okay." She started to slowly walk away with the two boba teas in hand.

As she got halfway down the block, she heard, "Yeah, lady. Happy Fucking Solstice."

❧

Read Any Good Books Lately?

Jeffrey Flanders had worked at the Brownsville library for 15 years. He enjoyed working there because it was quiet. He had tried working at the local bookstore, but there was always some sort of drama going on: angry customers, disgruntled employees, anxious booksellers. He found that after a day at the bookstore, it took him several hours to calm down. Wine didn't help. Chamomile tea didn't help. Lavender essential oil didn't help.

And then, there was an opening at the library. They hired Jeffrey on the spot. He was clean, mild-mannered, pleasant, and knowledgeable. Perfect. The last employee had apparently come to work inebriated once too often.

The library itself was old. There was a newer and larger one in the center of town. This one was on the outskirts, and practically no one ever came in. This pleased Jeffrey very much. He could just take any book off the shelf, sit down in one of the overstuffed, threadbare chairs, and quietly read while getting paid minimum wage. Heaven.

And then one Friday night, an hour before closing time, a woman he had never seen before came in. He had been sitting in the chair, reading *Lady Chatterley's Lover*. He didn't even hear the woman at first, so engrossed was he in the novel. When he felt her breeze past him, he jumped up, slammed the book shut, and hoped the blush in his cheeks would diminish. He put on his most pleasant smile and looked over at her inquiringly, putting on his most professional face.

The woman nodded politely and slithered over to the biography section. Just the week before, Jeffrey had lugged over the only other stuffed chair and placed it right in front of that section. *If someone were to read an entire biography*, he mused, *they might as well get comfy.*

He could see the woman from the back as he surreptitiously walked up and down the stacks nearby. She looked to be about 30 years old, give or take. Jeffrey had just turned 41. The woman's jet-black hair was pulled tightly into a bun. She wore a long blue dress that had tiny flowers on it. *What are they? Pansies? Petunias?*

Jeffrey couldn't help but notice that she had perfect posture as she sat erect in the chair, reading the book she had picked out. He wanted badly to know which book it was, but he couldn't very well peer over her shoulder. He also knew that he had better get back to his post at the reference desk, so as not to appear unprofessional.

At exactly 8 p.m., closing time, Jeffrey turned the lights on and off several times. He felt foolish using the microphone to announce the library would be closing soon. There wasn't anyone else in there. And then, there she was, clutching her brown shoulder bag and heading resolutely towards the door. She barely glanced at him as she walked out.

Who is she? It was a small town. Was she new? Did she have family here? There was no one Jeffrey could ask. It would seem odd that he was inquiring after a patron. And why didn't she check out the book she was so engrossed in?

The following Friday, Jeffrey kept looking at the front door. The woman hadn't come in all week. It had actually been an unusually busy week, though, because all the third, fourth, and fifth graders had come in for a field trip. That was exhausting. He hadn't even had time to read any more of his book. But the question now was, should he dare? What if that woman came in and caught him? Oh, but it was so good, so intriguing. Well, maybe he'd just read one chapter and then go back to his station. He remembered that she had come in exactly one hour before closing, so he figured he had better be at the reference desk by 7 p.m. And yes, it was true! The front door opened and the woman, a bit wet from the rain, came in, shook her coat, put her umbrella in the receptacle, shook her hat, and went over to the biography section again. As she walked by, he could smell a lovely aroma of—what was it? *Lilies? Roses?* Oh, how Jeffrey wished he knew his flowers. He'd have to look at those books during the day so he could maybe identify what scent this angel drifting past him was wearing.

Jeffrey couldn't help but creep down the stacks next to the one in front of where she was sitting, in the overstuffed chair. He peered through an open space between two books. Truth be told, he had made sure during the day that there was an open space, so that he could properly spy on her and not be seen. At least he hoped she wouldn't catch him.

And then he coughed. *Damn it! Why did I think to bring a cough drop?* He had a drawer full of them in his kitchen. He cursed his allergies.

Startled, the woman quickly closed the book and put it back on the shelf. Jeffrey had to pretend that he was shelving a book. He couldn't very well run over to the reference desk. Even if he walked quickly, that would look foolish. He coughed again. *Damn it!* Of course, he could feel his face turning that hideous beet color. Taking out his handkerchief, he patted his sweaty forehead and looked over at her, chagrined, as she glanced quickly his way, and then back towards the front door as she exited.

Why didn't she ever check out her book? Whose biography was she reading? He walked over to the section and looked at several possibilities. But he now knew exactly which one it was, because in her haste, she had put it back upside down. D.H. Lawrence. *D.H. Lawrence!* He was overjoyed. He couldn't think of a way to broach a conversation with her about it though. Yes, he was devouring the novel that Lawrence was most famous for, the novel that was not published openly in the United Kingdom until 1960 and was the subject of an obscenity trial against Penguin Books and had sold three million copies.

Jeffrey lay in bed that night thinking about Lady Chatterley and the woman. He tossed and turned. *That gamekeeper on the property was daring, wasn't he?* Jeffrey made up his mind. He would be daring too, for once in his life.

In his best penmanship, Jeffrey wrote: "I am reading D. H. Lawrence's book, *Lady Chatterley's Lover*. I would be honored if you would meet me for tea sometime so we could discuss it. If you would be interested, I am leaving you my phone number here. Please don't be offended. You can just rip it up if you prefer." Then, he poured a drop of the Old Spice that he kept in his bathroom cabinet on the note.

The next day, hands shaking, he placed the piece paper in the front of the biography. On Friday night, he watched, wringing his hands, as the woman walked towards the biography section. He heard her titter. Should he hide?

She walked over to where he was standing, leaned over and kissed him on the cheek.

Life began for Jeffrey that night.

Photos

Jack looked out the window after popping an edible. He may as well have closed his eyes though, as he wasn't focusing on anything outside at all. He mulled over different scenes from his childhood, trying to figure out if he really remembered them, or just thought he did because of the family photos he'd just sifted through at his mother's house. He thought about what a hot day it had been yesterday. Not atypical for Pleasantville in July. But still.

He recalled how stifling the conversation in his mother's kitchen had been, and how easily he had excused himself by declaring to his brother and sister-in-law that no, he didn't want any of her dishes or cutlery, nor any of her million-year-old appliances… none of it. He looked at his brother Jeremy and his difficult wife, Daisy, with her jet-black hair pulled tightly into a bun, and her penciled-in eyebrows arching higher than where her real eyebrows once were. *What did he ever see in her?*

Daisy was busily boxing up plates, cups, saucers, forks, spoons, basically everything in the kitchen. That sure didn't take her long. His mother had had only been dead for two days. He imagined his sister-in-law camping out in a sleeping bag outside the house, just waiting for the green light. His mealy-mouthed brother would just go along with whatever Daisy wanted. *Daisy*. What a ridiculous name. She was the opposite of a daisy. Maybe a Weeping Willow. Her name should have been Weepy. Or, he supposed, Willow would have done. Was his brother always this meek? Jack was the bad son, or that's what their mother had implied.

Jack thought back to the box of photos he found upstairs in the back of his mother's closet. Why did she hide them? He supposed it was because his father was featured prominently in most of them. He did stick around until Jack was ten and Jeremy was 12. Jack wondered if his father even knew their mother had died. And then, if he did, would he have the nerve to show up at the memorial? That could be creepy. Maybe he'd dance on her grave.

Jack found a couple of photos of his dad all dressed up in coat and tails, doing what looked to be a soft-shoe. What was the story? Oh, right. His mother had seen him in a musical and fell head over heels. She used to complain, right before he left forever, that he never was a part of his sons' lives. But those photos of his father seemed to tell quite a different tale. There was one with him on a swing on the back porch with both Jack and Jeremy in his lap. His long arms were around both their shoulders. All three had wide grins.

And then there was one photo where there was a ferris wheel behind them. Both boys had cotton candy and blue stuffed bears in their little arms. Their dad must have won those bears for them. Where was their mom? Maybe she was the one taking the photo?

And the lake; the photo of the two boys with their dad in a boat in the middle of a lake holding fishing poles. All smiles.

But then there were the photos of the brothers at their high school graduations. No dad there. Jack once asked Jeremy if he knew what happened to their dad or why he left them. Jeremy just shrugged. "Who knows? Mom just said he disappeared." How could a dad just disappear? Jeremy didn't seem to even care. Maybe his dad had a girlfriend? Or maybe his dad had some awful disease?

Jack felt the need to find his dad, talk to him, ask him questions. He imagined finding him on the streets with a bottle of wine in his hand, grubby, unfocussed, stinking of urine. He shook his head to erase that thought. Or maybe he was in a nursing home somewhere and had dementia. Jack would approach him, and his dad wouldn't know who he was. He would show him family photos and his dad would grin, sitting there in his wheelchair, nodding up and down, and then fall asleep. Or maybe his dad lived in a high-end apartment building in the middle of New York City, the kind with a doorman. Jack would explain over and over that he was his dad's son, but the doorman wouldn't believe him. Then, the doorman would buzz his father and describe Jack. Jack would hear his father say, "I don't have a son." *Oh God, that would be awful.* Jack shook his head again to get that fantasy out.

He forced himself to have a good fantasy. He and Jeremy would go to a Broadway musical, and his father would be starring in it. The audience would applaud him wildly at the curtain call. Then, Jack and Jeremy (Daisy wouldn't be invited) would wait for their dad outside the theater, where they would greet him with a big bouquet of fancy flowers, white and purple ones. Their father would graciously accept the flowers and then the boys would tell him who they were. Their father would be stunned. He'd stare at them, grab them by the shoulders and look at them, with tears in his eyes, memorizing them. He would then grab them and hold them, crying into their shoulders, saying, "I will never ever leave you again. Never. I promise. Thank you. Thank you. Thank you for finding me."

A voice came over the loudspeaker on the train. *What? What?* The voice was announcing the next stop. "Boston. Boston. The train will be arriving in Boston in 10 minutes." *Boston. Boston? Oh my God! Oh shit! I must have missed the last five stops! I can't go all the way to Boston! The memorial is in Pittsburgh. Oh my God! Oh shit! I can't miss my mom's memorial! Jesus H. Christ. She'll kill me. Well, she's already dead. But everyone else will kill me. They'll hate me. Jeremy will once again be the good son and I'll be the bad son. He and Daisy will be sitting there, glancing at the doors in the back to see when I would run in the door. I know. I'll tell them I was trying to find our father to see if he could come. Oh, sure. That's a good one. Jeremy always said I was a space cadet. He'll say I was too fucking stoned to get to the memorial. He knows damn well that I take edibles for my anxiety. I have a doctor's note.*

Well, I've got to get off in Boston and buy a ticket to Pittsburgh. Actually, I have a ticket that says Pittsburgh. Jesus. They better not charge me for going this far. I wonder how long it will take to get to Pittsburgh. The memorial is at 2 p.m. It's only 11 a.m. Maybe I'll still make it. Oh please, oh please. Let me make it on time. If I make it on time, I will look for my dad. I will look for him and I will find him. Please let me be a hero.

Obit

Ferdinand Costello (1934—2021) finally went on his pathway to hell on Tuesday, March 17th. His loved ones breathed a collective sigh of relief while bringing out several bottles of champagne. Their shouts of joy could be heard up to three blocks away, neighbors said. The fireworks, although understandable, were not appreciated. Sadly, the old buzzard did not die of cancer, Covid-19, liver, kidney, or heart failure. The physician who was called to the deathbed was at a loss to determine the exact reason for death, only the time, which was 9:58 p.m. Mr. Costello was standing on top of the dining room table, shouting obscenities, and collapsed mid-rant. His six adult children experienced a stunned silence before yelling "Hallelujah!" and embracing one another. There will be no service. Ferdinand's cremains will be scattered at the dump at the first opportunity.

Mr. Costello accomplished nothing in his unfortunately long life, other than bringing abject misery to anyone within his circle. He was a wealthy man who never had to work. His inheritance kept him in one of three mansions, with servants who quit most often within two weeks of being hired. His offspring lived in fear of his ill temper. On any given day, one might find one or two of them cowering under a table, or hiding behind another piece of furniture, until the rant seemed to subside. On several occasions, Linda, the only daughter, thought erroneously that she could placate him with interesting stories about her life. This never went over well, as poor Linda learned. She had been seen by the neighbors on more than one occasion, pulling her hair out and pounding the grass on the lawn.

One story that circulated the neighborhood was when a Mrs. Witherspoon moved in across the street and thought she would bring a freshly baked cherry pie over to Mr. Costello. When the servant let her in and she presented the pie to him, Costello grabbed it and threw it in her face, as the story goes. Mrs. Witherspoon moved away the following spring.

His eldest son, Ferdinand Jr., once asked his father if he would come watch him play in a tennis tournament. His father replied, "What? And be humiliated by seeing my son make a fool of himself?"

Their mother lived with the children in one of the other mansions. Ferdinand had forbidden her to leave the house and had guards stationed outside. Now and again, she made several pathetic attempts to try to please her husband, not to mention her children. As they sat at the dinner table, their mother, ever wanting everything to be all right, would ask them to hold hands, bow their heads and say, "Dear Lord in Heaven, when Father is no longer amongst us, life will be good again. We will once again be happy. Thank you for hearing our prayer. Amen." They would then wanly smile at each other and squeeze each other's hands. Several years later the prayer had another sentence added to it: "Please make it soon."

Two years ago, Mrs. Costello fell ill, gathered her children (now adults) around her, and reassured them that soon she would be in a better place. She asked them not to worry about her and to please continue saying the prayer. Her dying wish was that someday, the Lord would hear them, and her children would be freed from tyrant who was their father.

Her wish came to pass last Tuesday, March 17th, 2021, at 9:58p.m. The obituary stated that the main house would be open starting March 18th at 10:00 a.m. Any neighbors who wished to join the family in celebration of Mr. Costello's death were welcome. And if so desired, could accompany them to the dump to scatter his ashes three days hence. The family anticipated yearly celebrations.

Mabel Anderson

We are gathered here today to remember our dearly departed Mabel Anderson. Can you hear me? Hey, you in the back...move closer. There aren't that many people here, and I don't bite. I even used deodorant this morning. You're supposed to laugh at that, not look horrified.

What? What are you staring at? And you in the purple dress… are you fucking kidding me? I can't believe you are wearing that. What? No. That dress was in a box I took to Goodwill just last week. How much did you pay for it? No, really? Jesus! You know how much I paid for that piece of crap? Oh, never mind. No, I'm sorry. I didn't mean to insult you. You obviously have good taste. I mean I bought it too and no, it really isn't a piece of crap. And it looks quite lovely on you. It really does. It looks better on you than it did on me.

Well, where were we? Sorry, your attire distracted me. Oh, right. Mabel. Mabel Anderson. Well, she was high maintenance, wasn't she? Oh, oops. I suppose I'm not supposed to say that now. Motormouth, right?

How many of you really knew her? Raise your hands. Really? What the hell are the rest of you doing here then? What's with you? You just show up at a funeral in case there's a reception with food afterwards? Well, considering there are only ten of you, I think you'll be highly disappointed. There is a McDonald's just down the street, you know. You could even get a Happy Meal if they notice how immature you are.

Why isn't anyone sobbing? That's what you're supposed to do at a funeral. I almost said, "For crying out loud!" Isn't that a scream? For crying out loud!? Get it? God, you people are like a fucking oil painting! Did you ever hear of expressions on faces? I mean, to let the speaker, i.e., me, know you're really listening.

Oh, you in the back with the oversized…what the hell is that? A muumuu? And, oh my God, where are my sunglasses? Those big red flowers on your tent, or whatever it is are blinding me.

Oh, you're coughing now, are you? Well, cough away. Feel free! Just cover your mouth, thank you. After all, we are in the house of God. Okay, already. You can stop now. None of us here want to get whatever crud you have. What is it, walking pneumonia? It is? Well, why don't you just walk right out of here and don't let the door slam you on the back of your muumuu.

You probably think I'm mean, now, don't you? Well, wanna trade places? I didn't think so. And aren't you glad she left?

So, anyway, here we are amongst the living, unlike poor Mabel in that casket. If anyone would like to come up here and say something, feel free. No one? Really? You could make something up. No one would ever know. She certainly won't know. No? No one? Of course, in a scary movie, she'd sit right up and correct you. Oh, God, I'm cracking myself up.

Oh, lest I forget. If you'd like to hire me to speak at your funeral, or anyone you know's funeral, just let me know. I don't charge much and I'm usually available. You'd think I'd be totally booked, but alas, people haven't been knocking down my doors. And if you slip me a little note about the departed, I'll be sure to include it. I can even give you credit, if you prefer. A "for instance" would be, "According to Beth over there in the black dress and red shoes, So-and-so was always a generous and loving person." If you hand me something real snarky, though, I may be forced to tone it down a bit. Just saying.

So, how about you all just come up one by one and, oh I don't know, wave goodbye and be on your merry way?

See you at the next one, hopefully.

Love at Dusk

Cecilia sat under the elm tree in the backyard that her parents had just rented. *Why do we always have to move?* It was a humid day in the middle of July. Pretty soon the mosquitos and the fireflies would be out. She loved the fireflies and, of course, hated the mosquitos. She dreaded going to yet another new school. Being the only kid who didn't have a history with the others made her stomach clench. Would they like her? Would they think she dressed funny? Would they want to play with her? Would she have to pretend she was bad at reading like in her last school, so she could be in the same group as her friends? *I might not even have any friends here, ever.*

She could hear her parents in the new house, arguing. They were living in the downstairs part and another family lived upstairs. She wondered if they had any kids.

Looking around at the grass, Cecilia saw clover. Lots of it. *Maybe I'll find a four-leaf clover and have good luck.* She looked intently at the clover. No; after looking for about half an hour, there wasn't a four-leaf one. She leaned against the tree and closed her eyes.

She must have fallen asleep, because when she opened her eyes, she felt a weight on her lap. Looking down, she saw a grey, furry cat with yellow eyes. She felt its purr. Cecilia didn't want to ever get up. She wanted to sit there forever with this cat in her lap. Her parents had never allowed her to have a pet, even though she had begged them more than once. Almost every kid she knew had at least a dog, a cat, a guinea pig, a turtle, a parakeet, or even just a goldfish. But no, they said no.

The cat kept purring. *Do I dare pet it? Will it run away?* She gently and slowly put her hand on the cat's fluffy back and started stroking it. She held her breath. It didn't run away. It purred even more.

It was getting darker now. Firefly and mosquito time. No matter. No way was she going to get up. Never. If her parents called her, she wouldn't answer, she decided, but she could still hear them talking, although not as loudly as before. She saw a light go on in the room where her parents were, and then her mother pulled open a curtain and looked out the window at her. Don't, please don't call me. I won't come. Her mother seemed satisfied to having seen her under the tree, even with the cat on her lap. Maybe she didn't notice the cat?

Cecilia smiled at the cat as she continued to stroke it. "What is your name? Shall I give you a name?" The cat purred and purred.

Penny would have loved this kitty. She thought of her big sister, who didn't live with them anymore. Penny had run off with her boyfriend Frankie last year, when she was 16. Her parents didn't like him and told her she was forbidden to see him anymore. Penny would sneak out at night to be with him. Cecilia knew this because they shared a room, and she was sworn to secrecy. Penny put a bunch of pillows under her covers to make it look like it was her body in the bed; then she climbed out the window to be with Frankie. He was nice to Cecilia. He gave her Snickers bars and put his finger up to his lips to remind her to be quiet and not tell her parents anything. Cecilia liked how he smelled. He put some kind of stuff in his black hair and slicked it back. She also thought he looked cool with his chipped front tooth. Sometimes when Penny came home late at night, Cecilia would hear her crying into her pillow. When she asked her what was wrong, Penny just whimpered and said, "Never mind."

Penny had met Frankie at the movie theatre in the last town they lived in. She worked there on weekends, selling popcorn and candy. He was the manager or something. At least, Penny said he had keys to the place and could let them in whenever they wanted to see a movie. Cecilia didn't dare. She thought if her parents found out, they'd be really mad.

Two weeks before they moved to this new town, Cecilia heard Penny and her mother talking in whispers. Cecilia seemed very upset and was saying, "No, no, no!" And, "Don't tell Dad!" And, "I won't. I won't. I won't! You can't make me!"

That night, Penny sat on Cecilia's bed and said to her, "Don't tell Mom and Dad, but I'm going to run away with Frankie. I want you to know that I will always love you, and I will find you again someday. I don't want to move again. I love him so much. I just can't leave him. It's so unfair. Be a good girl. I will try and find a way to get messages to you without them knowing, okay?"

Cecilia just looked at her big sister and tried not to cry. Where would they go? Would Frankie be good to her? Why didn't her parents like him? She watched as Penny tore out a bunch of clothes from her drawers and stuffed them into a bag. And then, there was a tap on the window.

Penny leaned over and gave Cecilia a kiss on her cheek. "I love you!" she blurted through her tears as she fled out the window, lugging her bag.

Cecilia's parents were frantic when they realized Penny was gone. They went to the school and the movie theater. Penny wasn't there. She had written them a letter and left it on her bed. Of course, Cecilia had read it.

Dear Mom and Dad,
Please don't look for me. Don't worry about me. I know you hate Frankie, but I love him. I'm going to have his baby and we're going to go live with his relatives in Tennessee. His mom seems really nice, and they will take care of me. Once I have the baby, I'll write to you and let you know how we're doing. Please don't worry. And don't look for me.
Love,
Penny

Cecilia got a knot in her stomach. She didn't even want to see her parents react. Of course, they questioned her over and over again, but she really didn't know much at all. And then they moved to the new town. They told Cecilia if she ever heard from Penny, she was to tell them right away. She promised she would.

Cecilia thought about Penny's baby all the time. What would it look like? Would it be a girl or a boy? Would it have blonde hair like Penny's, or black hair like Frankie's? Would she ever get to play with it? *Maybe if they come to visit, I could show it the fuzzy cat with the yellow eyes.*

She could see the fireflies now, but she didn't want to move. The mosquitos were biting her bare arms and legs, but she didn't dare slap them away. She might scare the kitty, her new friend. The cat lifted its head so she could scratch under its chin. Cecilia looked into its yellow eyes that were closing now, contented. *Someday I'll be happy, just like you. You'll get to meet Penny and my new niece or nephew, and they'll pet you. You can purr for them and sit on their laps. Maybe even Frankie will come and want to pet you. Maybe they'll want to take you home with them to Tennessee. But I won't let them. No, you're my kitty.*

Just then, her mother came outside. "Oh, what have you got there? A cat?" She smiled. "Well, honey, it's time to come inside."

Cecilia didn't move. She just shook her head. Her mother crossed her arms across her chest and furrowed her brows.

"Okay, Cece. I'll ask Dad if you can keep it."

Cecilia looked up at her mom and down at the kitty. "Guess what?" she said to the cat, "I'm starting to feel happy now!"

She slowly got up as the cat jumped off her lap and walked off further into the backyard, flicking its tail. Cecilia, looking back at it, smiled, and then entered the new house, smiling.

I think I'll name you Penny.

Hello Out There

Ruby sat watching *Les Enfants du Paradis*— (*Children of Paradise*) in her film class. She was mesmerized by the character of the love-stricken mime during the time of the Nazi's in France. The actor was Jean Louis Barrault. The pain of unrequited love emanating from his tragic face. was frozen in her mind and her heart. Maybe it was the music? Who knows?

The next semester, she took an acting class. There were only 16 students. The instructor was a well-known director and playwright from Berkeley. The students hung on to his every word. But Ruby wasn't focused on him like all the other students were. No; she was focused on the strange student who looked so much like Jean-Louis Barrault, it was almost painful. Whenever she looked at him, the beat of her heart became erratic. They were assigned to each other as scene partners. They chose a one-act play by William Saroyan called *Hello Out There!*, about a young naïve girl who helps a criminal named Photo-Finish to escape from jail in a small Texas town.

In the play, Photo-Finish, mostly referred to as "A young man," puts his hands through the bars and caresses the girl's hair, telling her she's beautiful. After he finally convinces her to give him the keys, and he reaches through the bars to open the cell, he takes the girl's face in both hands and kisses her before he flees, leaving her behind.

The Jean-Louis Barrault look-alike didn't own a car. He lived in Hollywood, about a 20-minute drive away from Ruby's parents' house, where she was still living. They met at his mother's apartment to rehearse their scene for the first time. Ruby had a hard time concentrating. She just wanted every moment they enacted to be real.

His mother wasn't going to be home, so Ruby spent the night, sleeping next to him, fully clothed. They groped at each other and kissed a bit, but that's all. He seemed tense. She thought she was supposed to breathe at the same time as he did. She barely slept at all.

The next day, he called and told her she needed to make an appointment at the medical center.

"Why?"

"You might be pregnant."

She was incredulous. "But... but… we didn't do anything."

He waited a moment before saying, "I could have done it in my sleep."

She began to doubt her sanity, but said, "I'm not going to the medical center." She could tell he was angry. He didn't respond.

After that, they rehearsed at school. She felt like she had to walk on eggshells around him. He never kissed her outside of the rehearsals. She pined for him but said nothing.

The night before they were supposed to present their scene, he told her he couldn't live without her. She couldn't believe she was hearing those words. After rehearsing and an especially long kiss, he took a bus back to Hollywood. She got in her green and white '57 Ford Fairlane and drove home. Her room was an add-on in the back of her parents' house. She got into bed, thinking of him, and of *Children of Paradise*, sweet sorrow.

About 2 o'clock in the morning, she awoke to a sound outside her window. What?

"Ruby! Ruby! Ruby!"

It's his voice! Oh my God! What is he doing here? He must have walked all the way from Hollywood! That's insane! Unbelievable!

"Ruby! Ruby! I have to see you! I have to hold you! Please! Let me in! I won't stay long. I won't make any noise. I promise. I have to see you and kiss you."

She stood up on her bed and looked down from her window. There he was, in the driveway. Putting a finger to her lip to signal for him to be quiet, she motioned for him to use the back entrance. Her parents wouldn't hear him if he was very quiet. Shaking, she rushed to the back door and slowly opened it.

He scurried in and grabbed Ruby into is arms. Silently, she took his hand and lead him to her bedroom. She couldn't believe this was really happening. *This is so fucking romantic!* They groped each other, smothered each other kissing, and he ripped off his clothes. He lifted her nightgown up off her head. She'd never had sex before, only heavy petting. He reassured her he had done it many times before.

"I love you. I love you. I love you," he whispered into her ear. She wasn't exactly sure what was happening, but he was fumbling, and soon she felt a sharp pain. Seconds later, he bolted upright, threw on his clothes, and ran out the back door. She lay on the bed, stunned. Several minutes later, she looked out the window. He was gone. *Did he walk home? Does he really love me?*

In the bathroom, she saw the blood. *So, that's it. Just like that. I'm not a virgin anymore. Hmm. Was it great? No.*

The next day in acting class, he avoided her. She tried to catch his eye unsuccessfully. *Did I do something wrong? Why won't he look at me?* This went on for the entire rest of the semester. She wanted to die. One day she found herself in the library, unable to remember just how she got there. *I must be going insane. I have to get out of here. I can't bear it.* Feeling soiled, she asked and received a break from the university for one semester. She fled to New York City.

Three months later, he called her in New York. She didn't know how he got her phone number. "I want to apologize," he said. She didn't know what to say.

"It must have been awful for you, the sex, I mean." She still didn't know how to respond. It wasn't exactly memorable, but then again, she had nothing to compare it to. It certainly wasn't anything like the stuff she'd read about.

"I need to tell you that I was a virgin," he said. *Oh.*

Ruby wondered what he wanted from her. She supposed he wanted to hear that it was great, or that she forgave him. But it wasn't, and she didn't. She wasn't mad at him, just disappointed in herself. She lost her virginity to him because he looked like Jean-Louis Barrault. Plain and simple. *What a fucking idiot I was.*

She finally spoke. "Thanks for calling me," she said, and hung up. He called her again 10 years later to tell her his mother passed away and thought she'd want to know. Really?

Maybe she should watch *Les Enfants du Paradis* again, she thought. Or not.

Have Some More

Joanne's parents were known to throw afternoon parties on the weekend. They had a large backyard replete with Magnolia and Maple trees. Her mother loved to make canapes and to decorate the tables with ornate flower arrangements. She often hired caterers who made elaborate finger foods and fantastical alcoholic beverages, not to mention the desserts to die for.

It was the middle of summer, so the temperature was fairly perfect. The humidity was a bit oppressive, but bearable, especially after downing a few pear martinis, the mosquitos and heat were barely noticeable.

Normally, Joanne could ignore the tables full of enticing food, but for some reason, probably nerves, she sauntered out into the backyard and took a little delicious treat from each of the four tables. She tried not to disturb the design of the food, noticing the sideways glare of the caterers as she slipped one after another into her mouth. What could they say really? Her mother had probably paid them handsomely. Yum! This lox, cream cheese and capers on dark rye was scrumptious. And the crab meat and brie with a slice of casaba melon…oh, to die for. Of course, Joanne couldn't help but think about the dinner date she was supposed to have that night with that guy she met in the cafeteria at the university. Where was he from? Uruguay? Venezuela? Somewhere exotic. And he had on a powder blue cable sweater that looked squeezable. And then her bestie Barbara begged her to meet her at Pink's Hot Dog Stand in Hollywood. Really? Now? Why? Oh, some guy you want to impress? Why do I have to go? Oh, ok. He won't care if you're going alone. Oh, all right. Before she left, she popped a blackberry agave avocado pudding into her mouth.

So, Joanne hopped into her '57 Ford Fairlane, which, of late, had been sounding a bit off, and headed out to Hollywood. She parked on the side street around the corner from Pinks. As she walked in the door, she saw Barbara frantically waving her arms in were held two of the famous hot dogs, full of sauerkraut and mustard. Her mouth started to water.

"Listen, I'm kind of full. I ate a shitload at my mom's banquet just an hour ago."

Barbara shoved the hot dog under Joanne's nose. *Mmmm. Smelled so good.*

"Oh, okay. What? I'm supposed to look like we were just accidentally here eating when your heartthrob walks in?"

Barbara nodded, her mouth full of hotdog.

"How do you even know he's going to show up?"

Barbara swallowed. "Because, because he said he likes to go here in the afternoons on Saturday around 4 p.m. and get his hot dog before the crowds get here."

The door opened, and a rather scrawny looking guy with hair in a ponytail walked in. Barbara pretended to be surprised to see him.

"Oh, hi!" she waved and grinned.

"Oh, hi!" he responded.

Joanne was thinking, "A match made in heaven."

After Mr. Perfect got his hot dog, he walked over to their table and said, "Mind if I join you two ladies?"

Joanne practically flew out of her chair, announcing, "I really need to get back to my mother's house. She's expecting me. Nice to meet you!" She held out her soiled hand, adding, "I'm Joanne." A mouthful of food didn't stop this man from saying, "Oh, hi. I'm Christopher." He stuck out his bony hand, dripping with mustard. It was all Joanne could do to shake it, but she did.

Moments later, she was getting into her car, but not without noticing the couple in the car parked behind her, going at it. Did the girl have her top off? Really? In the middle of the day? Joanne rolled her eyes. Then, turning the key in the ignition, nothing happened. *Shit! My car won't start! It won't start! And I have that date with the guy in the powder blue sweater tonight! I'm going to have to call AAA! Where is a phone booth?* She saw one on the corner of the street about a block away. Walking quickly to the phone booth, Joanne started to feel queasy. *Oh no.* She put her hand on her stomach. Oh no. After explaining to AAA that she was parked on the side street by Pink's and describing her car, she walked slowly back hoping she wasn't going to puke. As she got to her car, however, not only was the couple still in the throes of passion, but the buffet at her parent's house and the Pink's hotdog decided to revolt. She puked right by the side of her car. *Oh, shit. Oh shit.* The couple didn't notice of course, but the AAA guy was sure to. She tried to make it all land in the curb. Most of it did.

After the AAA guy gave her a jump, he told Joanne that she would probably need to get a new battery one of these days. He also told her to keep the car running for at least 20 minutes once he started it. She just nodded; mouth tight, hoping there was no leftover vomit on the sides of her mouth. "Okay, young lady. Be good!" Was he grinning? Jesus! "Be good?" Did he think she had been drinking? Well, she did have 2 pear martinis, but she thought it was Pink's that did her in.

She got in the car and drove around very carefully for the 20 minutes the AAA guy suggested. She was still feeling pretty sick to her stomach. Oh God, don't let me puke inside my car. Please. Not inside the car. She looked down on the floor of her car on the passenger side. Oh. Those. There were papers strewn about from her classes. Some were marked, and some she hadn't yet remembered to turn in. Jesus! What if she puked on those?

When Joanne pulled up in her parent's driveway, she was thinking, *Oh, good. I can just take a nice hot bath and go to sleep.* But then she remembered. *Oh, no! That guy! That south American guy in the blue cable sweater! We're supposed to have dinner tonight! Dinner! Oh, sure. That's exactly my idea of a great time tonight. Dinner. Well, what am I going to tell him? I have to tell him something. I can't go. If I tell him my car broke down, he might say we should take a bus. I can't exactly tell him I've been eating non-stop since 2 p.m., although that's the truth. Maybe he'll think that's what all American girls do. We eat until we puke.*

Joanne picked up the phone and dialed his number, hoping his answering machine would pick up. "Hello?" No such luck. "Oh, Guillermo? Yes. So, I… I'm afraid I have to cancel for tonight. I'm not feeling well. I'm not sure what came over me, but I just can't think about going out anywhere. What? No, I'll be okay. I just need to stay home tonight. What? Well, yes, in fact I do have an essay I'm supposed to write for my English class. Oh, thanks, but no. I really have to do it myself. I can't concentrate if someone else is there. What is it about? Oh, cultural differences, I think. Yes, thank you. Maybe on Monday, if I see you in the cafeteria, you can listen to it and give me some pointers. Yes, I think it's mostly about the concept of time, but it could involve other things, I'm sure."

Joanne was starting to feel her stomach threaten her. "Listen, Guillermo, I really have to…" She hung up.

The following Monday, she was afraid to go to the cafeteria to see if Guillermo was there. She waited two full weeks to get up the nerve. She never saw him again.

Elevator Man

Yeah, so, Tony, listen…I gotta get my girl something you know, impressive-like. I mean, she says I never get her anything, that I'm a big nobody, that I don't take her nowhere, don't appreciate her, blah, blah, blah. So, I wanna blow her fuckin' mind, right? I wanna surprise her for her birthday next week and give her like diamonds or something.

So, here's the deal. I got this new job, see? Remember Frankie? Yeah, well, he kicked the bucket two days ago. Yeah, real tragedy. Nice guy. The thing is, he knew he was dying, you know, so he told me he'd recommend me for his elevator job at that fancy-ass apartment building on Park Avenue. Yeah. He said all them rich folks were real nice to him. All I got to do is look the other way, you know… mind my own beeswax when I take them to their floor. He said there's a real looker who lives in the penthouse. He said she's kinda old, but rich as shit and he thought she was horny too. He said she was always a little tipsy, leaned on him, even played with his goddam hair, can you believe it? But, you know Frankie. Yeah, he didn't want any part of it. His old lady woulda bashed his fuckin' head in if she caught him messin' around with any rich dame in that building. And besides, he had all kinds of shit wrong with him…high blood pressure, gout, diabetes… he was a wreck.

Anyways, before he kicked off, he told his boss about me, and that guy hired me on the spot as soon as I walked in the door. Easy peasy. Didn't even check my record. So yesterday was my first day on the job. Piece o' cake. And that broad Frankie warned me about? Jesus H. Christ, he wasn't foolin'. She was all over me with her fancy perfume, and her diamond bracelets, rings, and necklace. But I couldn't exactly rip the jewels offa her. Especially not the first day on the job.

So, this is where you come in. All's I'm askin' is, you go to Mr. Peterson, he's the boss, and tell him you're a window washer. It

don't matter if you never done it before. Listen to me. Just go borrow
some window cleaning shit from Jack. Tell him I sent you. Watch
him sweat. He owes me. Tell him to give you some pointers.

Yeah. Don't worry about it. You'll do fine. You afraid of heights?
No? Good. So, this dame lives in the penthouse, see? You go wash
her windows and figure out how to break into her apartment. Then
you just look around to where her jewelry box is, probably on her
dresser or something, and you grab a necklace or a ring and stash it
in your pocket. What's in it for you? Oh, right. Well, grab two things
and I'll give you half of whatever we can sell one of them for at the
pawn shop. Probably at least $500. Easy peasy. Then, you quit your
job, see?

No, you don't give the boss your real name or your real address.
That way he can't find you, see? It's simple. I can't wait to see the
look on Zelda's face when I hand her a diamond ring. She'll shit
bricks. Nah, don't worry about it. Nothing can go wrong. Call me
when you got the goods.

Hey, Charlie? Listen, we gotta talk. It didn't work out as
planned. Yeah, I borrowed the window cleaning shit from Jack. He
wasn't too happy about it neither. Yeah, Peterson said I could wash
the windows. The thing is, he asked me how much I charged. How
the fuck do I know? I didn't know what to say, so I says the first
thing that comes to my mind. I says, $500. No, I'm not shittin you.
And the fucker agrees!

Then, he says, who do I make the check out to? He got me
on that one. I didn't want to give him my real name like you said,
so I says, Jack Miller. I know that was stupid. I couldn't think of
any other name. So, what if Jack won't give me the money? Well,
anyways, that's just the beginning of what went down.

So, yesterday, I go to wash the friggin' windows. I don't know
what the hell I'm doin. I mean, Jack kinda told me, but I didn't even
know how to make sure I didn't fall off the friggin' platform. So,
anyways, I start on the first window and you know, you can't help
lookin' inside. These fancy ass people are eating some three-course
meal or something. Candles, tablecloths, the whole nine yards. They

have this maid serving them and some other dude pouring wine for them. Real classy.

The thing is, these rich people, they don't even talk to each other. They didn't say one friggin' word to each other. I swear to God. If it was my house, we woulda all been screamin' and laughin' or something. But nothin'. Not a goddamn word.

Yeah, so I don't want 'em to know I was starin' at 'em, so I move up to the next floor. They have the friggin' curtains closed. I hear thumpin' and moanin' though, so I pretty much guess what kinda party is goin' on there. Hold your horses. I'm getting' there.

Yeah, so the next floor, these two dudes are dancin' together. Nah, I don't care what people do. It was just kinda weird watchin' them is all. They looked happy. Yeah, it's a free country. Yeah, I'm gettin there.

So, I go to her window. The rich old lady. Yeah. So, I kid you not, the second I start washin' her window, she comes right over and opens it up. I tell her I can't wash it if it's open, and she just grabs me and yanks me inside her place. So then, get this, she offers me a glass of wine. Me. I can't fuckin' believe it. Yeah, I took her up on it. Of course, I did. This was like a fuckin' dream. Some rich old lady offering Tony Paccione glass o' wine in her hoity-toity apartment. And the wine was good too. Didn't even bite back.

So then, this broad starts, like, touching my hair, and she tells me I have pretty eyes. I didn't even take offense at pretty. I mean, she coulda said handsome, but what the hell. Then she starts rubbin herself all over me. Yeah, she's old, but so what? I mean, a man's gotta do what a man's gotta do, right?

I'm gettin there. Hold on! So she asks me if I can cook, and I tell her I can make ravioli like you can't believe, and cannoli that'll knock her socks off. So, she says, "Tony, can you come over tomorrow and make me ravioli and cannoli?" I say, yes, ma'am. I sure can.

So, yesterday, I go over there. Hey, you weren't in the elevator. Why not? What? They fired your fuckin' ass? What? You looked suspicious? Yeah, well. So, sue me. You do look suspicious. There was some old lady there. Yeah, they hired an old lady to run the elevator. Sign of the times. Women's lib. No, she wasn't no looker. She looked like the back of a bus. And let me tell you, you wouldn't want to mess with that bitch. No way. She looked like she could chew you up and spit you out in no time flat.

So, anyways, gettin' back to Betty, that's her name, the rich lady… I make her my killer ravioli and cannoli, and she practically has an orgasm. After we kill off a bottle of her wine, she invites me to come live with her. No, I'm not kidding. I'm moving in tomorrow. No, I didn't get the friggin' diamonds. What do you take me for? You think I'm gonna filch off the old lady? I mean, my old lady? Yeah, that's right. Cry yer eyes out. Yeah, maybe if you're real nice, we'll invite you up there sometime. But, you gotta promise to keep your paws off her diamonds, capeesh?

Dollface

Dolores dreaded visiting her aunt in Calgary. The only reason she was going was to bring her eleven-year old daughter Celia for her aunt to dote over and hopefully offer her a good sum of her inheritance early. Aunt Ida was the last living relative of the three sisters. She was childless and known to fawn over the children she could never have. She lived alone in an upscale apartment in a gated village for the elderly. Her husband had died years ago of a sudden heart attack. He had been an antique dealer and was well known in the community for his collections of rare and beautiful items. One reason he became so wealthy was because he offered to make life-sized dolls for clients who would send in photographs of their children. He had sent Dolores one such doll when Celia was nine. As far as Dolores was concerned, this doll was hideous. For one thing, it wore a lacy powder blue bonnet, and a lacy blue and white dress with white bloomers underneath. It also had black patent leather shoes with frilly white socks bedecked with tiny roses. Celia hated the doll as much as her mother did. Celia, much to her mother's delight was a tomboy. Not only would she never be seen wearing a dress, but heels and a bonnet were simply unacceptable. Laughing, Dolores and Celia stuffed the doll into the furthest end of the walk-in closet in their shabby apartment in Winnipeg.

Dolores knew only too well that her Aunt Ida was getting on in years. She dutifully if not regretfully, called her once a week to pretend to check up on her well -being. The conversation usually ended with, "When are you and your lovely child going to visit your poor aunt? What was her name again?" And the reply was "Oh, soon. As soon as school is out. Her name is Celia, Aunt Ida. Celia."

Now school was out. It was August, the most humid month of the year. Dolores, having had no child support checks for the past year, as the father of Celia was a deadbeat, found herself thinking about all the antiques in her aunt's house and the possible money that was stashed away. She figured she'd just make herself and Celia look as presentable as possible and lather on the compliments to her aunt. Her aunt was quite vain and loved to hear things like, "Oh, Aunt Ida, you don't look a day over 50!" In reality she looked like an apple doll. Or "Oh, Aunt Ida, that necklace is so becoming. Did Uncle Frederick buy that for you?"

Then, she and Celia would have to listen for the hundredth time to where and when Aunt Ida had received the garnet necklace or how her latest trip to the cosmetologist was so expensive, but worth it.

When Dolores broke the news to Celia of the pending visit, she was greeted with a temper tantrum.

"I hate her! She smells bad! Her house is gross! There's no one to play with."

"Yes, dear. But she may give us some money. A great deal of money. And she has dementia. She might not even remember who you are or who I am for that matter."

"So what?"

"Well, if she gives us money, I can buy you fine things."

"I don't want fine things… like what, for instance?"

Dolores had to think about it.

"A new baseball cap and uniform."

Celia's eyes lit up.

"And Converse? Red ones?"

"Sure."

It was decided then, Dolores reluctantly doled out the $70 dollars for the train tickets. She had to buy seats in a sleeper car. She couldn't imagine Celia not running up and down the train, disturbing everyone. She packed them tuna sandwiches and a couple of orange sodas.

When Celia came out from her bedroom the morning of the trip, she was carrying a large suitcase.

"Why are you bringing that? It's very big. We're not going to be gone that many days."

Celia grinned.

"You said she might give us a ton of money. This is for all the baseball gear I'm going to buy in Calgary."

Dolores raised her eyebrows and laughed. Her daughter was definitely planning on taking advantage of this trip, as was she.

When they got to their seats, Celia jumped up and down on the bunk bed and climbed to the top one.

"I want this one, mom."

"But.."

"Please? Pretty please?"

Oh, that Celia could be a charmer when she wanted to be.

"Well, okay. Just go to sleep when I ask you to. I want you to look presentable for Aunt Ida."

Celia made a face, but soon thought better of it. She really wanted the top bunk.

"I will. I promise, Ma."

After they ate their sandwiches and drank their sodas, Dolores gave Celia permission to climb up to her bunk bed early. Celia jumped up and down at least 30 times, until Dolores said,

"That's enough! Now go to sleep. I'm just going down the hall to see if I can buy us any crisps and to see if there's a coffee machine. I'll be right back."

"Okay, mom."

Dolores was grateful to get away from the jumping and was curious about what else there was on the train. She secretly hoped there might be a handsome available looking man who might rescue her from her drudgery. Maybe she could even have a quickie in his room. She laughed at herself. *Oh my God, you are so desperate. When was the last time you had sex? Five years ago?* Robert left when Celia was one and Dolores was too exhausted being a single mom to think about men.

Dolores went into the dining car. She saw a family with two children about her daughter's age but thought better of going back and getting Celia. *No, I don't want to take any chances.* And then, sitting by himself, she saw a rather dapper looking gentleman reading a paperback. She was trying to read the title, when he looked up abruptly and said, "Oh, hello. Yes. I'm reading a book I should have read a long time ago, I'm afraid. It's *Lady Chatterley's Lover*. I saw the movie, but I never read the book. So often they're so different, don't you think? Have you read it?

"Um. Yes. A long time ago."

Dolores had a flash memory of having masturbated while reading it. She flushed.

The man patted the seat beside him and said, "Do have a seat. I'd love to discuss it with you."

Dolores looked at her watch, worried about Celia, but thought, *Oh, what the hell. This may be the chance of a lifetime.*

An hour and a half later, Dolores could be seen slithering out of a compartment that wasn't hers and rushing towards her own with a big grin on her face.

She didn't want to wake Celia, so she just looked at the lump under the covers. She got into her bed, pulled up the covers and fell fast asleep, the best sleep she'd had in years.

In the morning, it was rather noisy in the train. She awoke with a start.

"Good morning, luv."

No response.

"Celia! Wake up!"

No response.

Dolores stood up and put her hand up to the covers in the bunk bed above hers. Something was wrong. It didn't feel right. Celia's body wasn't warm. In fact, it was cold and hard. Dolores climbed the couple of rungs and threw off the covers. It was then that she screamed. The life-sized doll in the exact replica of Celia was lying there with a permanent smile on her face. How did that doll get here? Dolores was sure they had stuffed it into her walk-in closet. Dolores frantically stormed through the train rudely opening all the compartments looking for her daughter. She startled several people in various stages of dress. And one other couple in a rather compromising position.

This is my punishment. This is what I get for allowing myself a slip.

She finally found her in the baggage car, sitting cross-legged next to group of suitcases.

"What are you doing here? And why did you bring that doll?"

Celia was frowning.

"Mom. I really don't want to see Aunt Ida. She's so awful. I thought maybe you could just bring the doll in and pretend it's me."

Dolores looked at her daughter in disbelief.

"Well, that's very inventive, but no way. There is absolutely no way I'm going to do that."

Celia crossed her arms over her chest and glared at her mother.

"I'm not going to move from here. If you want me to come, let that stupid doll go in my place."

Dolores turned to hear the door opening to the baggage car and saw the man from the night before.

"Hello luv. I've been looking all over for you! Are you trying to hide from me?"

Celia looked back and forth from the man to her mother.

"Who's he?"

Dolores blushed.

"Just a friend. Never mind."

She watched as her daughter plastered an evil grin on her face.

"I bet Aunt Ida would like to hear about him, wouldn't she?"

Dolores inhaled deeply, grabbed her daughter by the elbow and whispered in her ear.

"Shut up. Okay. I'll bring the doll instead of you. You can wait outside for me."

Celia triumphantly skipped back to their compartment.

Three hours later, they were dropped off in front of Aunt Ida's apartment. Dolores gave the cab driver extra money, asking him to wait for her, that her daughter was going to wait in the cab and that it would only be about 45 minutes.

Dolores then asked the cab driver to grab the large suitcase for her. She smiled wanly and lugged it up the steps. Outside of the Aunt Ida's apartment, Dolores unzipped the suitcase and extracted the replica of Celia. She brought it inside and sat it beside her on the green couch facing Aunt Ida and the Earl Grey tea and raspberry crumpets she had prepared. After several minutes of pleasantries, Dolores announced that she and Celia had to catch the train, that it had been a lovely visit and she was so happy to see Aunt Ida looking so youthful and well.

Aunt Ida beamed.

"What a perfectly obedient child. She's just lovely! Thank you for taking the time to visit me. I'll be sure to include a great sum in my will to the both of you. What did you say her name was again?"

"Celia. It's Celia."

"Promise me you'll bring her again soon."

"I will, Aunt Ida. I will."

Dolores ran to the window and looked out at the cab. Yes, it was still there.

She gave Aunt Ida two quick pecks on either cheek and waved goodbye.

"Isn't Celia going to kiss me too?"

Dolores held her breath.

"Oh, Aunt Ida. She's very shy. And she's been exposed to a friend who just had a bad cold. She doesn't want to pass that along to you."

Aunt Ida put her hand up to her mouth. Dolores couldn't help but notice the large ruby ring on her left forefinger.

"What a thoughtful child. I congratulate you on doing such a good job of raising her on your own. Don't forget to bring that lovely child again."

Dolores grabbed the doll by the waist and managed to lift one of its arms to wave goodbye to Aunt Ida who waved gaily back. As she descended the steps with the suitcase and the doll, she saw the cab driver standing outside by the car, smoking. He looked up just as she was stuffing the doll into the suitcase.

How am I going to explain this?

Celia had been watching from inside the cab. She looked at her mother's face and knew she had to come to her rescue. When her mother was seated and the driver was at the wheel, she said,

"My aunt just loves dolls. Especially life-sized ones."

She felt her mother relax, put her hand over Celia's and then try to keep a straight face. A face as straight as the doll's.

Cafeteria Hero

Freddie slumped in the chair that he was so used to sitting in. Yes, here he was in Principal Johnson's office. As always, Freddie just looked down at his ragged tennies. He wasn't about to make eye contact.

He heard Principal Johnson sigh as he shuffled papers on his desk.

"It says here that you were seen selling some kind of pills on the playground."

Freddie grunted.

"Well? Well, young man? Were you selling drugs?"

Freddie looked up. "You tell me. Was I? Can you prove it?"

"Listen, pal. If you were really selling drugs on our campus, you will be taken directly to juvenile hall, understand?"

"I ain't got nothin' on me." Freddie stood up and emptied the pockets of his jeans. Two quarters and one dime fell onto the wooden floor.

"I was also told that you had snuck into the cafeteria after hours and stole some of the food. What do you have to say about that?"

Freddie shook his head. His black hair badly needed to be washed. He had an image of his mother at the kitchen table the night before, sitting there in the same yellow dress she always wore, with the apron that his grandma used to wear, full of stains.

"Ma. Don't look so sad. Look, I brought you something." Freddie took some cheese, bread, and a banana out of his backpack. He pushed them onto the table in front of her.

"Where did you get this?" She looked up at him, both fearful and grateful.

"They gave it to me, Ma. I swear! Mr. Jackson, the janitor, said I could have it. He said that they throw away a lot of food every week and that it's a damn shame."

Freddie's mother wanted to believe her son.

"Come on, Ma. Make something. Cook something. Make something for both of us."

As she stood up, Freddie's mother held onto the kitchen table and clutched her heart. She swayed back and forth.

"Ma! Ma! Are you okay? Where's your meds? Sit down. I'll get them."

His mother obediently collapsed into the chair as Freddie rushed into the bathroom and opened the medicine cabinet. He pulled out a bottle of pills, hoping they were the right ones. Rushing over to her, he held out the bottle in front of her face.

"One of these? Ma? Answer me! One of these?"

She nodded, breathing erratically. Freddie opened the bottle, took out one pill, and handed it to his mother. He watched as she put it under her tongue and closed her mouth. He stared at his mother, not knowing what he should do next. Should he call an ambulance? No. They could never afford that. Should he walk her to the couch? He pocketed the pill bottle, walked over to her, and put his arms around his mother's shoulders. She had started to breathe in a regular way now.

"You okay now, Ma?"

Freddie's mother looked over at her son, smiled and nodded yes. Then she slowly stood up, grabbing the cheese and bread. She placed two slices of bread with two slices of cheese in the toaster oven. Freddie watched her, so relieved that she was okay enough to make melted cheese on toast.

Later, once he saw her go into her room and lie down, fully clothed, on her bed, Freddie bent down beside her, took her hand and said, "I'm glad you're okay, Ma. Let me know if you need me."

Freddie got up extra early the next morning to check on his mother. She was already in the kitchen, making her instant coffee. She had the radio on and was humming to one of the songs.

"See you later, Ma!"

"Why so early, sweetheart?"

"I have a test I have to study for," he lied. What he really wanted to do was to get to the cafeteria early, so that Mr. Jackson would give him more food. It was Friday, so Freddie was hoping they'd have even more left over than yesterday. He'd emptied his backpack of all his books to make room. Like his mother, Freddie had slept in his clothes. He hoped they didn't smell too bad.

The sun had just come up as Freddie ran the 12 blocks to school.

He loved the way the sky looked in the morning, so pink. When he got to the school, he saw the light to the cafeteria was on. He knocked on the door. He didn't hear Mr. Jackson. He knocked again. Nothing. Then he looked in the window. Mr. Jackson was on the floor, face down. Freddie panicked. What was he going to do? The door was locked!

Freddie tried the window. It was locked. He ran into the schoolyard and found a rock. He threw it hard against the window, smashing it. Mr. Jackson didn't move. Freddie crawled in carefully through the broken window and knelt down beside Mr. Jackson. He was afraid to touch him. *What if? What if?* Freddie then remembered that he had those pills in his pocket that worked for his mother. *What had she done with them?* She had put them under her tongue, he thought. He didn't see her swallow them. He opened the bottle, took one out and opened Mr. Jackson's mouth.

Freddie was shaking. He put the pill under the janitor's tongue and closed his mouth. He waited. Then he heard the bell ring. *Oh no! First period!* He heard a key in the door. Mrs. Steinmetz, the principal's secretary was standing there looking at both Mr. Jackson on the floor and at Freddie.

"Oh my God!" Mrs. Steinmetz exclaimed. "What's happened here? We buzzed for Mr. Jackson and he didn't answer!"

Mr. Jackson stirred, sweat dripping down his forehead. Slowly, he sat up, resting his hands on his head. Mrs. Steinmetz was dialing someone on the wall phone.

"Yes, come right away. We have an employee who is hurt."

When the paramedics came, they asked Freddie what had happened. He told them everything, including the pill that he had put under Mr. Jackson's tongue.

"You save his life, son. You saved this man's life."

Instead of juvenile hall, Freddie was given a coupon for food from the cafeteria for the year, and got his picture in the local paper. "Local Hero," the headline said.

Better Not to Know

Donna had her map opened up on her lap as she looked out at the scenery from the train car. The familiar sound of the train chugging along had seemed to speed up quite a bit. In fact, it was rather zipping along quite rapidly. She loved to take the train, because as it passed peoples' homes, she liked to look into their backyards and wonder about who they were. Sometimes she'd see someone in their garden or working on their car. Now and then she'd see a woman hanging up clothes on the line, with a toddler in tow. She wondered what it was like for them to have a train pass by in their backyard. She figured they probably didn't even notice it. Or maybe this was how they knew what time it was?

She had gotten used to the absurdity of her childhood. Her father, for who knows what reason, had gotten a job at a drive-in movie theatre. It was a double-screened affair where the screens came together in a triangle, with a tiny apartment at the top. The only way to get to their apartment was to climb a 20-foot stepladder. The bathroom was the same one shared with the 50 or so cars in a building down below. On the men's side there were five stalls, and seven on the women's. She never understood why that was, until one of her father's girlfriends told her that women took longer to pee, so they needed more stalls.

From Donna's bed, she could hear the movie playing on one side very clearly. If she walked over to her father's side, she could hear the other movie. If she stood in the middle of the room, where they put the couch, she could hear both at the same time.

"How can you stand it?" asked Alice, her dad's latest girlfriend.

"Stand what?"

"The noise!" Alice said in frustration. Donna just shrugged. "Oh, that? I don't even notice it."

Alice was one of many girlfriends who didn't last long. Her dad tried to explain to them that this was his job and he had to be available 24/7, in case the projector broke down, or something went wrong with the bathrooms, or the concession stands. He didn't take kindly to their suggesting he find another job. He would say, "Hey, it's free rent, and I get paid, too!"

Donna's mother was long gone. According to her father, she had run off with a carnie. Her mother had tried to entice her to go with her, but the idea of traveling from town to town, being the new kid every month or so, didn't really appeal to Donna. Besides, that carnie guy smelled like herring, cigars, and whiskey. *Gross!*

Just when Donna was about to graduate high school, her dad told her that the town had decided to tear down the drive-in. He was going to have to look for another job and a place for them to live. They had distant relatives in Canada somewhere, so he suggested they pack their bags and hop on a train to go visit them. Since Donna had to stay two more weeks in order to graduate high school, they slept in an abandoned car near the train tracks, with all their belongings in two duffle bags. That was weird and cold. Donna was miserable.

When Donna woke up on the morning of her graduation, her father wasn't there. She walked around outside looking for him, with no success. Combing her hair as best she could, she walked the mile to her high school and stood with everyone else. At least they loaned her a cap and gown, but her fellow students kept their distance. She didn't blame them; she hadn't been able to bathe for a few weeks. She went back to the car, certificate in hand, hoping her dad would be there to at least congratulate her. Instead, she found a note inside.

Sorry, honey. You're on your own now. I'm just a failure of a father. I know that. I'll try to make it up to you some day.
Love,
Dad.

Donna bit her lip, the tears flowing. She then found an envelope with $200 in it and two addresses: one in Winnipeg and another in Calgary. On the outside of the envelope, her father had written, "I think these are the addresses of our relatives. Maybe they can help you get on your feet. You can probably buy food and a train ticket with this money."

On her way to the train station, Donna wondered if those two cities were near each other. At least it wasn't too far of a walk to the station. Once there, she washed up as best she could in the station bathroom.

After asking at the front ticket counter, Donna found out that those two cities were practically on opposite ends of Canada. She figured she'd go to the closest one first. That was Winnipeg.

Sitting on the train, she watched as other people got on. There was one distraught-looking mother with two toddlers, a rather stern man wearing a pinstriped suit, a grey Fedora, and shiny black shoes. There was also a 20-ish couple with dyed blue and purple hair, rings in their noses and lips, and silver bracelets. The mother sat down with her two children and opened a wicker basket. She took out two large sandwiches dripping with mayonnaise and attempted to offer them to the kids, who were whining and hitting each other. Donna tried not to stare. Her stomach was grumbling. The little girl looked to be about four years old, the boy about seven. The mother's shoulders were up to her ears, her hands in tight fists.

Donna heard herself saying, "Can I be of any help? I could tell them a story about where I used to live." The children turned to her, wide-eyed. "Where did you used to live?" The mother nodded gratefully.

Donna began to tell the kids that she lived inside of the two movies at one time. The mother looked both amused and grateful for this absurd story. She noticed Donna looking at the uneaten sandwiches.

"Would you like a sandwich? My kids don't seem to want them. I'd hate for them to go to waste. Julia, Arthur, give this nice lady your sandwiches please." Donna nodded and tried so make herself eat very slowly, so as not to show how hungry she was. She devoured both sandwiches.

"Tell me the story of the movie where you used to live again" begged Julia. "Yeah, was there shooting in the movie? Loud guns?" said little Arthur.

"Oh yes," Donna replied. "It was very noisy. I could hardly sleep!" The children looked at her in delight. About an hour later, they fell asleep, leaning against each other.

The mother asked Donna where she was going. "Oh, Winnipeg. I have some relatives there, I think. I will be looking for work."

The mother eyed Donna. "Might you be interested in being a nanny? We are going to Stony Mountain. It's near Winnipeg. We could offer you room and board in exchange. You could visit your relatives on the weekends."

Donna looked at the sleeping angels and back at the mother. She wanted to ask where their father was but didn't dare. *Better not to know*, she figured. By the looks of their clothes, and the offer of this job, she figured this family wasn't poor. How did she get so lucky?

There wasn't a station at Stony Mountain. They got off together at Winnipeg. It was a very big city. The little girl, Julia, insisted on holding Donna's hand. The mother directed them to a cab, which whisked them away to a large mansion at the top of a hill.

Donna was shown to her own private room by a butler. She even had her own bathroom with a shower in it. The butler gave her a long look and opened a closet. In it were about 20 dresses and 20 different pair of shoes. "The last nanny left in rather a hurry. You may wear any of these clothes. It looks as if they'd fit you." Donna tried unsuccessfully to read his face.

"Dinner is served promptly at 7 p.m." the butler continued. "You are expected to be there to help with the children." Donna stared at him as he briskly left the room. In the shower, as she stood under the deliciously hot water, she mused, *I wonder what made the last nanny leave so quickly?*

Feeling clean for the first time in months, Donna donned a bright yellow dress from the closet and floated down the staircase to the dining table. The aroma of roast chicken and candied yams made her delirious.

The table was set for five. Donna wondered if the children's father was going to join them. The mother bowed her head and mumbled a prayer of sorts that Donna couldn't hear. Then the mother turned to the empty chair and spoke to someone who, as far as Donna could tell, wasn't there.

"Darling, I do hope you approve of the chicken Mazie made today. And we have your favorite yams." The mother smiled sweetly at the empty chair.

The children also piped up. "Daddy, when are you going to get me a pony?" Julia whined to the empty chair. "Daddy, you promised you'd play polo with me tomorrow!" demanded Arthur.

Donna sat at the table, staring at the mother and two children. She didn't dare ask what was going on. She thought about the 20 dresses and pair of shoes. She thought about having a real room and a real shower. *Do I really have relatives in Winnipeg?*

After dinner, Donna read the children part of *Huckleberry Finn* and tucked them in. She couldn't help but ask them, "Did you enjoy talking to your father?" They both smiled in unison, "Oh, yes. We always do."

Tossing and turning in bed that night, in the light blue flannel nightgown the last nanny had left (or had it belonged to several past nannies?), Donna wondered if she were losing her mind. She listened for any familiar sounds. There was no hum of the speakers that she had grown used to at the drive-in. She couldn't hear her father opening a can of beer. She strained to hear something, anything. Nothing. Not even crickets.

Early the next morning Donna left the mansion, closing the door quietly behind her. The butler saw her and gave her a brief nod of understanding. He didn't seem to mind that she was wearing the yellow dress, as well as a warm winter coat. She wondered how far it was to the bus station. It took her about 30 minutes to walk there. She was told that the bus to the train would take another 30 minutes. No matter. She still had some money left. Thinking about the night before, she thought, *Better not to know*. On the way to the big city of Winnipeg, she opened up her map.

Bad Boy

John had spent the whole day in the movie theatre with a clicker. His job, for which he made $8.30/hr. was to count the number of people who went into each of the three rooms where different movies were playing. He hated this job, but as his parole officer said, he was lucky to have one at all.

Once a week his P.O. would stop by the movie theatre to check on him. John found this irritating, but the alternative was worse. He hated prison. The food was bad. You couldn't sleep. People would scream. There were fights every few hours. His mother was so happy when he got out.

"Oh Johnny! Oh Johnny!" She cried and hugged him to her bosom. "I made the peanut butter cookies you like."

John loved his mother. His sweet, suffering mother. After his dad ran off forever when John was five years old, his mother did all she could to keep them from living on the streets. She cleaned houses. Some of her clients took pity on her, and would give her hand-me-downs from their children, so John would have some decent clothes for school. He dropped out before high school. He wanted to help his poor mother who always looked so tired. He had a paper route, getting up at the crack of dawn that helped some, but it was never enough.

His mother let him come with her to her cleaning jobs. She figured she could at least keep an eye on her boy. But she didn't always. John would meander through the mansions and find something here or there to stuff into his backpack. His mother never caught on.

But one night she saw him playing with what looked like a diamond necklace.

"John, where did you get that?"

John looked at her quietly.

"It's for you, mom. You could sell it."

His mother started to cry. When she brought it back to her

employer the next day, the police were there waiting to take John.

And now, six months later, he was out. It was Friday night, his dear, sweet, mother's birthday. He needed to give her something. Anything. Something to keep her warm. Something beautiful.

Sitting on the subway, he saw a woman knitting a rainbow-colored afghan. He knew he had to have it. He had to give it to his mother. She deserved it. She deserved everything. He tried to grab it from the woman.

"I need this. Give it to me!"

They had a tug of war. No one on the subway paid much attention. But now, this horribly cruel woman, who understood nothing, had stabbed him in the eye with her knitting needle. It hurt so much. As he ran off the subway, clutching his bleeding eye, he could only think that on her birthday, his sweet mother would now have to clean the blood off his shirt. He was a bad boy.

An Evening of Thanks

Florence Barkley had been a widow for the past two years. The first year was difficult for her, but she soon realized she could do several things that were forbidden by her late husband now that he wasn't around to chastise her. They had never had children. This was not her idea. She had grown up in a large family, ten to be exact, and she missed the din of conversations, laughter, even anger that would burst forth during the day in her home. But Charles told her he couldn't bear the thought of feeling responsible for other little humans. And what if a child they brought into the world were imperfect? What then? When she questioned him about the meaning of that, he simply shrugged. The third and last time she brought up the question about having children, he looked out the window, stroked his beard and said, "My nephew James is a mongoloid."

Charles came from a prominent family in the town. His father had been the mayor. He had one sibling with whom he never was seen. Charles was the manager of the bank. Florence was a customer. When Florence looked over at the office of the manager and saw Charles sitting there, he looked so lonely to her, so sad. She read in the paper that his mother had passed away the month before. She went to the memorial. There were only a handful of people there. She asked after his father. The news was delivered in a hushed tone to her by the man officiating at the memorial that his father was in an assisted living home and was unable to come. Florence decided that the bank manager needed to feel as if someone cared, so she brought him some of her renowned banana cream pie the next time she went to the bank. She felt a bit foolish about it, but her mind was made up. The sermon the previous Sunday was about reaching out to the poor and needy. The bank manager wasn't either of those, but she thought, can't rich people need to feel that they are cared for? So, with her weekly check from the local supermarket where she worked at the cash register, she carried the freshly baked pie. She asked the teller if she could speak to the manager.

"Do you need a loan?" the teller smiled benevolently at her.

"No, thank you. I'd just like to give him something."

The teller raised her penciled-in eyebrows. She eyed the bag in Florence's hand.

"It's a pie."

The teller couldn't hide the look of amusement. She shrugged her shoulders and nodded in his direction.

Florence saw through the window on his office door that he was on the phone. She waited patiently. When he put down the phone, he looked over at her and furrowed his brows. When she didn't move, he stood up, walked over to the door and opened it, motioning for her to come in and sit down in the big brown leather chair opposite his enormous desk.

Florence sat down and put the pie, which was in a brown paper bag, on her lap.

Charles looked over at her, cleared his throat and said in a slightly annoyed voice, "Did you have an appointment?"

Florence felt like she did in grammar school when she was called on and didn't have the right answer.

"I... brought you something," she said looking down at the bag.

Charles looked incredulous. Florence reached into the bag, lovingly took the pie out, stood up, walked up and placed it on his desk. He just stared at it.

"It's a banana cream pie."

They stared at each other. She watched as his face began to turn red. "I... don't know what to say," he blurted out. "Why did you bring me a pie?"

Florence found herself twisting and untwisting her hands. "I... thought you might like one."

She heard him exhale.

"That's very kind of you."

"I'm sorry about your mother."

"Thank you."

They were married 3 months later.

After several years, Florence began to regret ever bringing him the banana cream pie. He was never forthcoming in affection, never remembered her birthday, any of the holidays. He never visited his father. Florence was the one who did every week until his father passed. She would take long walks during the day while he was at work, stopping at the playground to watch the children with their mothers.

When she got the news that Charles had had a heart attack in his office and wasn't expected to make it, she wondered what her life would be like after that. She knew she wouldn't need to work. She would inherit the big house and he probably, although he never told her, had plenty of money.

And this year, when Thanksgiving was imminent, she decided she wanted to have a big Thanksgiving dinner. Who could she invite? Her family had moved too far away, so she couldn't invite them. What about Charles' relatives? He did have a sister in town who they never socialized with. Maybe the poor thing was lonely? She wasn't even sure she had ever met or seen her, even at the memorial for Charles' mother, father or Charles himself. Florence decided she would do the right thing and invite his sister Hannah and her family.

Hannah seemed shocked when she called her. But, reluctantly she agreed to come.

"What can I bring?" she asked.

"Oh, anything you want! I'm planning on roasting a turkey, baking yams and making a banana cream pie. Maybe you can bring cranberry sauce?"

She agreed right away. And then she said, "May I bring Jimmy?" Florence wasn't sure who Jimmy was, but said, "Of course! Bring whoever you want!"

Florence was very happy planning her first Thanksgiving with more than just Charles. And how nice to invite his family! The house felt very warm and inviting, the aromas wafting through her kitchen.

When she opened the door, Charles' sister walked in pulling the arm of her son, Jimmy. He had a big smile on his face. It was immediately obvious to Florence that Jimmy had Downs Syndrome. That brought back the conversation she had had with Charles. Jimmy looked so happy and sweet. He was carrying something in a small cage.

Florence stared at the cage. Hannah looked apologetic.

"This is Jimmy's best friend. He's a very gentle rat. I had to let Jimmy bring him. I hope that's okay with you?"

What could she say? It was most unusual, but if it brought harmony to the table, so what?

Florence motioned towards the table which was set with her finest China, a white tablecloth, white candles, and polished silverware. There were appetizers on the table. She had splurged on the fanciest cheeses she could find at the new gourmet supermarket in town and bought delicate crackers to go with it. Then she arranged red and green grapes around the cheeses. She was very pleased with how it turned out.

"Oh, it's beautiful! Isn't it Jimmy?" Hannah looked over at her son, while he slowly opened the cage, took out his pet rat and petted it as it climbed onto his shoulder."

Florence held her breath. While it was very endearing watching Jimmy and his rat, it was unnerving wondering just how trained the rat might be.

Florence poured herself a larger glass of wine than usual. Then another, then another. By the end of the evening, Florence, Hannah, Jimmy and the pet rat were splayed out on the Persian rug, feeding cheese bits, turkey, yams and cranberry sauce to each other. The din of laughter and love was emanating from this evening of thanks.

A Cold Glass of Water

There it was again, the old beige Ford truck, slowing down by the assisted living place as Laurie walked her dog. The first time she had seen him—the old man—he was just leaving the building. He must live there, she thought. Grasping a small ball in his hand, he squeaked it, and smiled at her as he tossed it out onto the sidewalk as close to her dog as possible. She bent down, picked up the ball, and put it in her pocket as the man got in his truck and drove slowly off.

The next time she saw him, he stopped his truck, rolled down his window, smiled sweetly, and waited until she got closer. Then he leaned out of his window and said, "Would your dog like a ball?"

"Sure! Thanks!" she said as he threw the ball. Laurie knew that her dog wouldn't pay any attention to the ball, but she didn't want to turn down such a kindly offer.

The following day, she was walking down a street she hadn't walked on before, and she thought she recognized the old man's truck. It was parked in front of a nondescript duplex with a manicured lawn in the front. Very orderly looking. She couldn't help but look in the picture window, because she thought she saw the man slumped in a chair. He looked like he was asleep, perhaps, but she couldn't really tell. *I wonder if he's all right?* She saw the newspaper on the front porch and thought that maybe she could just knock on the door with the pretense of giving him his paper.

As she walked close enough to see inside through the bay window, newspaper in hand, she saw photographs on a mantel. One was a wedding photograph. Now she wondered if it was his wife who lived in that assisted living building. Another was of him as a much younger man in a military uniform. Then there were several photos of a German shepherd. She wondered if he missed his dog, but she knew he was too old to get another one. *Maybe that's why he always gives out balls to dogs walking with their owners?* He was still slumped in his chair, not having moved an inch. Laurie took a deep breath and knocked on the door. Her dog was wagging her tail, excited to see a new house. The man hadn't moved.

This was how we found Dad. Fifteen years earlier, she and her sister Lily decided it was about time to visit their estranged father. After they had gotten the confession out of him that yes, they had both been adopted, he refused to speak to them again. "What's wrong with him?" she had asked Lily. Turning a troubled face directly to her, she answered, "I know what's wrong with him. He should be ashamed." There followed a long silence before Lily whispered, "He would come into my bedroom when you were asleep and do stuff to me. I was afraid to tell Mommy. I thought they'd send me back to Korea."

After that, their father moved into a rented apartment 50 miles away, refusing to answer the phone or any letters; not that they called him or wrote to him, but they had heard from one of their aunts about his lack of communication. One day, feeling guilty after hearing a church sermon about forgiveness, they decided to surprise him with a visit. They brought his favorite foods: baked beans with ham hocks, black eyed peas, and an apple pie. Laden with these gifts, they knocked on his door, but he didn't answer. There was a light on inside, so they figured he might be awake. The knocked for about ten minutes until finally, they gave up.

"Should we ask the neighbor?" Lily asked. Laurie shrugged, but agreed. The neighbor told them she hadn't seen him in days and suggested they call the police. They sat in their car, waiting for the police to arrive, and watched as they eventually had to break a window to get into his apartment. Lily and Laurie were still in their car when the ambulance arrived. They watched as their father was carried out in a body bag.

And now, she was at this old man's front door, hoping he was okay. She looked again now through the window and saw a bucket full of multi-colored balls. *How sweet.* This time, she knocked as hard as she could. She realized she was trembling. *Oh please. Oh please. Don't be dead. Please don't be dead.*

Then she saw him slowly get up from his chair, look at her through the window, and wave. He wore a big grin as he opened the door.

"Oh, young lady. How kind of you to visit me with your little doggy. You don't know how happy this makes me. My name is Arnold. I'm so happy you came to visit me. Please come in," he waved gallantly with his right arm. She walked in, holding the leash.

"I'm afraid I have nothing to offer you, unless you'd like a glass of ice-cold water?" He looked dismayed.

"Oh, Arnold, a glass of water would be perfect!"

The man ambled over to his kitchen. Laurie's dog tugged at the leash, trying to follow him, hoping for a treat. She looked over at the photos on the mantel again. What a dapper-looking young man he had been. And then she saw a photo of another young man in a military uniform. She wasn't sure if it was him or not.

When the old man came back with her drink, he saw her looking at the photo. "Oh, that's my son, Adam. He was killed in Vietnam. And that was his dog, Buster."

She didn't know what to say, except to blurt out, "Oh, I'm so sorry."

The following week, Laurie brought her sister with her, and knocked on his door again. This time it was around 5 p.m. She was carrying a big bag.

As the man opened the door, Laurie said, "Oh, I hope you don't mind, but my sister Lily and I brought you a home-cooked meal. I was hoping we could eat dinner together. Our father used to like ham hocks, black-eyed peas, and apple pie. We hope you do too."

She watched as his face turned red and his eyes got watery. "Why, that's very kind of you two young ladies. I'm overwhelmed." He motioned again for her to come in and put her bag on the kitchen table. "It smells delicious!"

As they sat down together at the table, he looked over at them with a sad face. "I hope I'm not intruding, but I take it your father is no longer with you." Laurie gave Lily a quick glance. Lily was looking down at the table.

Laurie felt the need to answer. "No, he passed 15 years ago."

Arnold looked over at the two sisters. "He must have been very proud of his daughters."

Laurie squeezed Lily's hand under the table. Neither said a word. The silence that followed was uncomfortable.

Arnold stood up and said, "Well, I'm very grateful to you two."

They watched as he walked over to his cupboard and took out three plates and three cups. He turned to them and said, "I'm afraid I still only have ice-cold water to offer."

"Oh, that will be perfect!" they both said.

American Customs

"Guess what? I got invited to a New Year's party at that fancy Victorian on Third Street. Yeah! And, you know who I'm going to invite? That cute Middle Eastern guy, Rashid, we were talking to in the cafeteria. Yeah. I am. I'm going to hopefully show him, oh, I don't know, American customs. Not that I really know any. I mean, these people probably do stuff I've never even heard of. But, what the hell.

"Yeah, I'm supposed to bring something. It's a potluck. What? Oh…remember Tracy? Yeah, that Chicana who works in my office. She made this thing called albondigas—that's meatballs—that was to die for. I asked her today for the recipe. She wrote it down on a 3-by-5 card. Yeah, I'll just walk down the street when I get off work and get the ingredients. No, I've never made it before. It can't be that hard.

"Wear? Hmmm. I guess I should wear a dress. I only really have one. What shoes? Oh, the red jelly shoes. They're cute. No, he doesn't have a car. Duh. I'll pick him up."

Carla hopped out of her VW bug and walked into Safeway. She pulled out the 3 by 5 card. Rice, grape jelly, ground beef, ground lamb, tomato paste. Okay, sounds easy. Too bad Tracy didn't write down exactly how to make these meatballs or how much of each ingredient for that matter, but it can't be that hard, right? She bought a package of rice, a small can of tomato paste, ½ pound each of ground beef and lamb, and an 8-ounce jar of grape jelly. Looking at her watch, she realized she had better get a move on it. The party was starting at 7 p.m., and it was already 5:30.

In a bowl Carla put in all the meat, half the package of rice, the entire jar of grape jelly, and all of the tomato paste. She stirred the ingredients and tried unsuccessfully to make meatballs. Shit! Now what do I do? The mixture seemed a bit runny. The meatballs weren't forming. Hmmm. Maybe I should add cornmeal? Would that make them stick together? She added about a cup of cornmeal. Nope.

Shit! Now what? Well, fuck it. I'll just put this mixture into a glass container and bake it. Hmm. 350 degrees for a half-hour? Why not? She shoved the gooey mess into the oven and went to her closet to get her dress and red jelly shoes.

After spraying her curly hair with water, Carla admired herself in the mirror. She thought she looked pretty good in the green velvet dress and the red jelly shoes. They were so comfortable., and there was something so unique about them. She especially liked the ridges on the bottom of the shoes. They made her a half-inch taller.

The oven timer went off. She looked at the clock. 6:30 p.m.—I'd better hurry up. Pulling the culinary gunk out of the oven, she was more than a bit dismayed at the visual. It looked like a meatloaf disaster. The rice hadn't cooked and the cornmeal was an all-too-obvious thread of yellow throughout. I guess I should have cooked the rice first? Oh well. What the hell do I do now? Maybe he'll think this is a typical American dish for New Year's Eve? God, it looks awful. Kind of like dog shit. Well, I'll just put a sprig of parsley on the top for decoration. That'll look festive.

Carla covered the dish in tin foil, then put on some oven mitts to hold it while she skipped down her front steps to her car. She put the dish in the back seat, checked the address she had written down, and started up the car. Sniff, sniff. Sniff, sniff. What's that smell? It can't be the failed albondigas. It smelled rank. Driving down a few more blocks, she realized the odor was coming from her jelly shoes. Her jelly shoes with the high ridges. She pulled over to the curb, got out of the car, and slipped off one shoe.

Oh no! Oh no! Oh, fuck! It was dog shit. Dog shit! Dog shit that she had stepped in and because of the high ridges and the pebbles, it had stuck to the bottom of her shoes. Jesus fucking Christ! Now what? She was halfway to Rashid's house. She couldn't be late. She decided to pick him up, drive back to her house, and tell him to wait in the car while she skipped up the steps, tearing off her jelly shoes, tossing them into her front yard, and going back into the house for another pair of shoes. Maybe he'll think this is another American ritual on New Year's Eve? "Oh, yes, we always step in dog shit, toss off our shoes for good luck, and change before a party. This is what we do." She thought if she just kept talking exuberantly in the car, he might not notice the stench. Maybe he had a bad sense of smell.

During the ride, Rashid was very polite, basically just grinning at her. Once she had done her little shoe-exchange dance and gotten back into the car, off they went.

The party on Third Street was very elegant indeed. The old Victorian house was exquisite, as were the various dishes people had brought and placed on the kitchen table. Carla tried surreptitiously to put her dish at the far end of the table, emove the tin foil, and leave the kitchen as quickly as possible.

The party was festive enough. Fancy canapés, crabmeat and cream cheese on crackers, caviar and lox. Champagne. Neither Carla nor her hot Middle Eastern date partook of the alcohol. Maybe she should have. Someone was playing some kind of New Year's Eve tune on the piano that everyone—except Carla and Mr. Hot to Trot— seemed to know. And then there was a scream from the kitchen.

It was easy to decipher whose very high-pitched scream it was. It was Larry, the drag queen.

"Oh my God! What is this shit? Who made this awful shit? Oh my God! I've never seen anything like it?"

The piano player stopped playing. Everyone looked around at everyone else to see who would confess to bringing this disaster to the party. Luckily, Larry didn't "drag" it out of the kitchen.
Carla hoped the red in her cheeks would look like she was just tipsy and thrilled to be with her new Arab hunk. She looked around wide-eyed at everyone else. Of course, no one else admitted to bringing the dish.

For the next hour, lyrics were passed around to songs that everyone seemed to know except Carla, and of course, Rashid.
But they bravely played along, the way she did when she attended Catholic churches and sang hymns. Carla was more worried about how she could leave without her pièce de résistance. Near the end of the evening, as the other guests said their goodbyes, she tiptoed into the kitchen. Looking at the table, she saw that most all of the dishes had been devoured, with one notable exception. Hers, at the end of the table, had one dent out of it about the size of a tablespoon.

Running swiftly from the kitchen, Carla put on what she hoped was her most appealing smile and motioned to her date that they should be off. Saying goodbye to the hostess—"Thank you, what a lovely party"—she practically fled out the door, leaving behind her culinary catastrophe.

In the car, when her date asked her about her food, she shrugged gaily and said, "Oh, it's okay. I'll just get it tomorrow."

Two weeks later, she saw Larry in the park. She braced herself for the ensuing discussion.

"Oh my God! That was so much fun, wasn't it?" he screamed.

"Yes. Yes." She waited.

"And who was that stud you brought?"

"Oh, some Middle Eastern guy."

"Are you seeing him?"

"Um, no."

"Didn't he like the party?"

"Oh, I think he did."

"Oh my God, and did you see that gross food in the kitchen?"

"No. Not really."

"You didn't?"

"No."

"Oh my God! It was so gross, I almost puked! I wonder who brought it?"

"I don't know. Never saw it."

"Well, darling. Do bring that stud muffin to the next party."

"Okay. Sure. Although I think he may have gone back to his country."

"What? Didn't like the American customs?"

Carla sighed and looked over at an oak tree.

"Maybe not."

Seventh Grade Hero

All the kids going into the seventh grade hoped they wouldn't get Mrs. Carothers. She had been teaching at the school for at least the past 25 years; no one was really sure how long. But they were sure that she was very, very strict, and very religious. She had long, thin arms with bony fingers. Her permed hair was kept close to her scalp. The cross she wore around her neck was prominently displayed. She wore polyester dresses several inches below her knees. Her oxfords were black and polished. One thing all the students knew was never, never to be late to her class. She stood behind the door staring at her Timex watch, and at 8:01 a.m., she simply locked the door and marked the student absent. If they were late three times, a note went home to the parents.

One day, Tony Miller had come rushing toward school, hoping to make it to Mrs. Carothers' class on time. His mother's car wouldn't start, so he had to run to school. It was 8:03 a.m. when he got to the locked door. This would be his third time late. Now he would just have to wait outside the classroom, or somewhere else in the school, until the bell rang. This is so not fair.

I wonder if Mrs. Carothers lives alone, and what neighborhood she lives in? Tony decided to follow his teacher after school. Maybe if he found out something about where she lived and with whom, he'd know why she was so mean. It was a weird thing to do, but the next day at school, Mrs. Carothers for sure would be handing him the note to give to his mother, who was stressed out enough and didn't need any more bad news. Tony's dad had been gone for over a month now, and they didn't know where he was. His mom didn't get home from her job until at least 7 p.m. She cleaned houses for some rich people on the other side of town, and sometimes she stayed to cook for them for extra money. He knew his mother had enough problems and didn't need any more bad news.

Tony hid behind the big oak tree near the parking lot and watched as Mrs. Carothers got into her Oldsmobile. It was such an ancient car; he was surprised it even still worked. Luckily, she drove very slowly. He ran from behind one tree to another, keeping his eye on her loud blue car. She finally pulled up in front of an old house clear across town. Tony hoped he could get back in time not to worry his mother. He watched Mrs. Carothers sit in her car, take out something, and drink from it. That's weird. What is she drinking and why isn't she going into her house? He stayed watching her from behind a pine tree across the street for what seemed like forever, as she continued drinking whatever that was. Then she finally slowly opened the door of her car and started to get out. He saw as she fell onto the sidewalk in front of her house with a thud. Oh no! She's not getting up! I'm going to have to help her, and I'm going to get in big trouble! What should I do? She's not moving!

Tony ran over to Mrs. Carothers. She was lying face down. "Mrs. Carothers? Mrs. Carothers?" he blurted out, hoping she'd respond. She didn't. He leaned over and tapped her on the shoulder. "Mrs. Carothers? Are you okay?" She groaned then and turned over on her side, staring up at his anguished face.

Tony looked at his teacher and around at the houses on either side. No one seemed to be home.

"Can I help you up, Mrs. Carothers?" He hoped she would tell him in that mean voice of hers to leave her alone, that she was perfectly fine… but she didn't.

Tony watched as she tried to get up unsuccessfully. He knew then that he had to help her. Just the thought of touching her long, bony arms and fingers gave him the shivers. Her eyes looked bloodshot and wild. Oh, please, let this be a bad dream.

Tony reached down and lifted his most hated teacher up to her feet. Then he slowly walked her to her front door. She gave him her normal withering stare, but he was relieved to see that. Very relieved. Then, she reached into her purse, fiddling around for the keys, stuck them in the lock, and opened the door. The odor coming from her house was an odd mixture of sweat, old food, and cigarettes. Tony stepped back a few feet.

She continued to give him her most chilling look as she saw the expression on his face. "Still, I've been a good mother," she said, and closed the door abruptly in his face.

Tony took off faster than he'd ever run in his 13 years. He got home just as his mother was pulling up.

"Mom! Mom! Mrs. Carothers fell, and I helped her."

It took a while for his mother to get the whole story. "Did she thank you?"

"No."

The next time Tony was one minute late, though, Mrs. Carothers did not lock the door.

Lederhosen

Bertrand looked at his face in the mirror. *You're not ugly. You're not. All you have to do is go back to that café, bring a book so that you look like you have a purpose and order something. Just look at what other people order and order the same thing. Stop it!* Bertrand put his hand over his heart and ordered his heart to stop beating so fast. He practiced a smile in the mirror, then took a whiff of his armpits.

Walking into his room, his tidy room, he sat down on his bed, his head in his hands. On his desk was his jar of quarters for the washing machine and dryer. He had just enough for maybe two more loads. He had washed his clothes four times this week using a different soap each time. Sitting in the orange plastic chair, pretending to read one of the magazines, he snuck a look at which brand of laundry detergent the different men were using: Tide, All, Arm & Hammer, Seventh Generation. Last week he noticed that the men who used Seventh Generation and All had women with them. *Important*, he thought. One man who was muscular and used Tide looked like he was in a very bad mood. Bertrand tried hard not to let his hands shake. The man was wearing lederhosen and combat boots. Bertrand tried not to think about the reason for this.

After shoving his clothes into the washing machine, the muscular man stormed out, slamming the door of the laundromat. Bernard considered not returning for fear of seeing that man again, but his clothes were in there, being washed for the fifth time that week. He couldn't just leave them. He pretended instead to read the *National Enquirer* that had a picture of Elvis Presley in his casket. The door swung open and in stomped lederhosen man with a lit cigarette dangling out of the corner of his cruel-shaped mouth. Bertrand peered over the magazine as lederhosen man lifted the lid of the washer, slammed it down again and kicked it as hard as he could with his steel-toed boots. Then, to Bertrand's dismay, the man called out to him, "Hey, hey you!" Bertrand looked around quickly hoping to see another person in there, but no, he was the only one. "Yeah, you. Listen, my girl is coming here to meet me in a few minutes and my fucking clothes aren't ready. Can you just tell her I'm sorry, but that I had to run, give her this change and ask her to finish my laundry. Tell her I'll be back in an hour." The he-man shoved some quarters into Bertrand's shaking hand and stormed out the door.

Maybe she won't come. I can't just leave. I have to put my clothes in the dryer. Maybe she won't come. But what if he comes back and I have to tell him she never came? Will he blame me? I don't even know what she looks like.

And then the door opened. *Oh my God.* A tall stunning redhead walked in. She was wearing tight hot pink pants and a low-cut blouse that had red and pink blossoms all over it. Her toenails, he couldn't help but notice, were painted dark red and had tiny sparkly things on them. He could smell her perfume from across the room. He was afraid to make eye contact with her, but he knew he had to. She looked all around, obviously searching for someone. It had to be the lederhosen man. She didn't have any laundry with her. *Oh God. Oh God.* He forced himself to breathe slowly. And then there she was, standing over him. He almost passed out from the exquisite aroma of her perfume. "Hey there, cutie. Have you by any chance seen a big, burly guy doing laundry here a bit ago? I was supposed to meet him here. He gets really pissed off if I'm late."

Bertrand forced himself to look up into her beautiful face. *Oh my God! She has green eyes.* "Um… um…" he swallowed… and held out his hand full of quarters. "He asked me to give these to you and to ask you to finish his laundry."

"Oh, he did, did he?" She burst out laughing, her head thrown back, her earrings tinkling. All Bertrand could do was nod insanely up and down, up and down, his hand still thrust out with the coins in her direction. "Well, you sweet little man," she said as she plucked the coins from his shaking hand. "Why don't you show me which washing machine is his?"

Bernard pointed and in a high, squeaky voice said, "That one… the third one from the left." She grinned as he watched her saunter over to the machine. It was done. She grabbed the wet clothes, looked back and forth to all the dryers and back again to Bertrand, who was staring at her. "Oh, sweetie, can you show me how to use one of these? I've never done it before." *Oh my God... she called me sweetie.* Bertrand stood up, suddenly feeling stronger than he had ever felt. He took the clothes out of her hands, walked up to the dryer directly opposite the front door and shoved them in. Then, clearing his throat, but still feeling like a new man, he managed to not squeak while saying, "You just put $1.75 worth of quarters in this slot and it should be dry in about 45 minutes." Grinning, she started putting the quarters in. "That's right." He tried to sound reassuring. "That's right." Standing by his side, she put her hand on his bony shoulder.

"Oh, thank you, darling. You're such a dear! I don't know what I would have done without you."

"Glad to help," he managed to choke out.

The next night, wearing the clothes that he had washed in Tide, Bertrand sat in the café sipping a latte. He was holding a young woman's hand and looking directly into her eyes.

Cecille Brunners

Charles was afraid to make the first move. He was inexperienced in almost every way, having led a quiet life being homeschooled in his teenage years and then caring for his elderly and infirm parents until their deaths last year.

When his father keeled over in the garden while shaking out a container of ladybugs onto his rosebushes in July on a particularly hot day, Charles was sitting in the dining room, doing the New York Times crossword and looking out the bay window. He smiled as he watched his frail but chipper dad bending over with the ladybugs. Charles was just answering (in ink) "post dryer chore" with "folding the laundry," when he saw his father take a nosedive right into the Cecile Brunner roses. Charles leapt up and ran out the door to find his father face down and inert. His mother had gone to her bingo game, so Charles hesitated about whether to call her first or the ambulance. Knowing how much his mother loved bingo, he decided to call 911.

His mother got her usual ride home ten minutes after the ambulance carried his father's body away. Not terrifically good timing. The ambulance driver had asked if he wanted to come along, but Charles said he'd wait first to tell his mother. His mother's reaction when he told her was etched into his memory.

"How did it happen?"

"Well, I was doing the crossword and looked out to see Dad keel over right into the Cecile Brunners."

"The Cecile Brunners? Oh no! Not the Cecile Brunners! The Danny Boys or the Fire Princesses would have been much preferable.

Charles blinked and stared at her. "I imagine the hospital will be calling you soon." He then grabbed the crossword and went into his room. The phone rang twenty minutes later. Charles knew where to find her. She was inspecting the damage to the Cecile Brunners.

Three months later, on a crisp October evening, Charles got a call from the bingo parlor.

"I'm afraid something quite awful happened tonight," was the way Mrs. Gunther put it.

"Something awful?" Charles had just finished answering "Utopia" in the puzzle.

"Yes, dear. I'm afraid it's your mum."

Charles rolled his eyes. These bingo ladies never got to the point.

"Yes, well, the good news is that she won tonight. $35."

"That's not awful. She must be very happy."

"Well, yes, one supposes so, doesn't one? I don't believe your mum has ever won. But I'm afraid she got too excited about winning."

Charles snuck a peek at the crossword. What could be the answer to "German deli meat"? Fourteen letters. Hmmm. Maybe two or three words?

"Yes, well, we were very happy for her at first, you know. She had brought her lucky peppermint pig, like usual."

Charles hated that stupid pig. It was a ridiculous Irish tradition in his opinion… You say what you're grateful for and then break the pig and eat a piece for good luck.

"What did she do? Choke on it?"

"Um, well, yes, I'm afraid so, dear."

"And…?"

"Well, none of us knew how to do the Heimlich maneuver, but Bertha tried."

"And…?"

"Well, you know, your dear mum choked and choked and then turned an awful haze of blue, you know, kind of like the sea on a dark day."

Charles took a deep breath. He was mulling over "German deli meat."

"I'm afraid you're an orphan now, dear. We're very sorry."

"What? An orphan? You mean...you mean she died?"

"Yes, I'm afraid so."

"Black Forest ham!" Charles found himself blurting out.

"What?"

Charles felt as if he were just waking up from a dream.

"Oh, sorry. I'm not myself."

"Of course not, dear. We understand. It must be quite a shock. It was for us."

The following day the bingo ladies came by with cakes, pies and cookies. Charles was focused, however, on the daughter of one of the ladies who was helping bring over the dishes. Not only was she toting a shepherd's pie, but she had a crossword puzzle tucked under her arm. He saw it as she placed the shepherd's pie on the table in the dining room and immediately plopped herself down onto the stool in the kitchen. She saw him looking at her and unabashedly said, "I'm sorry, but might you have an extra pencil with an eraser? I'm almost finished with this puzzle, and I just have to finish it. I know it's rude and I'm sorry for your loss, but crossword puzzles are an addiction of mine. Charles looked at her unkempt brown hair, her mismatched blouse and skirt, her tennis shoes with holes in the tops and her overbite. He was in love.

"Um, not only do I have a pencil with an eraser, I have an erasable pen! And I've just finished the very puzzle you're doing. Just ask me anything and I'll give you a hint. I won't, of course, tell you the answer. But," he said charmingly, "I'll give you a great hint."

Their eyes met. He ferreted around in the drawer of the end table and gallantly handed her the erasable pen. Then he watched as this woman, this delicious woman, stuck her lovely hand into her handbag and pulled out a small plastic baggie with something in it. He couldn't tell what it was. He watched as she took something out and began crunching on it.

Seeing him watching her with rapt eyes, she cooed, "Would you like one? They're quite scrumptious."

Charles couldn't tell what they were, but he was certainly game.

"Try one," she said in an enticingly throaty voice.

If she had said "Dive headfirst into the Cecile Brunners," there would have been not one second of hesitation. He took the greenish, crunchy thing from her extended hand and took a bite. Not bad, he thought. Chocolate covered something. He swallowed, cleared his throat and, with his heart beating rapidly, said, "What are these delicious treats?"

"Chocolate covered grasshoppers."

Charles suddenly felt the need to go into another room, even the room with all the bingo ladies. He collapsed into the overstuffed chair, his head in his hands, hoping not to upchuck. They all circled around him, the aroma of cheap perfume and cigarette smoke wafting in the air. "Oh, you poor dear. You must be overwhelmed."

He was.

Takeout

Terrence kind of liked this shelter-in-place thing. He didn't really like people. Never really had. He was the oldest of ten, and had been forced to take over as both father and mother for his siblings when his parents were killed in a car crash when he was 15. His grandma was there, but she was pretty useless. There were days she didn't recognize him or any of the other kids.

Once his little sister, at barely 14, ran off with her good-for-nothing jerk of a boyfriend, and Grandma had been properly buried, Terrence decided to get the hell out and be a hermit. He figured he had paid his dues and then some, and since he was now 18, he figured he was more or less considered a man.

He found a shack on the outskirts of town which suited him just fine. He mostly lived on beans, rice, and beer. For money, his parents had left a hefty inheritance that was divvied up amongst the siblings. Grandma, cheapskate that she was, had also left them a nice wad of bills. If he found himself low on funds, he went into the city and sold his sperm. They paid $100 each visit. He filled out reams of paperwork full of half-truths. No, he didn't have a college degree, but said he did. He didn't disclose his mother's mental health hospitalizations either. But he had stupidly checked the box saying it would be okay if his offspring wanted to contact him when they reached adulthood. That would be 21, he figured. Now, in middle age, he lived in dread of ever meeting any of them. *What the hell was I thinking?*

In his shack, he had one family photo that included his parents. He also had a picture on his wall of Bela Lugosi as Dracula. He found that picture satisfying.

Today was his 42nd birthday. He didn't feel like rice and beans. Beer, yes. But hell, he wanted something different. In the mail, he had just gotten an ad for the new pizza place in town. Pizza? Why not? It was late. 10 p.m. Were they even open? He called. "Yes. Open till midnight." Wow! He ordered ham and pineapple. Yum! Forty-five minutes? Geez. Good thing he wasn't starving.

Terrence sat down in his only chair. It was pretty beat up, but he loved it. He fired up a doobie and waited. He must have dozed off, because the knock at the door startled him.

He bolted up and opened the door. A young woman, maybe 20, with curly black hair pulled tight into a ponytail under her hat with the Pizza logo, was waiting there with the box in her arms.

"Here's your pizza, mister, and if you want, I have three extra ones. No charge." It was raining hard outside and she was drenched.

"Three extra ones? C'mon in out of the rain."

He held the door open as he took the boxes. She looked hesitant, but stepped in. He tried his best not to notice the distraught look on her face. She just stood there looking miserable.

Terrence cleared his throat. It felt odd to talk. He hadn't really talked to another human being in quite some time, except when he ordered the pizza.

"Listen, um, this is going to sound crazy, but if you don't have to go back to work right away, wanna share some of this pizza with me? There's no way I can eat all of it." Her eyes grew wide.

"It's my birthday," he said. The woman started to cry. "Hey, don't cry. It can't be that bad."

"They just fired me. I'm so bad at everything I do."

He motioned for her to sit down. "Well, take your raincoat off and stay for at least a slice of pizza or two with me. I'm not a pervert, I promise. Why did they fire you? What did you do wrong?"

"I couldn't find the last two addresses. So, they didn't get their pizzas. That's why I have these extra ones. My mom will kill me. We really need the money. I can't go home. I just can't." She stared sobbing, bent over with her head in her hands.

Terrence's heart was being pulled in two directions. He felt sorry for her and afraid for her, but he couldn't really let her stay in his shack. He was probably 20 years older than her. He'd be in deep shit. "Listen, I'm really sorry. I'd like to be able to help you, but I can't." To his surprise, she grabbed his legs, looked up at him and pleaded.

"Oh please. Oh, please. Just tonight. I promise I won't make any noise. I'll sleep on your floor in the corner. I just can't go home."

Terrence pried her arms from his legs and said. "What about your dad?"

She stiffened and looked off into the distance. "I don't have a dad."

"What do you mean? Your parents are divorced?"

"I don't have a dad," she repeated.

"You don't know who your dad is?"

"No."

"Have you ever tried to find him?"

"No."

"Why not? Maybe he'd want to help you out?"

"I was a sperm donor baby."

Their eyes locked. "Oh. I see." Terrence swallowed hard. "Did you ever think he might want to know who his daughter is?"

"Oh, right. I'm just a piece of no-good shit. That's what my mom says. She says she's sorry she ever had me. So, why would my dad, whoever he is, want to meet me?"

Terrence walked over to his chair and fell into it. After several minutes, he said. "Okay. Yes. You can stay here tonight."

Augustus

There was something about the alphabet, the A-to-Z alphabet, that made Augustus calm down. Nothing else really did. When he first learned it in grammar school by singing the song, it made his little five-year-old body hum. He sang it over and over, grinning and tapping his chubby little fingers on whatever he could find: desks, chairs, walls, cabinets. Because he was an only child and had been conceived through IVF, his mother let him do whatever he wanted. His father had been out of the picture; in fact, he had run off with one of the local librarians a month after Augustus was brought home.

At first, his mother was distraught about being left alone to parent the child, but soon decided if he wanted to sing that song incessantly during breakfast, dinner, his bath, whatever, it was okay with her. "Oh, you darling boy. You just love the alphabet, don't you?"

His teachers sent notes home about his annoying insistence on singing the alphabet song. She ignored them. But soon it became obvious that something had to be done. She took Augustus to a therapist, who suggested finally, in frustration, that the boy learn to hum the alphabet song quietly.

Augustus reluctantly complied, which seemed to satisfy the therapist, if not the teachers. They delivered an ultimatum that his mother simply could not, would not, comply with that he had to stop. His mother finally had to home school him. She sat with him as he did his homework, while he happily hummed the alphabet song.

For Augustus' eighth birthday, his mother went to the local educational store and bought five-inch letters of the alphabet that glowed in the dark. Together they tacked them onto the walls of his bedroom. When he turned 12, the home school curriculum committee suggested that a weekly trip to the local library would be a good idea. His mother was a bit taken aback by this, thinking she might see her husband's paramour there, but her child's education was more important than a silly encounter with a woman foolish enough to fall for her husband.

Augustus happily went on this field trip with his mother. When they walked inside, Augustus humming happily away, his mother took him over to the children's section. She watched as he slowly went over to the first stack and lovingly ran his hands across all of the books. Then, she watched him walk over to the next stack and do the same thing. He grazed his hands over all the books in the next stack. His mother soon became aware of one of the librarians standing close by, arms akimbo, staring at Augustus. The look on her face was of amusement, concern, and annoyance.

"What is your son doing?" the librarian said in a pinched voice.

"He's humming the alphabet."

"No, I mean, why is he caressing each of the spines of the books?"

"Augustus? The librarian here doesn't want you touching the books like that. If you want one, we can take it home."

Augustus stopped humming and looked at both of them. "I wanted to feel how they felt. Isn't that okay?" He seemed puzzled. The librarian raised an eyebrow and shook her head.

His mother answered, "No, dear. Not really. Why don't you choose a book, and we can take it home and read it."

Augustus blinked. "It has to start with A."

His mother beamed at him and looked over at the librarian. "He loves, loves, loves the alphabet. I'm going to help him find a book that starts with 'A'."

The librarian walked resolutely over to the stack closest to Augustus and quickly found a book that started with the letter A. "Here you are!" The librarian held the book out to Augustus. The title was Adventures Are Awesome!

Augustus held the book in his hands, smiling and humming the song. "It has three A's, Mom! Three!" His enthusiasm placated the librarian, who sent them home with a library card and the book.

Augustus and his mother began to come in every week for a book with the next letter of the alphabet. Word soon got out to the other librarians, one of whom was Augustus' father's girlfriend. Several weeks later, when they were on the G's, the librarian, who was now living with Augustus' father, approached them.

"Augustus, your father and I would like to invite you and your mother to our house for dinner someday soon. Would you be interested in that?"

The librarian looked over his mother, expecting her to be upset. To her surprise, his mother, thinking that a night off might be just what she needed, happily agreed to drop him off at their house, and pick him up afterwards. Augustus looked up uncomprehendingly at his mother.

"We have lots of books at our house, Augustus," the librarian said. "Lots. Would you like to see them? And of course, you can touch them! Oh, and you can call me Leslie." Augustus resumed humming.

The following Friday, Augustus' mother piled him into the car. "We're going to that librarian Leslie's house, Auggie. Remember her? She said you could touch their books. She said they have lots of them. Oh, and your father will be there. I don't know if you remember him, but be nice."

The house looks decent enough. She squelched any thoughts of Augustus' father and that librarian in any compromising embraces. As she walked Augustus to the front door, holding him by the hand, he hummed. Before she knocked on the door, he looked up at her. "When will I get to touch their books, Mom?"

"Oh, I don't know dear. Probably right away," she said brightly, thinking about the massage and the facial she was about to get. When the door opened, Leslie, the girlfriend, stood there. His father was nowhere to be seen. Perhaps he was hiding? Leslie warmly greeted Augustus as she led him to the living room with the bookcase full of books. Augustus ran to the bookcase and caressed the books' spines. Then he frowned.

His father had just come in and saw his son for the first time in almost 12 years. "My, my, my! You're a big boy! Your mother said you love books! That makes me very proud. But son, why the frown?"

Augustus started pulling the books out of the bookcase one by one, looking at their covers. Soon he had them all living room rug, rearranging them.

Leslie and his father looked at each other, shrugging their shoulders. Augustus was humming the alphabet song. Then, happily, he looked up at them. "I'm putting them in alphabetical order, see?"

"Ohh," they replied in unison.

Fifteen minutes later, Augustus, mid-hum, looked up at them, and said unhappily, "The R's and U's are missing!"

"Ohh," they replied in unison.

When his mother came to pick him up after her massage and facial, Augustus beamed at her. "They're going to get R's and U's for me soon, Mom! R's and U's!"

His mother grinned at Leslie, who looked a bit haggard but at the same time, self-satisfied. Augustus' father must have been in the other room, because he wasn't at the door. "When would you like us to come again?" asked his mother.

"Um…" said Leslie, glancing past the vestibule towards the living room. "I'll check and get back to you."

I Know You

Henry was not well liked in school. Ever since he started Kindergarten, the kids had made fun of him. One reason was that his head was so large, compared to his body. The other reason was that he was cross-eyed. His father was in denial that anything was wrong with him. "Of course, nothing's wrong with my son. How dare anyone insinuate that?"

Henry's mother Sara, on the other hand, was frantic to make the kids stop teasing him, and to try and figure out what to do about his huge head and crossed eyes. The pediatrician was no help; she said Henry's body would grow bigger soon enough. The eye doctor suggested putting a patch over Henry's "good" eye to see if the other one would right itself. Henry's mother thought this would be too humiliating. Life was hard enough for her little boy.

So, Henry continued to be tortured by the kids daily. When his mother picked him up from school, the look on his face was heartbreaking. She took him to the school psychologist, who said Henry needed to develop some defense mechanisms. "Like what?" Sara questioned the psychologist.

"Oh, like saying, 'leave me alone.' Or 'does it make you feel good to say mean things about me?'" Henry's mother looked at her son, who was staring out of the window. She just shook her head, picked up her purse, took little Henry's hand, and walked out the door.

Several months later, Henry's mother's best friend Gina called her. "Sara? Listen, I have an idea. You and Henry need to get away. Go somewhere different where nobody knows you. John was going to go with me to Veracruz this summer, but he can't leave work. He just got this new job, and he doesn't want to push his luck with his new boss. Why don't you and Henry go with me? It'll be an adventure. Don't worry about the money. I already booked the flight, the hotel rooms and everything. I just need to add Henry on the flight."

Sara didn't know what to say. She had never really traveled, especially not with her son. Besides, what would her husband

Douglas say about them leaving him alone for two weeks? She told Gina that she had to think about it.

At the breakfast table, she looked over at her son, who was bent over his cereal, as usual dreading having to go to school.

"Henry. How would you like to go on a vacation with Gina and me?" Even though she felt doubtful, she put a half smile on her face.

Henry looked up from his cereal. "Where?"

Sara said, "Oh, Mexico."

"Is it far away?"

"Pretty far."

"Will people be there that we know?"

"No, not really. Just you and me and Gina."

She watched as her six-year-old son contemplated this. "What about Dad?"

"Oh, he has to stay here." Sara got out her cellphone and showed Henry pictures of the people in Veracruz. He stared at the photos.

"They have big heads," he said.

Sara looked closer. "Well, yes, I guess they do." She smiled. Henry's eyebrows furrowed.

"So, do you think you'd like to go?" Henry shrugged. Sara took that as a yes.

When Sara picked up her son from school the next day, he didn't look as miserable as usual. "How was your day today?" she ventured.

"I told the mean kids I was going somewhere where people had big heads."

"Oh. And what did they say?"

"They didn't say anything."

A month later, they were in the sweltering heat of their hotel room in Veracruz. There was no air conditioning, and the fan was broken. They were sipping a drink made of tamarind, sugar, and water. It was refreshing.

"Tomorrow we're going to a museum, Henry. We're going to see things made by the people from a long time ago." Henry kept staring at the ocean and the short, dark-skinned people walking on the sand.

As they entered the museum at 10 a.m., the first thing that they saw was the huge, Olmec head, with crossed eyes made entirely of jade. Henry's mother and Gina just stood there, mouths agape.

As Henry ran up to the colossal head, a guard shook his finger at him, admonishing him not to touch it. And then, the guard looked at Henry more closely and smiled. He nodded towards the two women, not able to speak English, but with a gesture that was obvious. He winked at Henry and pointed toward the Olmec head.

"Mom! Mom!" Henry was pointing, smiling and jumping up and down.

Sara put her arms around her son. She knew her eyes were welling up. Looking over at Gina, she gave her a grateful smile. "Did you know?"

Gina shook her head. "I wasn't totally sure. I knew about the big heads, but I never knew about the eyes. I wonder what that was about?"

At the museum store, they bought ten postcards depicting the jade Olmec head. Henry begged his mother to buy him a tiny replica. It was way more money than she had intended to spend. She shook her head no.

"Mom! Please!" Henry grasped her hand and pulled on her purse.

"It's okay, Sara," Gina ferreted around in her purse. "I set aside extra money in case of an emergency. I believe this is entirely justified," she said, as she pulled out her ATM.

Henry's mother sent one of the postcards from Mexico directly to the school, addressed to Henry's new first-grade teacher. The teacher announced on the first day of class that they would be studying the Olmec civilization. There was the postcard on the wall in front of the classroom.

When the teacher asked the kids to talk about how they spent their summer, Henry raised his hand. The tiny replica of the Olmec head was in his pocket.

2

Alternate Realities

sci-fi & fantasy

The Patient in Room Two

It was after 5 p.m. when the office should really have been closed. The doors should have been locked. Dr. Bellwether grimaced as she heard the whistle. *Whose idea had it been anyway to install a whistle? That was insane!* They used to have some nice sounding bells as she recalled. But she had hired a new company to try to streamline her business. She was constantly finding herself staying until way past 7 p.m. There was never enough time to make dinner, let alone relax afterwards. And then, James, dear, sweet, suffering James was always so patient with her coming home so late from the office. *Well, I'll probably stop by Whole Foods and get a nice soup. And then, maybe some brownies. Oh, and they did have a nice selection of wine.* She sighed.

Dr. Bellwether opened the door to her office and went down the hall. The medical assistant, bless his heart, was looking rather guilty, his head hanging down so far that the bald spot on top was showing.

"I'm sorry. I'm so sorry. I tried to tell the patient that we were closed, but he begged in a peculiar voice."

"A peculiar voice?"

Gerald screwed up his face and lifted an eyebrow. "His voice, I think it was a male, didn't really sound human. He sort of buzzed."

"Buzzed?

"I don't know how else to put it. I put him in room two."

"Did you take his vitals?"

"I… I… I don't know what to say, Doc, other than it proved to be rather difficult."

Poor Gerald. He looked frazzled. He was such a good medical assistant. He always stayed late to help her, but she knew that his husband was getting impatient lately. And she saw the bouquet in the back office.

"It's okay, Gerald. Just go on home. I know Steve will appreciate the flowers and you two need time together."

Gerald's head righted itself. "You sure, Doc?" He was smiling now.

"I'm sure. Go on. Have a nice evening. I'll see you in the morning."

He scrunched up his face again and scratched his head. "Listen, Doc. This patient is a bit odd. I'm not sure you should be alone with it."

"It?"

"Yes, it."

Oh God, Gerald was so theatrical.

"Just go, Gerald. I'll be fine. You know I was a black belt in Tae Kwon Do in my day." Doc Bellwether winked at him.

"Okay, okay. Thanks, Doc." Gerald ran to the back staff lounge and grabbed the bouquet. He flew out the door.

Doc Bellwether smirked to herself as she knocked on the door to room two. There was no response. She knocked again. No response. And then she thought she heard a low buzzing sound. Maybe "it" had fallen asleep and was snoring. She plastered on her pleasant doctor face and slowly opened the door.

There was no patient on the table. There was no patient on either of the two chairs. But there was a resemblance of a patient perched on the counter. Doctor Bellwether blinked. She couldn't recall ever having seen anything like this in medical school. What was it? There were two very skinny legs dangling off the counter, two skinny arms flitting about, two enormously bloated looking eyes, no discernable nose and yes, were those diaphanous things coming off its back wings? The patient had a greenish tinge to its visage. It seemed to be humming anxiously.

"Hello. I'm doctor Bellwether." She decided not to reach out her hand in greeting. Doctors didn't do that nowadays anyway, what with Covid being so rampant. She just nodded in what she hoped what a professional demeanor. She felt her heart beating rather erratically. Clearing her throat, she said in her most calm and reassuring voice, "What can I help you with today?"

The patients little skinny arms and legs began to flap and rub against each other.

"I have a growth problem."

"A growth problem?"

"Yes," it buzzed.

Dr. Bellwether's mind was racing, mentally turning the pages of the medical journals she had read and the Physicians' Desk Reference. She cleared her throat.

"When did you first notice this growth problem?"

"About an hour and a half ago," it buzzed.

Dr. Bellwether wasn't sure just what to ask next.

"And where were you?"

"In Whole Foods."

Dr. Bellwether found herself gripping the chair and fiddling with her stethoscope.

"In Whole Foods?"

"Yes." the patient nodded gravely.

"Where in Whole Foods?"

"By the soup."

"What were you doing by the soup, if I may ask?"

"I was hungry. I wanted some soup. Someone had carelessly left open the top to the butternut squash soup. It sounded so delicious. I just thought I'd take a little sip."

"Oh."

"Well, the patient continued, the sip turned into a gulp and then another gulp and then another. Pretty soon I had emptied the entire vat."

"The entire vat?" Doc Bellwether felt as if she was becoming a parroting fool.

"Yes, doc. And with each gulp, I grew and grew until I hurt from eating so much."

"Did anyone else notice?"

"Oh, yes. Lots of people screamed, but they didn't know what to do. I tried to fly away, but I was too big! I couldn't fly! It was very distressing."

"I see." That's what Doc Bellwether said, but no, she didn't see at all.

"So, I crawled over here to your office. I saw your light was still on, so I thought I'd take a chance and knock on your door."

"Hmm. Well, I've never really seen a case like this before. I'm afraid I really don't know what to do. I'm sorry. It's getting rather late as well, and my husband is expecting me."

The patient looked very forlorn.

"I'm really sorry. But I can't help you. You'll have to leave."

The patient hopped off the counter and slowly crawled on the floor following the doctor out the door. It watched as the doctor walked across the street to Whole Foods and shuddered.

The doctor came out 15 minutes later with a bag. She got into her Prius and drove the ten minutes it took to get to her house.

"Hi, honey. Sorry I'm so late. I brought dinner. I hope you didn't starve to death waiting for me."

Her husband gave her his usual sweet smile. "I set the table, put some candles out and wine glasses, just in case."

"Oh, you're such a dear."

"What's for dinner?"

"Oh, I just grabbed some soup. They didn't have any of the butternut squash soup you like, but I got tomato soup. It looks good."

"They were out of the butternut?"

"Well, yes, dear. If I told you about it, you'd never believe me."

He smiled his benevolent smile. "Hard day at the office?"

"Most unusual."

"What's the buzz?"

Doc Bellwether, who had a mouthful of tomato soup, spit it out.

The Lawn

Harold looked forward to his writing group every Wednesday night. The prompts that people took turns giving were usually enough to get him going on a fun ride. The prompt was sort of science fiction-like, which wasn't his forte, but well, why not? He figured he'd write about a couple of extraterrestrial beings wandering around in his next-door neighbor's backyard. *Boy, she'd shit her pants if that really happened.* Harold chuckled to himself at the thought of it. He could just see her in that stupid powder blue bathrobe she wore when she went outside to get the morning paper.

He decided to get up and look out the window so he could properly describe how the aliens landed, what they looked like, what their spaceship looked like, how they moved around…when he noticed a huge shadow enveloping his yard. Four chartreuse figures bounded about near the maple tree, and then appeared at his side, having somehow walked through the outside walls of his house.

Their bodies seemed to coagulate into a form that had a head, arms and legs; and then melted into a squishy ephemeral grayish tissue, and back again into the slightly humanesque form, which smashed through the bay window. *This is downright fascinating. Oh boy, I'm going to have to remember this and write this down*, Harold was thinking, when all four creatures started making sounds at him.

"X8d0w4kdgg8eldutig. Dkwldyidsldkdss skdeilgdesl," they said all at once. Harold had just enough time to realize he wouldn't be able to decipher this language before he felt himself grabbed and yanked towards the wall.

Ow! Shit! They are trying to pull me through my wall. That's not going to happen. Apparently, the foursome realized this, changing strategies as they pulled and pushed him out the bay window by which they had entered. *Ow!*

The creatures were making noises again: "3093oajdsofnge3 wo48thldtlgh dlkfjeoigh." He hoped they were having second thoughts. Maybe they would be repelled by his profuse bleeding? His arms and head had been cut by the glass remaining in the window frame.

Wait a minute, Harold thought. *Is this a dream?* Then, they yanked at him again and dragged him onto his lawn.

Mrs. Fenderhoff, the neighbor, came out of her house. Of course, she was wearing that stupid bathrobe. But this time, Harold was very happy to see her. *Oh, God! She'll save me! She'll call the police! She loves to call the police. Or she'll call an ambulance. She loves to do that, too. She'll do something!* But for some reason, she wasn't even aware that he was lying there bleeding to death on his lawn, nor that there were aliens responsible for this nightmare.

"Fsalot7ro39e. W984tfnghf. Dhowdsjty dowygtft!" The aliens seemed to be arguing. Harold was aware that his head and his arm hurt a lot. Was he going to die out here on the lawn while Mrs. Fenderhoff was totally unaware of his suffering? Normally, she would be nosing around, asking him all kinds of questions. "So, when are you going to find a woman to take care of you? Do you ever see your ex-wife? Your kids? Do you even call them?" She was so annoying. He purposefully avoided her whenever he saw her. But now, at this moment, he wanted her attention badly. *Ask me anything Mrs. Fenderhoff. Anything. I'll even tell you my social security number. Just notice me! Talk to me! Please!*

The Chartreusians (that's what Harold decided to call the extraterrestrials) seemed to have settled their argument. He felt himself lifted off the grass and into what he guessed was a spaceship. It smelled like French Onion soup inside, his most hated food odor. The color of the walls was turquoise blue and pulsating, as if he were inside a discotheque.

Harold felt one of the Chartreusians tapping on his head and his arm. It hummed an annoying tune over and over. He stared as the wounds on his arm healed and the pain magically went away. And then, he felt the ship ascend at a very high speed.

Oh God. Oh no! What will I tell them at work tomorrow? What will I tell my kids? "Oh sure," Mr. Richards, would say. "Sure, you were abducted by aliens. Uh huh. Hitting the bottle again, are you?"

Belinda, his ex-wife, would probably say, "Good riddance! Don't ever come back." His kids? "Dad, be real. Don't be an asshole."

"Fkdw394h dhojddisgy9y. Dljfwiudth!" The Chartreuseians were arguing again. They seemed very excited about something.

Then Harold saw a door open, and to his great dismay, Mrs. Fenderhoff was being led in. The look on her face was unmistakably serene.

"I tried to tell you. I tried to get your attention for the past week, but, as usual, you wouldn't give me the time of day. I picked up a piece of paper that had fallen out of your recycling bin." She looked over at him with a satisfied grin on her face. "No, I didn't go rummaging around in it. I swear. It was on the lawn. I couldn't help but read it. I mean, I know you're a famous writer. Well, I don't know about the famous part. But I know you're a writer, so I picked it up and read it. I suppose I shouldn't have. I know that now. But when I read the part about one of your characters, who I suppose is really you, saying, "I wouldn't spend time with her if she was the only person on a spaceship and I was in there with her," I decided to take this matter into my own hands and prove you wrong." Harold looked at her, stunned.

"I wasn't too sure how to go about finding aliens," she continued, "But I found a crystal ball at Goodwill and rubbed my hands all over it, wishing to talk to aliens. On the third day, the ball lit up and these chartreuse-colored creatures appeared. Of course, I couldn't understand them, but I showed them pictures I'd taken with my cellphone of you, your house, and your lawn, and made hand gestures and a few rather risqué movements with my hips as well. They jumped up and down and seemed to sing a little song. The crystal ball flashed like a disco ball and went dark. That was the night before last. And now, look! Here you are at last! You're here with me and you can't escape. I don't know how long we'll be here, so you might as well resign yourself to it."

Mrs. Fenderhoff sniffed the air. "I'm not sure what they have for food here. I think it's French onion soup. I can smell it. Yum!" Harold pinched himself hard on his good arm.

"Don't bother, Harold. No, this isn't a nightmare. This is a dream. A dream come true. At least for me. I suppose you should be careful what you write. Or at least rip it to shreds before putting it into your recycling." Mrs. Fenderhoff emitted a deep throaty laugh.

Pretty soon, "Flkerjy02yr. Dhoweujth dhowd6tfy!" was heard throughout the ship. They were now surrounded by a gaggle of aliens, their big, bulging eyes spinning in circles. Harold found that very unnerving.

"Aren't they just adorable?" Mrs. Fenderhoff gushed. *Not the least bit adorable*, thought Harold. *Rather repulsive if you ask me. And that high-pitched sound they're making in no way adds to their appeal.*

"Scldklytydci cljkdfetto ckejdf6te…." Harold felt like yelling *STOP IT!* But unsure of the consequences, he refrained. And then from the ceiling of the spaceship, a red, pulsating light came beaming down surrounding Harold and Mrs. Fenderhoff in a circle.

"What the hell?" he blurted out as Mrs. Fenderhoff undid the tie on her shabby blue bathrobe, looked at him, winked, crossed her legs coquettishly, and ran her tongue over her lips. He watched as she turned to the Chartreusians one by one and gave each of them a conspiratorial smile.

"You are fucking kidding me," Harold said, teeth grinding in a panic.

"No, darling," she drawled. "I'm going to give you something to write about." The red beam pulsated, and the Chartreusians ululated as she grabbed him.

Weather Report

Chelsea and Donald had made the big move from LA to San Francisco. Everything was different: the weather, the way people dressed, the way people talked, the types of stores. They figured it would take a few weeks to get used to it.

Sitting in their apartment in Noe Valley, they felt like they were in a movie. That should have been a good feeling, but it really wasn't.

"We haven't made any friends, have we?" Chelsea looked over at Donald, a glass of Chardonnay in her hand.

"No, dear. We haven't. People are different here."

Chelsea sighed. "I wish it were like the good old days in LA, when we would throw parties every weekend. Those were fun, weren't they?"

Donald walked up to the bay window and looked down at the people walking in the street. "Yes, they were fun."

Chelsea walked over to the kitchen and poured herself another glass of wine. A smile soon crept over her face.

"Hey, I've got an idea! Doesn't Sam have an airplane?"

Donald looked over at her. "Yes, why?"

"Well, why don't we throw an apartment warming party and invite all our old friends? If they don't feel like driving, they can ask Sam to fly them here."

"Hmmm. That's a good idea! How fun! I'll look at the weather report for this coming weekend."

"Great! Check the weather report for LA too, just in case."

Donald was on it. He reported back. "Well, it'll be good weather here… at least, people from LA might not consider it good, but it won't be raining. It'll be foggy. And, yup, they're expecting somewhat of a storm in LA. I bet they'd be glad to get out of there!"

"Well, I hope that won't be a problem for Sam's little plane. How many does it seat?"

"Oh, I'm not sure. I think it can seat six. That's pretty good. And Susan and Jonathan will drive for sure. They just got a Tesla. They haven't stopped talking about it."

"Lovely! I'm going to invite them all now. How about Saturday at 4 p.m."

"Perfect!"

Saturday morning looked pretty good, although the weather report said the storm from southern California was moving north. At 3:30 p.m., Donald looked out the window again and saw the sky darken. Really darken. He turned on the TV to the local weather station. The anchor was laughing and holding his stomach. He couldn't seem to get any words out. He just kept pointing to the map behind him.

"I don't know what to tell you folks," the anchor finally blurted out. "It.. it... appears..." he started guffawing. "It appears… Well, it's coming down in buckets. Yes. Buckets… the storm from southern California has rapidly moved up our way and it's… it's…" He collapsed into his chair, head in hands, pounding his fist on the desk in fitfuls of giggles. Donald turned off the TV.

The doorbell rang. Donald ran over to answer it, but as soon as he opened the door, he jumped back several feet. Susan and Jonathan were standing there in trench coats that appeared and smelled as if they had big globs of shit on them.

Donald motioned towards the coat tree, while holding his nose.

"Um, you can hang up your…your…."

"Yes, it's awful, isn't it?" Susan said apologetically. "We certainly didn't expect this. I mean, it started to rain pretty hard in LA, but then it started coming down in clumps. I mean, big clumps."

"We thought we could drive away from it," said Jonathan, "But it seemed to be following us. It smells pretty bad, doesn't it?" Donald nodded vigorously while holding his nose.

Chelsea who by now had come to the door and smelled the stench, put on her most charming hostess face. "Yes, well," she replied, "But it's not your fault. Um… if it's not too much trouble, would you mind shaking out your raincoats outside?"

Susan and Jonathan, properly chagrined, took their raincoats outside. Five minutes later, they opened the door, looking dismayed.

"It's still coming down pretty hard."

Chelsea, Donald, Susan, and Jonathan looked out the window. The sill was filling up with dark brown globs of fecal material.

"I think I'll close the blinds, unless there are any major objections" declared Donald. Everyone nodded in agreement. They could still hear the thump, thump, thump of shit landing on the outside of the window.

"Let's put on some music, shall we?" said Chelsea, in an attempt to seem cheerful.

"Good idea. Maybe something to do with sunny skies?" Susan said, trying to be helpful.

Donald's phone rang. He put it on speaker after he heard Sam's voice.

"Um… it's been a bit of a difficult flight. We just landed, thank God. I don't exactly know what to tell you."

Donald offered, "I think we know."

Sam's voice was heard throughout the apartment. He sounded hysterical.

"You do? You do? You can't possibly know what we've gone through!"

"Well, Susan and Jonathan are here. They drove up."

"Did they…? Did they…?"

Donald held the phone out to the others. They all answered at once. "Yes. Yes. Unbelievable!"

Donald said, "Well, grab an Uber and come on over. Just leave your raincoats outside."

"An Uber? An Uber!" Sam was now yelling. "Can you imagine an Uber driver letting us into the car? No fucking way!"

Chelsea offered, "Pay him triple!"

Sam hung up.

Twenty minutes later, they heard a knock on the door. Donald opened it, quite woozy from having drunk an entire bottle of wine by himself. He watched as their friends dutifully shook off their raincoats outside.

"Hurry up, you guys. The stench… is…"

"We know. We know," they all mumbled simultaneously.

Once inside, not one of them spoke for several minutes. They had plopped themselves down onto the couch after having carefully examined their clothes for any remnants of the weather.

Donald was the first to utter an opinion, albeit a slurred one. "Well, I had heard that people in San Francisco hated LA. They said it was a shithole… but…"

There were no objections.

Sam had been looking intently at the floor like everyone else.

"Should we check tomorrow's weather?" he offered.

Vitamin B6

Curtis sat at his kitchen table stirring his coffee with his favorite spoon. The spoon was from his last marriage; marriage number five. Shanti had quite a taste for antiques, and Curtis was only too happy to indulge her. This spoon was the only thing she had forgotten when she had angrily packed up all, or rather most, of her things and left, slamming the door behind her.

Curtis sighed as he looked out the window. The maple tree was covered in newly fallen snow. His attention went back to the spoon as he remembered how happy Shanti had been when she came running in the door, her long, dark curls flying, her scarlet heels clicking.

"Oh, honey," she had said while she wrapped her arms around him. "I found the most exquisite antique cutlery today. You can't imagine how happy this makes me."

Curtis loved it when she was happy like this. Most often, or at least starting three months after they were married, she looked despondent. Why did he always have to pick complicated women? His therapist had told him he liked to find difficult and damaged women so that he could save them and appear as a hero. Well, maybe so. He guessed he wasn't performing so heroically all that well, considering all five of the women he married had left him.

"What's the matter with me?" he had asked his therapist. "I'm kind. I have money. I buy them whatever they want. What am I doing that's so wrong?"

All of his ex-wives had eventually gone on psych meds: Zoloft, Paxil. He couldn't remember all of the names. They did seem to help, at least for a while. Eventually, all of the exes told him he was too controlling. *Too controlling? What was wrong with wanting to know where they were going, when they would be home and who were they with?* So what if he texted them a few times every hour to tell them he loved them? Wasn't that what a husband was supposed to do? And they got so defensive when he asked them what medications they were taking. Didn't he have the right to know?

It was getting chilly. Curtis decided to get up and go into the bedroom where the walk-in closet was. He picked out a navy-blue cardigan. His first wife, Beanie had given it to him. He smiled when he thought of her button nose, her freckled face and how tightly she hugged him. It was almost a desperate hug. A clingy, claustrophobic hug. What was she taking? Something with a long name. Well, that marriage lasted all of three months.

The next one (Susan), the third, oh God, he hated to remember Susan. She was a yeller, a screamer. She broke things, like plates. And then there was Joan. *Oh, Joan. Why did you ever agree to marry me?* She told him her therapist said to marry a man who was gentle like a woman. Her therapist thought that she was just faking being a lesbian. Well, so much for his presumption.

And of course, Stephanie. Stephanie, the nurse who was always taking his temperature. She was very thoughtful. Maybe she wasn't disturbed enough? She only stayed with him two months. He was actually relieved when she took off.

And Shanti. Shanti who was in his yoga class. Shanti with the black hair and green eyes. Shanti, who was a vegan. Shanti who would do sun salutations every morning and run from the room with her hand over her mouth if she saw him eating meat.

Curtis put his hand into the left pocket of the cardigan. *What's this? A pill bottle?* It said, Vitamin B6. He googled B6. Sounds healthy. Supposed to calm you down. Why was it in his pocket? Had Shanti accidentally slipped it in there, hoping he would take it? Weird. He noticed on the side of the vitamin bottle in green ink, it said "electric." *What's that about? Electric?* He looked at the expiration date. Still good. It was a couple of months before it would expire.

Well, he thought, *I'm going to say a toast to my five ex-wives, have a glass of champagne and pop a vitamin B6. Maybe if I'm calmer, I'll be able to figure out why my marriages have failed.*

Curtis walked into the living room, popped a pill from the bottle, poured himself a glass of champagne, and sat down on the red velvet love seat. He raised his glass, and said aloud, "To Beanie, Joan, Shanti, Susan and Stephanie, my damaged, neurotic ex-wives…"

And then Curtis began to feel weird. The walls seemed to be vibrating. No, melting. And where was the floor? He could hardly get up and walk to the bathroom if there was no floor beneath his feet. He looked at his image in the mirror on the wall to his left and saw his canines descending. What? Was he turning into a werewolf? His hands had grown fur. His toenails were now long and curled. His throat hurt. He tried to talk, but it came out like a growl. He got down on all fours and started sniffing his antique Persian rug. Why am I doing that? He then fell to his side and felt the need to roll back and forth on the rug, getting the odor to seep into his… his what? His fur? He felt his side. Yes, it was fur! *Oh God, Oh God!* Now he knew why they had left him. Of course, they left him. He wasn't a man at all. Perhaps he never had been, and they sensed it. He crawled to the kitchen, opened the refrigerator with his hairy paw, pulled out a raw steak, and ate it in one bite.

Venturing Out

I'm walking in a neighborhood I'm not accustomed to. Why, you may ask? I'm basically sick of always going down the same streets, greeting the same neighbors, looking at the same gardens. So, today, I decide I'm going to shake up the old routine. Of course, being the lazy ass that I am, I drive for 20 minutes so that there will be no possibility of seeing anything that I've seen before.

This neighborhood—well, at least at dusk—looks fairly elegant. I look at the vast green lawns, the large brick mansions covered in ivy, the neatly trimmed hedges, the flowering dogwood trees. No one, and I mean no one is outside.

I notice how quiet it is. There is birdsong, but I can't see the birds. There are no sirens blaring, no glass breaking, no drunk people screaming at each other or their kids, no helicopters circling. I notice lights on in people's houses, the blue glare of TV screens, Teslas and BMWs parked in driveways.

I walk to the end of the block. It's a cul-de-sac, and I see a house that looks different from the other ones. The house looks like it is embarrassed to be there, its color indistinguishable. The yard is not kept up, the oak trees (there are three) have a look of desperation, their leaves brown and curled. Perhaps these trees need water. Then I hear a distinct sound coming from them. I have a hard time believing what I'm hearing. I think I'm losing my mind. Perhaps I am, because there is no light on inside the house. I stand there and stare. And then, I feel a fluttering around my head. From what seems to be the branches of the trees, hundreds of moths are suddenly buzzing around my head. I try unsuccessfully to swat them away. They keep returning in their crazed dance around my head. I want to scream, but I don't dare open my mouth for fear of swallowing one.

And then I hear that sound again. It's coming from the moths. Again, I think I'm losing my mind, because I hear them saying, "Help us. Help us, please. Save us from the man inside the house."

I put my hand up to my forehead. No; no fever. I look around, hoping to find a human. But no, just hundreds of moths circling. I'm afraid to open my mouth even slightly.

Then I see it: a light goes on inside the house. The moths fly towards the light in unison. The front door opens slowly. An old man with long, disheveled white hair, wearing a dark blue tattered robe, holds a kerosene lantern in his hand. He has a toothless grin. As the moths flock to his light and sizzle in the flame, he laughs a deep echoing laugh that shakes the ground beneath me and the oak trees.

I run back to my car, turn on the ignition, and drive fast. I vow never to try to walk somewhere new again.

Under the Covers

The first thing I usually notice at my mother's house is the familiar smell. It's so weird how the places I'm accustomed to being in, like work, or certain department stores, or my kids' room, have a certain smell.

My mother always washed her clothes and the bedding in Tide detergent. She also used Downy fabric softener. Those smells, though familiar, were not my favorite. Today, as I walk inside, those smells aren't there.

"Mother? Mother?"

She doesn't answer. I hear laughter coming from her bedroom. That's not normal.

"Mother?" More laughter.

I hesitate before I slowly open the door and peek inside the room. I don't see my mother. I see a lump in her bed. I hear giggles coming from under her covers that no longer smell of Tide and Downy.

What is that smell? It smells like Old Spice. *Old Spice?* That's the aftershave my dad used to wear. But he's been dead for 10 years.

I can't decide what to do. Do I walk up to the bed, grab the covers, and throw them off to the side?

More giggling. *Hmm.* That actually sounds like my dad's silly giggle. The giggle he made when he's winning at Scrabble. The giggle he made when he's just won a game of Hearts.

That's crazy. That can't be my father.

And then I look at the bed again. *Wait!* The lump is gone! The blanket is entirely flat. *What the fuck?*

I must be going insane. And where is the giggling? That has stopped too.

Oh my God! The smell of Tide and Downy has returned. *That's nuts!*

Now I'm staring at my mother, who has appeared from under the covers. She's wearing those pink pajamas with the elephants on them that I got her last year.

"Oh, hello dear. Have you been here long?"

I don't answer. I'm frozen in place.

"What's wrong? You look like you've seen a ghost!"

"Mom? Um, can I ask you a question?

"Of course."

"Was, um…. Oh, never mind. You'll think I've lost my mind."

"What? What is it?"

"Was um, Dad just here?"

"Dad?"

"Yes, Dad."

"Oh!" My mother put her hand over her mouth and tittered.

"Well…?"

"But, Mom…" I try to recover from the shock. "Dad is dead."

Mom giggles. "Not entirely."

I am incapable of saying anything. She looks at me.

"You don't usually come on Tuesdays."

Driving home, I try to decide whether to tell my sisters.

No. Definitely not. This did not happen. These three sentences become my mantra for the 30-minute drive home.

Tickle Feather

Sara sat on her back porch, looking out at the bougainvillea. It cheered her up somewhat. She had decided that since she had been sheltering in place for the past three months, it was time to pretend that she had somewhere to go, people to see.

She had just washed her hair, rinsed it, and put conditioner, hydrating conditioner, and forming gel on it. It really did feel good. Smelled good too. She had also shaved. She ran her hand along her newly shaved leg. Smooth. That was nice. If she had not been clean and sober for the past 25 years, she might have considered a nice cold glass of white wine, but that was out of the question.

Now what? She went back into the bathroom, which now smelled so nice, and picked out a bottle of blood-red nail polish. *Might as well.* She got out the emery board and nail clippers. *Those poor women who own the nail salon... how are they ever going to pay their rent during this quarantine?* It wasn't easy doing her own pedicure. What a luxury she had gotten used to.

After clipping and filing her nails, Sara shook the bottle of polish and commenced painting them. She kept missing and getting polish all over her toes. *Pretty sloppy. Oh well, who's really going to see this?*

At that moment, Sara's cat, Otis, made his warrior sound. He dropped a lizard from his mouth which scampered behind the toilet, cowering.

She waved her hands at Otis. "Leave the poor lizard alone!" Otis sauntered off in search of a tasty mouse, his orange and white tail flickering in anticipation.

Sara leaned over and gently picked up the lizard. Its little body and legs felt weird to the touch. "See? I saved you!" she said happily as she carried the lizard down the back stairs into her garden, where she placed him safely under the lemon tree.

As she walked back up the steps, she turned and noticed the lizard following her. *What?* As she sat back down, it jumped up on the table, startling her. Then it jumped right onto her lap. She froze.

This is bizarre. Lizards don't do this. The lizard then crawled up the front of her blouse and sat on her shoulder.

She couldn't move. It tickled. She almost brushed it away.

The lizard whispered in her ear, "Sara. That pedicure looks like shit and you know it."

What? I must be going insane. Did that lizard just talk to me? Really? And anyway, how does it know my name? I've been sequestered too long.

"I'm not kidding, Sara. It looks really bad. You're just not good at putting yourself together. You never have been."

Sara put her hand up to her forehead trying to take her temperature while not disturbing the lizard still situated on her shoulder, close to her ear. *What if it shit on her?*

She did feel hot, but maybe that was just the shock of having a talking lizard on her shoulder, putting her down. It actually sounded like her brother, Preston, who had died of AIDS 25 years ago. He was the one who used to help her pick out outfits, put on makeup, all while humming show tunes. He was so good at it! Well, after all, he was a drag queen. Pretty famous, actually. Tickle Feather was his drag character. *What a name!*

Sara looked out at the bougainvillea again. That usually calmed her down. The lizard was still on her shoulder.

This is nuts! This shelter-in-place thing is making me lose what little mind I have left.

The lizard then jumped down and started deftly flicking his tongue over her toenails, cleaning up the sloppy mess. Then it started doing pushups. Lots of them.

Okay. Pushups, yes. But cleaning my toenail polish? Lizards don't do this. It must be Preston. But… Preston as a lizard?

She bent over and gently picked up the lizard, held it in the palm of her hand, and said, "Preston? Is this really you?"

"Of course it is, hon. Who do you think I am? Judy Garland?"

"Okay. Okay. Oh my God! Preston! But, why a lizard?"

The lizard jumped up on her shoulder again and spoke into her ear.

"Well, hon, there was a long line of spirits waiting to choose what to come back as. Because I've always been so damn accommodating, I let almost everyone else go in front of me."

"You didn't."

"I did. You know me. Always wanting to please everyone. Be everyone's best friend."

"Well, yes, that's true. You even gave away your best feather boas, and those gold lame open-toed heels with the diamonds imbedded on them." *Wait a minute. Am I seriously talking to a lizard?*

Yeah, well. I thought he was going to marry me."

"Instead, that fucker probably gave you HIV and killed you."

"No, sweetheart. I can't be sure it was him. It could have been a thousand other guys."

"A thousand?"

"Well, I don't know. Several hundred at least. After the shows, I pretty much went home with anyone who asked. I was as slutty as they come… no pun intended."

"But, Preston. A lizard?"

"I like their tongues. How they flick. And their beady eyes. And did you see how many pushups I did? I can do 100 a day, easy. I'm going to be very buff."

Sara laughed.

"Oh, Sara, hon. I've missed your laugh. And I've missed helping you dress yourself, you poor dear. You always managed to look like such a bag lady."

"Preston, where have you been? Hiding under a rock? Oh, oops, you may very well have been. But we have this shitty, scary virus, tons of people are dying, and we can't go anywhere. At least not without a mask. This is the first shower I've had in a couple of months."

"Stop! You're killing me! Oh, oops. I'm already dead. I do need to tell you, hon, that when I knew I was going to die, I just decided to make the best of it. You know, appreciate what I had, play music, tell people I love them. I didn't know, of course, that I was going to get to come back."

"Yeah, as a lizard. Ms. Tickle Feather, lizards can't wear boas or bright red lipstick. And look at your feet. You'd never get heels on those claws!"

"Oh, I'll figure something out. I always do. Hey, Sara, remember Jon? You know, hunky Jon? Yeah, well, he was fighting with someone in the line because the next choice was to come back as a flamingo. Jon just shoved that poor guy out of the way and started screeching. He made quite a scene. But then, he always did."

"Well, did he get to come back as a flamingo?"

"Sure did. Next time you see one, yell out his name and see if it turns around!"

"Oh, God, Preston. You haven't changed one bit."

"Of course not, Sara. Just bigger biceps. Hey hon, open the door. I'm going into your room to open your jewelry box. I think there's a tiny red silk ribbon in there. I want you to cut it for me and tie it around my neck. I think it might even have a teensy bell attached to it."

"Okay! You know what? I think I can even find an itty bitty red feather from a Halloween costume too. I'll attach it to the ribbon."

Preston flicked his tongue at Sara's cheek. She smiled.

"Preston. This is the most excited and happy I've been in forever. Thank you for coming back."

"It's entirely my pleasure, sweetheart. My pleasure."

The Netherlands

Today was the 30th day in a row that I went to the Museum of Natural History. The guards have gotten know me. One thing I have been doing, which is disingenuous, is pretending I'm looking at anything else other than the big ape in the panorama on the third floor. I don't want them to get suspicious, you know. I mean, the other exhibits are very well done and quite informative, but honestly, they don't hold my attention. Oh no. Not like the ape does. Now, if I told you the truth, which I would really like to do, although I'm sure it's impossible, given that your reaction will most probably be that of scorn, derision, disbelief or skepticism…the thing is, I wasn't really expecting this to happen at all. I've tried to be nonchalant about it. I wanted to appear like a tourist, and able to say, *Oh, yes. Of course, I visited the Museum of Natural History. Doesn't everyone?*

I'm pretty sure I've seen tourists just walk in and go straight to the souvenir store, buy something, and never even look at anything inside. I even contemplated doing just that, but the guard was always eyeing me suspiciously. I felt like he was reading my mind. So, I begrudgingly started to wander through the third floor, where there is an enormous statue of an African Bush Elephant, or maybe it's stuffed? I didn't really know.

Then I walked up the marble stairs to the second floor. It had something to do with a tropical forest. That was kinda cool. Lots of piped-in sounds of birds and water. But what I really wanted to do was just sit down on one of the benches and figure out what I was doing with my life. Kind of a weird place to do that in, I mean a museum and all, but there you have it. The truth of the matter was, I was sick of being on my own. See, my mother hadn't been in the picture since I was 12. We never found out where she had gone. My dad said she was probably strung out somewhere. Sad, I know, but that's the hand we were dealt. And then, my stupid brother… well, he thought he was badass and stole a bunch of stuff from REI… what a dimwit. Of course, he got caught. And since it wasn't his first offense, shall we say, he's now doing time for a while. I think he'll be out in ten years.

And that leaves my dad. Well, he tried. I know he did. He was a big, hairy guy and worked on the docks. When he came home, he was usually drunk and basically beat to hell from the hard labor. Sometimes he'd tell me bedtime stories about his hippy days in Amsterdam. He told me that weed was legal there, that everyone was open-minded, non-judgmental. When he would talk about Amsterdam, he'd get this far away look in his eyes and smile. He talked about the boats on the canals, and the cobblestone streets, the nightclubs, the hash. I liked it when he'd talk like that. It was the only time he wasn't grumpy or angry.

One night when he was drunker than usual, he winked at me, saying that because he was such a hairy guy, if I ever couldn't find him, to look in the Museum of Natural History. The look on my face made him laugh, as he crushed another PBR can in his palm and said, "I'm just a big hairy ape. That's what my boss calls me. A big hairy ape. So, if you ever need to find me, I'll be in one of those exhibits of apes in the museum."

And then last month, he totally disappeared. He didn't come home. When I went down to the docks, they said they hadn't seen him at work. It was so weird. He didn't leave a note or anything. I was scared that maybe somebody had offed him at the docks, and they were keeping it quiet. But I don't trust the cops, so I didn't go to them. I have this part-time job typing shit in an office so I can still eat and pay the rent. At least there's that. But it gets lonely. It really does.

So, there I was about a month ago, walking right past the Museum of Natural History, when my dad's words came back to me. When I walked in, I saw that the man at the information booth looked friendly enough, not like he would put me down for a stupid question, so I asked him if there were any ape exhibits. He smiled and did an odd little bow, while pointing to the staircase, saying, "Why, yes, young lady. We most certainly have ape exhibits. Third floor. Enjoy!"

I saw him right away. My dad. My dad, the ape; I mean, that ape really looked exactly like my dad. It really did. It might have been a bit larger, but he had the same eyes, the same twinkle. I could just hear him talking about the canals.

I found myself sitting on the bench right across from the exhibit and staring at that ape. That ape that was my dad. What I really wanted to do was to talk to him, but I knew that wouldn't be possible. Not unless the guard or the tourists weren't looking. I thought if I came every day, every single day, that I might just get the chance. I don't know what we'd talk about. I'd probably ask him how it felt to be behind glass. Or what about the other apes in there with him? Did he like them? Did they move around after hours when no one was there? Or… I don't know. Maybe I'd ask him if I should quit my job. Yeah. Quit my job and go traveling, like he did. In my mind, I told him that if I ever did, I would come back and give him a detailed report on how everything was, like the food, the people, the music, whatever. Shoot, I might even bring him back a souvenir. I'd slip in over the top of the glass in his exhibit. He could show it off to his exhibit mates after hours. This idea made me very happy. I felt like I now had a purpose.

So, today, believe it or not, there was a small gap of time when no one was watching me, no guards, no tourists. I was just alone there with my dad. I quickly whispered my plan. And I swear to God—you might not believe me, but I swear to God his head turned towards me and he blinked. I saw him blink! I knew it! I absolutely knew it all this time. From inside that glass, he knew I was there, and he could read my thoughts. I practically skipped out of the museum.

Running up the steps to my apartment, I flung open my door, grabbed my checkbook, wrote out a check for a month's rent in advance, packed my suitcase, hopped on a bus, and went straight to the airport.

The House in the Field

Genevieve and Arthur had been hitchhiking for five hours. The last old truck dropped them off in a field and sped off. Looking at each other perplexed, Genevieve spoke first: "Did we say something to offend him?"

Arthur shrugged his shoulders. He never was much for talking. They both looked out at the landscape which was fairly barren and put down their backpacks.

"I feel filthy," she said, looking at her soiled dress and threadbare shoes. Arthur grunted. He looked determined to make the best of it as he unrolled his sleeping bag onto the wet earth. It had sprinkled a few hours earlier.

And then she saw it in the distance: a house. A large, dilapidated house. It looked like there were lights on in the windows. Thoughts rushed through her mind. She didn't relish sleeping outside on the ground. What if it rained again? And she was hungry. Very hungry. Looking over at Arthur who was turned on his side, she saw that his red hair needed a trim, as did his beard. Maybe that house had a bath? Oh God! A bath! They could get clean. What a luxury. Maybe she could wash out the dirtiest of their clothes in the sink, and hang them out in the bathroom, or any room for that matter. And, if the people in the house were kind, perhaps they'd be hospitable. She had heard that people in this country were often hospitable, and they might offer them a hot meal. Genevieve hugged her knees to her chest in anticipation.

"Honey! Honey!" she nudged him. Arthur apparently had fallen blissfully asleep. She watched him as he opened one eye at her.

"What? What?" He sounded annoyed.

"Look at that house over there."

"What house?" he sat up.

"That one." He looked towards her pointed finger.

"Hmm." He grunted. "What of it?"

"Well, I thought we could maybe just go knock on the door, and maybe they'd let us stay there tonight." He looked incredulous.

"Well, they might. And they might let us take a bath."

His eyebrows furrowed. "A bath?"

"Yes. A bath! Can you imagine? They might. And even offer a hot meal."

"Right."

"Well, "she started to whimper. "It's worth trying, don't you think?"

Arthur hated to see Genevieve cry. He felt responsible for this bad turn of events, after all. What had he said to the truck driver? Oh, right. He had asked him not to smoke cigarettes because Genevieve was allergic to them. He probably shouldn't have done that. That big tub of shit had gotten royally pissed off and started speeding. Genevieve had grabbed the dashboard and further pissed him off. Then he just dumped them off in the middle of nowhere. Asshole.

Well, he supposed they could walk over to that creepy old house. It was probably abandoned. If it was, they could maybe break in. Oh, but no: he saw the lights in the windows. Sighing, he rolled up his sleeping bag and stood up, ready to trek over there.

Genevieve looked pathetically hopeful. He wanted to put his arm around her shoulder, but with her backpack, that was impossible. He took her hand instead, and they started walking on the uneven earth towards the house. It looked to be about half a mile away.

As they neared it, he thought they might hear dogs barking, but there were no animal sounds at all. Oddly enough, not even birdsong. The sun was setting, the temperature dropping. Arthur began to hope there was someone in the house. The weeds were high near the front of the house, the trees looked as if they had been unattended for a long time.

"Shall I?" Genevieve looked over expectantly at Arthur, her arm raised with a soft fist, ready to knock on the heavy front door. Arthur grunted approval as his heart quickened.

Knock, knock, knock. Her knocks started out quietly and got slightly louder. They listened for footsteps but heard nothing. She knocked again. This time, slightly louder. No footsteps. "Maybe you should," she said to him, feeling the wind picking up and the sky darkening.

Arthur knocked with what he thought were three manly knocks. Nothing again. Then, he looked at her and turned the giant knob. The door was easy to open. He opened it slowly as it squealed. It wasn't totally dark in the front room as they carefully and quietly tiptoed in. They noticed several lit candles.

"Hello? Hello?' Genevieve called out. There was no response. Arthur cleared his throat and tried. "Hello? Hello?" No response. They looked at the lit candles and at each other. Then they saw a door that led to another room. Genevieve looked questioningly at Arthur. He nodded approval.

They walked through the swinging wooden door into what appeared to be the kitchen. On the stove, there was a pot that smelled as if it had some kind of stew or soup in it. Genevieve lifted the lid cautiously; a delicious aroma filled the room. It was a meat stew of some kind. Rabbit? Lamb? She felt faint from hunger and anticipation. They looked around and again called out, "Hello! Hello!" Arthur tried to increase the volume of his voice. They heard nothing.

Genevieve spied a spoon on a counter. Gripping it, she dipped it into the stew and took a bite. "Oh my God, Arthur. It's heavenly." She took several more bites while standing at the stove. Arthur obediently walked over and let her spoon-feed him standing up. They waited to hear footsteps again. They heard nothing.

Genevieve looked over at the counter where she had found the spoon. On it was an empty jar. She picked it up. "I wonder what was in this?"

Arthur shrugged. "Smell it," he suggested.

As she lifted off the lid, a sudden gust of wind and smoke emanated from the jar. She let go of it, almost causing it to fall to the wooden floor. They stood there, frozen.

"Hello," said a voice seemingly coming from the vapor. It was a deep, echoing kind of masculine voice. "Welcome to my humble abode."

Genevieve and Arthur's eyes got wide. "Don't be afraid," the voice echoed. Arthur gripped Genevieve's arm. "I've been waiting half a century for someone to come into my home. I mean you no harm. An evil spell has been cast upon me." Arthur and Genevieve trembled.

"I was informed that until a man with red hair and a woman came into my house, tasted some of my rabbit stew, and opened the lid to this cookie jar, I would not be set free. You have saved me."

Genevieve slumped down into a rickety chair, her hand on her heart. Arthur, suddenly feeling brave and grateful at last for his red hair, said, "But sir, why can't we see you?"

"Yes, that was part of the curse. Even if I was freed, I would remain invisible forever."

"But you can see us," Arthur ventured.

"Yes. I can see you both very well. In fact, I could see you as soon as you were abandoned in the field. My vision is fairly extraordinary. I saw you with your red hair and this lovely young lady with her rosy cheeks and dark brown braided hair. I hoped my house would look inviting to you. You look like you've been traveling for quite some time. I heated up the stew, just in case."

Arthur was intrigued. He cleared his throat yet again. "But sir, are you allowed—I mean now that you are free—are you allowed to leave your house?"

"I'm not sure. I would like to give it a try, though. Do you think I could put myself into one of your backpacks and travel along with you both?"

Arthur looked over at Genevieve, who nodded enthusiastically. "Let's try it tomorrow morning," Arthur said.

"There's a bedroom upstairs," bellowed the phantom. "Feel free to settle down for the night. There's even a bath with hot water if you'd like."

The next morning, Arthur and Genevieve went downstairs, happily cleansed. Arthur called out, "Hello! Hello!" There was no response. "Hello!" he tried again. They looked over at the empty cookie jar. The lid was still off. "Hello! Hello, kind sir," Genevieve called to the phantom voice.

On the stove, there was hot porridge. They each ate a bowlful and waited for their host to appear. After several hours, they decided to leave.

"I guess he couldn't wait for his freedom." Arthur said.

"Can't blame him." Genevieve agreed.

Hand in hand, they ventured out into the field, smiling. What would today bring? Whatever it was, it would be worth it.

The Good Stuff

God, she hated Halloween. She had thrown together a stupid costume at the last minute. It wasn't as bad as a sheet with holes for the eyes—you know, the two-second ghost costume—but it was almost as bad. She had put on black leather boots, a black leather jacket, black leather pants, a big black '40s-looking hat with a giant red feather stuck in the band, a small silver mask for her eyes, and a big shocking pink Afro wig.

She had written down the address on a slip of paper and shoved it into the left pocket of her leather pants. She pulled it out and squinted at it. She couldn't really see it very well without her cheaters, but she figured, how wrong could she be? The first letter was a "P". Pine? Pennsylvania? Oh well, fuck it. There were shitloads of parties. If she went to the wrong house, it probably wouldn't matter. No one would recognize her anyway. The numbers looked like 531, or was it 582?

Walking up to the Victorian house with the lights on inside, she knocked on the door. Nothing happened. She knocked again. Nothing. She felt the door handle and turned the knob. Looking into the living room she saw that there were some people, all in in costumes, drinking what looked to be champagne.

One of the ghosts was seated in a corner, playing the cello. When he saw her, he stopped playing, and smiled a broad smile with his skeletal-looking teeth.

"Why, hello June," he said in a deep and echoic voice which reverberated off the walls. "We've been expecting you."

"You have?" June held onto the back of a chair so she wouldn't keel over.

"Why, yes. We have, haven't we?" He turned and nodded to each person, each ghost, in the room. They in turn nodded in agreement. June was suddenly aware that she could see through their ghost costumes to the walls behind them.

"You never gave us the good kind of candy when we came to your door, did you?" The ghost cellist was reprimanding her, a grimace on his face.

"I… well… I…" June was stunned, unable to think. Who were these apparitions?

The cellist read her mind. "We are the children you only gave chewing gum to on Halloween. Not M&M's, not Snickers, or anything good. That killed us, you see. Now we demand that you go to an ATM, get cash, and go buy us the biggest bag of good chocolate treats from Costco that you can find… or we'll haunt you for the rest of your life.

"Costco?"

"Yessss," he said in his hollow, echoic voice. "The good kind."

"But, Costco isn't open at this time."

June was trembling as all the ghosts, five of them to be exact, began to laugh in deep, threatening voices.

"Too bad, June. Too bad. Too bad."

Talent

It was the first day of Junior High. Deirdre sat in the back of the classroom, hoping she wouldn't get called on. She couldn't see the board very well, but she didn't really care. She figured if she kept her head slightly downward and she looked distracted, it might just work.

As she looked around the classroom at the kids she was seeing for the first time, she realized she didn't have the same clothes as the other girls seemed to have. Her hair wasn't right either. She hated being the new kid, but she was almost used to it, having moved six times already in her young life.

She was grateful that the boy in front of her had a very large head, body, and especially neck. If she looked straight ahead, she couldn't even see the teacher. She could see from the back of his blue t-shirt that he was sweating. Maybe he didn't want to be called on either? If she could just see the clock, she could figure out how long until the bell rang, but lately her eyesight seemed weird. Even if she squinted, it didn't seem to help much.

What was that teacher droning on about? Something to do with California history. Her family had just moved to California from the East Coast, and she knew nothing about California. She hadn't paid much attention in her history classes in New Jersey either, but she sure couldn't fake this subject.

"Deirdre? Are you paying attention?" she heard the teacher say. She sounded mean, like her Aunt Betty, whose mouth looked like she had just taken a bite out of an unripe persimmon. She looked at the image that was the teacher at the front of the classroom and arranged her features into what she hoped was a respectful and interested look on her face.

"Deirdre? I said, are you paying attention?" Now the teacher sounded like she was a badly injured crow. Deirdre forced herself to stare at the teacher. Her vision was doing this bizarre thing again. It was kind of making the form that was the teacher disappear while the outline of the teacher was still there. As well as making the teacher mostly disappear, it made the volume of the teacher's words get softer and softer until they could be heard no longer.

One kid said, "Hey! What happened to Ms. Foster? She disappeared! Wow! I guess we don't have class anymore!"

"How did that happen?" another kid said.

"Should we tell Principal Harler?"

"No!" was the consensus.

After a few minutes of talking back and forth, grabbing their backpacks, and standing up excitedly, they noticed that Deirdre was the only one still at her desk.

"What's up with the new kid?"

"You mean the freak?" This was pronounced, arms akimbo, by a girl who looked like she was the most popular in the class. She had perfect hair, shiny, blonde, set in the bouffant style that was popular at the time. Her clothes looked new. She had on a pink angora sweater and a pink plaid skirt. Her tennis shoes were even pink, with white, lacy socks.

Deirdre felt the tears well up and her cheeks flush. As her lips trembled and the girl laughed, Deirdre stared hard at her. She could feel the instant energy coming out of her eyes as the outline of the girl remained, but the rest of her disappeared. As Deirdre continued to stare, the girl completely disappeared.

"Hey! Susie disappeared! Just like Ms. Foster!"

"Oh my God! What's happening here? I think that new girl is doing it. She's a total freak!"

"Watch out! Don't piss her off! She'll make you disappear, too!"

After the bell rang, Deirdre walked home slowly. Her mother was doing the dishes and singing to herself. She could tell her mother was angry because she always sang that song when she was upset.

I didn't know the gun was loaded
And I'm so sorry, my friend.
I didn't know the gun was loaded
And I'll never, never do it again.

"What's wrong, Mom?"

Her mother took her hands out of the sudsy water and turned to her. "Nothing dear. Just life. How was your first day of school?"

Deirdre looked away from her mother. She didn't really want to tell her what had happened. Her mother probably wouldn't believe her anyway.

"Oh, it was alright."

"What did you learn about?"

"Oh, I don't know. It was kind of boring. California history."

Her mother looked at her with a knowing look. "Yeah. What do we care about California? I never wanted to move here."

Deirdre looked over at her mother. This was news to her.

"Oh, I shouldn't have said that," her mother said. "It's just that your father is never satisfied with where we live. He's always looking for a better job, a better location. Frankly, it's exhausting."

"Would it be easier if he wasn't here, Mom?"

Her mother let out a sharp laugh. "Honey, sometimes you're very perceptive beyond your years. I sometimes think that. But, well, I'm afraid we're just stuck with him."

"No, we're not."

Her mother laughed again. "Yes, we are, dear. We are. He's the breadwinner."

"Couldn't you get a job?"

"I don't have any job skills. I can't type. I can't sew. I'd be a terrible waitress." Deirdre watched as her mother's posture sank into itself.

"There must be something you could do." Her mother just shook her head. "But you said it would be easier if he wasn't here."

Deirdre watched her mother as she looked out the window. With her back to Deirdre, she said, "Don't ever repeat that."

"I won't."

Just then they heard Deirdre's father's car pull up in the driveway. As he opened the door to his Ford Fairlane and got out, they could hear him swearing. He looked angry; so angry that he slammed the car door. The front door opened, and he burst in.

"Well, that was worthless." Her father's voice sounded strangled. Deirdre and her mother stood there frozen, waiting for the explosion that was sure to come.

"What are you two staring at? Can't you find something better to do?"

They looked away as he headed toward the liquor cabinet, fixed himself a martini, went over to the TV and turned it on. He then sat down. There was some kind of talent show on. It was a rerun.

Her father was snarling at the TV. "Look at that girl! She can really sing." He turned to look at Deirdre. "Why can't you sing or dance or something? What the hell can you do?" Deirdre looked down at her hands.

Her mother approached him gingerly. "How was work, dear?"

"They fired me, if you really want to know."

"Fired?"

"You heard me. Are you deaf? Fired. They said they didn't like my attitude!"

"But..."

"I don't want to talk about it. That guy's a complete jerk. I hate Californians. I drive all the way out here, 3,000 miles, to get insulted? I don't think so. No, siree, Bob. Not me. You can't push me around like that. Pack our bags. We're going to move to Nevada. I heard it's great there."

"But honey…we just got here. I just finished unpacking everything. This was Deirdre's first day of school."

"So what? She can have another first day of school. Right, Dee?"

As her father turned to look at her, martini in hand, Deirdre stared at her father hard. Within seconds, there was an outline around him. A minute later, poof! He was no longer there.

"Dee, what just happened? Your father was just sitting in the chair and now he's gone!"

Deirdre shrugged. "Well, you said you'd be better off without him, Mom. I took care of it."

Her mother looked at her, mouth wide open. "Did you do that?" Deirdre nodded.

Deirdre watched as her mother wiped her hands on her apron, walked over to the blaring TV and turned it off. She started at her daughter. "You made him disappear?"

"Yes."

"You've done this before?"

"Yes."
"Can you teach me?"
"I can try."
Her mother smiled. "Maybe I won't need to get a job after all."

Pink Lady Apple

There once was a beautiful young woman with black shiny hair and green eyes. She was, in fact, the most beautiful woman in all the land. A few decades earlier, that honor had gone to the Queen, who was now well into her 60s. Upon hearing about this lovely young woman, the Queen was insanely jealous of her.

Looking in the mirror one morning at the wrinkles around her mouth from smoking Galois's, her brow furrowed from the disdain of many years, the Queen was appalled. Every day, she spent over an hour putting on cosmetics: eyeliner, powder, concealer, mascara, lipliner, blush, and ruby-red lipstick. That particular morning after she had, in her estimation, sufficiently beautified her aging face, she approached the mirror, the famous truth-telling mirror. But first she dimmed all possibly offending lights and lit candles.

After she had given the mirror her good side, she cleared her phlegmy throat a few times and croaked, "Mirror, mirror, on the wall, who's the most beautiful of all?" She waited. And waited. And waited.

"Excuse me, mirror," she finally said sternly. "I asked you a question I believe."

To her dismay, the mirror began to crack into a million pieces, but not before saying, "Let's face it, darling. You are butt-ugly. Everyone knows that the young lady with the black hair and green eyes is hands-down the most beautiful young woman in the land. Get a grip."

The Queen was devastated. She made a mental note to have her servant purchase a new mirror first thing in the morning.

Meanwhile, she asked her pet monkey, Zander, to whom she paid a handsome salary, to find a way to make that young woman, really sleep; like, for a long, long time. Zander jumped up and down on the Queen's Persian rug, doffed his red fez, and said, "Oh, my generous Queen, just give me a few extra quid and several ripe bananas, and I'll find a Pink Lady apple worthy of your request. This apple will not only appeal to that young woman, but when she bites into it, as long as she swallows, she will be stoned out for at least 50 years. Without her around, you definitely will be the most beautiful in the land. The new mirror you get will attest to that, I guarantee you.”

The Queen clapped her hands and, as was her custom, touched her lips to Zander’s forehead as she slipped the money into a secret pocket in his fez. She then unbuttoned her red velvet blouse to reveal three ripe bananas which he grabbed, peeled, and greedily ate.

“Oh, my Queen, do you aim to please. You will soon be very happy.” With that, Zander bowed deeply, tipped his little red fez, spun around, and danced sideways out the door.

The next morning, the kingdom was all a buzz with the news that the beautiful young green-eyed woman had fallen into a deep stupor and no one was able to wake her. Upon hearing this, the Queen rushed upstairs to her bedroom and grabbed her new mirror, holding it firmly in her aging hands.

“Mirror, mirror… um… mirror, mirror…” The Queen was suddenly unable to remember the rest of the question. No matter how many times she tried, she couldn’t remember the end of the question. After several more attempts, she threw the mirror against the wall, smashing it to smithereens.

Zander found her splayed out on the rug in front of her white canopied bed. “Oh, my Queen. What has happened? Did the mirror not tell you what you wanted to hear?”

The Queen opened one eye, turned her head towards her monkey, and said, “Please, Zander. Give me the rest of that Pink Lady apple. All I’d like is to sleep for 50 years.”

Me! Me! Me!

The family room, or that's at least what they called it at Pleasant Manor, was full of senior citizens. There were 25 of them. June was not pleased. She had just been hired a week ago and felt deflated when she saw the listlessness of the residents. They sat there in their wheelchairs or with their walkers, eyes downcast, not conversing with one another. Dinner had just been served, mashed potatoes, boiled-to-death green beans, gluten-free bread with the edges cut off, pork roast, applesauce, and butterscotch pudding, each serving replete with two blueberries on top.

Gross! No wonder they're miserable.

June went out to her car and opened her trunk. She hauled out a black suitcase, dragging it into the family room.

"What holiday is coming up next weekend?" she chirped to the uninterested audience waiting to be wheeled up to bed. There was no response.

"Might it be Halloween?" she asked cheerily as she opened her suitcase full of costumes. "These are special costumes. When you put one on, you literally become the character." No heads looked up.

"Okay. Okay. I can see you don't believe me. I'm going to have to demonstrate," said June as she put on the witch's hat and cloak and picked up the broom. Straddling it, the broom lifted itself off the floor and she began circling above the heads of the now suddenly interested old folks.

"Hey!" yelled Maybelle. "Look at her! She's flying around the room!"

Mr. Johnson adjusted his bowtie, took off his spectacles, and cleaned them on his shirt before he put them back on and looked at June with a big, toothless grin. "Well, well, well."

June kept flying around the family room, almost smashing into the chandelier. Within a few minutes, she had everyone's attention. She alit onto the game table and faced the residents.

"So, does anyone want to try on a costume?" There were

murmurs of assent. June jumped off the table and pulled out a Tinkerbell costume, holding it up.

"Me! Me! Me!" yelled Mrs. Witherspoon, wheeling herself over at full speed. June helped her put on the wings and tutu, handing her the wand. Within seconds, Mrs. Witherspoon was flying around the room, giggling. "A whole new world..." she sang out, over and over again.

Next, June pulled out a pirate costume and held it up. Mr. Smithers raised his good arm, pleading, "Oh please. Oh please. I want to be Captain Hook." After helping him put on the costume, he walked around the family room with his cane, belting out, "It's not such a good thing to be young, you know. Not good at all."

Then June pulled out a huge blue lamp and a genie costume. She heard several oohs and ahhs. Mrs. Pearlman, who was known for grumbling about everything—from her room, to the food, to the choices of movies, to the games, to the décor—piped up. "Me! Me! Me!" she begged, her bejeweled hand outstretched.

June dutifully helped Mrs. Pearlman on with the genie costume and handed her the blue lamp. She watched as Mrs. Pearlman violently rubbed it. And then, poof! Where was Mrs. Pearlman? June looked around the room. "Mrs. Pearlman? Mrs. Pearlman? Where are you?" Within minutes, the room was abuzz with questions as to where Mrs. Pearlman had gone.

The staff was alerted. They searched Mrs. Pearlman's room. They combed the gardens outside. Finally, June was forced to call the woman's son and daughter-in-law. "I'm afraid your mother is missing." The response was not what she expected.

"Good riddance," said the daughter-in-law. "I hope you don't find her." June held the phone away from her ear and stared into it.

"What did she say?" the night manager asked.

"Um, I don't think you want to know."

"Well, call again and talk to her son."

June called again, asking to speak to Mrs. Pearlman's son. "She's missing? Hmm. Will I be charged for this month? Can I stop payment?"

June covered the phone with her hand and shook her head.

"Well?" the manager asked.

"Let's just say, they're not particularly upset," said June.

June stared at the night manager, who had begun to sweat profusely. The residents watched the two of them expectantly.

The manager grabbed the phone from June. "I'll have to check on that, sir," he told Mrs. Pearlman's son. "I hope you realize we are as surprised and upset as you are. We have very strict guidelines about locking the premises and watching out for our residents—"

"Upset? Who said I was upset? Surprised, maybe. Just between us," said Mrs. Pearlman's son, "Don't worry about looking too hard for my mother. As I'm sure you know, she's a royal pain in the ass. My wife and I just popped a bottle of champagne."

The manager held the phone away from his body and stared at June. He pointed to the phone and made hand gestures circling his head and rolled his eyes.

"Sir, I'm afraid we are obligated by law to look for any missing clients."

"Yeah, well. You'd like a good Yelp review, wouldn't you?"

"Yes, sir."

"Then don't look too hard." The phone went dead. The manager swallowed hard and looked at June. He shook his head and threw up his arms.

June smoothed out her uniform pants and put on her most reassuring smile, the one she had practiced in the mirror when she applied for the job. Turning to the elders, she said, "Well, I guess we've had enough excitement for today. I'll help you get out of your costumes, and we can call it a night, shall we?"

Mrs. Witherspoon continued to fly around the family room, refusing to give up her costume and come down. Mr. Smithers held his sword up high and said, "Arrrrghhhh! You will not get me to give you anything, Matey!"

June glanced at the manager and looked back at the residents, costumed and not. She closed her suitcase, grabbed it by the handle, and slowly dragged it into the parking lot. Then she hoisted it into the trunk of her car. As she pulled out of her parking space, in her rearview mirror, she thought she saw a genie with a lamp, perched up in a nearby pine tree.

"Good for you," June called out to Mrs. Pearlman as she rolled down the window and drove off.

I'm Such a Dick

If I had known it would be like this, I would've OD'd sooner. I wonder how long it's been? I mean I kinda remember being lowered into the ground. Kinda. This is the most fucking cool thing. It's not hot, it's not cold, I'm not hungry, not sleepy. I can see and hear. This is fucking incredible. And I'm now I'm back at Denny's! How did that happen? What a trip. This must have been where I kicked the bucket. Where are my homies? They must have split the second I keeled over. Now I bet they're chickenshit to come back here. What a bunch of losers. I wonder if they squealed on Frankie? He sold me that shit.

This is going to be interesting. I mean, I feel like I have a body. I wonder if people can see me? No one is looking up at me. I must be invisible! Far fucking out! Hmmm. I guess I'm a ghost. A freakin' ghost. There's some fat dude eating a Grand Slam. *Wow!* Look at him shovel it in! *You better watch it, pal, or you'll have a heart attack.* Hmm. Still shoveling it in. I guess he can't hear me. Well, if he can't, I guess nobody can. That's kinda good, I guess. Kinda.

I wonder if I can like fly or something? Or walk or run. *Ooooh.* Maybe I can walk through walls! That would be way cool. I'm gonna try it. *Whoa!* Far fucking out! I just walked through the outside wall of Denny's! I walked right through it, bricks and all. I didn't feel a thing. And, what's even weirder, there isn't even a hole or nothing where I walked through. Trippy! This is way better than any high I've ever had. Fuck ecstasy. Fuck acid. Fuck heroin. Even cocaine can't beat this.

Man, I wish I could tell people. I mean you know, my homies, and my girl. She must be broken up. *Shit.* We were gonna, like, tie the knot and everything. I promised her. I wonder if I can, like, fly or walk or whatever the hell I'm doing over to her apartment. Maybe I can let her know I'm okay, and that I still love her, that I'm sorry I lied to her about hanging with my buddies again, even if it was just for one night. What a fucking loser I am.

Whoa! I guess I can sort of fly in that weird ghost way. It's kinda like swimming and moon walking at the same time. *Yo, Michael! I look like you!* Maybe I'll even see him around? I haven't seen any other ghosts though. Bummer. I'd really like to. I mean, I'd like someone to show me the ropes. I wonder if I'll ever get hungry, or tired, or horny? Yeah, will I get horny? I'm not really feeling much of anything really. That's kinda good and kinda not so good. *Hmmm.*

Well, here goes. I'm floating in the direction of Linda's apartment. It's not too far away, I guess. I mean, I'm not driving exactly. Not taking a bus neither. This is cool seeing into people's houses. I can fucking see through walls! What a trip. There they are…mom and pop, the kids, eating their dinner, watching TV. Oh look, the dad is yelling at the kid. *Fuck you, asshole. Don't yell at your boy.*

Hmmm. I think I'll teach that dad a lesson. I'm gonna take his car keys out of his pocket and throw them across the room. That'll freak him out. No, I need to think of something better than that. I'll crush his PBR! *Here ya go, buddy. Ha ha ha!* His eyes practically popped outta his head. He keeps looking around, over his shoulder, opening and closing the front door, locking it over and over again. *Ha ha ha!* Maybe I can do that every time he yells at his kid? That would be fun.

Yeah, but now I want to go over to Linda's. Oh, wait. I'm just going to meander upstairs in this dude's apartment to see if his old lady has some hot jewelry that I can take for Linda. That would be way cool. *Hmm.* I wonder which room is hers? Oh, here's her dresser. A pearl necklace! Score! Linda always wanted a pearl necklace. I told her the last time we were together that I would get her a pearl necklace that she could wear to our wedding. What a dick I am. But here goes! I've got it! Now I'll go through the wall up here and float (I guess that's what I'm doing) to her apartment.

Awww. That's so sweet! She's lit candles and has pictures of me all over her dresser. Where is she? Oh, there she is! She's in the kitchen, sitting at the table, bawling her eyes out. *Awww.* What a dick I am. Well, I wonder if she'll feel it, if I put the pearls around her neck? They don't feel heavy or cold to me, but hey, I'm a fucking ghost. Of course, they don't feel like anything. Nothing does. She looks so beautiful, tears streaming down her face, her eye makeup smeared, saying my name over and over. What a fucking dick I am.

Well, here goes. I'm being very careful and gently putting the pearls around her neck and clasping the necklace in the back. She just bolted upright. Both her hands, her beautiful hands, are touching the pearls. Now she's pacing around the kitchen, looking out the window, going to the front door, checking to see if it's locked. She's looking at herself in the mirror, touching the pearls. She's crying my name.

"Louie, where are you? Honey, is that you? Have you come to visit me? Louie? Louie? How did you get these pearls? You fucking good for nothing slimy bastard! You die and then you get me pearls?" Yeah, well, she's right.

Now the poor thing is going to the bathroom and getting out the thermometer. *Ha!* She thinks she must have a temperature and is hallucinating! I wish I could hold her, but I don't want to freak her out any more than I already have. Now she's on the phone, calling her mother! Listen to her. Poor thing. I totally freaked her out.

"I know mom. I know. I saw them lower his body into the grave, just like you did. I saw him at the coroner's. It was horrible. And then, these pearls? How do you explain this? I'm going insane, I really am. Yes, come over. Come right over. I am definitely losing it."

Well, I guess that's my answer. I can't play any games with people dear to me. It's not fair. I need to stop being a dick. This is my big lesson, I guess. Damn! Well, hopefully she won't really go off the deep end. But if she does, I wonder if she can join me here in ghost land, or wherever I am. How would that work? I haven't really seen any other ghosts. And if we can't feel anything, how great could it actually be? I shoulda been smarter when I was like a real person. A living, breathing, person.

I guess I'll just go back to Denny's and watch people stuff their faces.

I Love These Birds!

"Honey?" Ginny called out to her husband, Bob, "I read in this magazine in the doctor's office that certain animals have ESP."

"Yeah, right. And do they speak English too?"

"Well, according to the article, yes, they do."

"And what animals might these be, pray tell?"

"Oh, don't be such a downer. Bob. Remember Rachel?

"Of course, I remember Rachel. Our obnoxious next-door neighbor who would sing 'Oh What a Beautiful Morning' at the top of her lungs every morning at 6 fucking a.m.?"

"Yeah, that was pretty bad, wasn't it? Well, I ran into her at Safeway yesterday. She said she works for the SPCA now."

"Oh, she'd be good at that. Didn't she also bring in every stray cat, dog and bird in the neighborhood?"

"I know," said Ginny. "Jesus! At one point, she had seven cats and three dogs… and a parakeet, right?"

"Yep. That's when she got evicted."

"Poor animals."

"Yeah. I wonder where she put them after they kicked her out?"

"I guess she must have had to give them up to the SPCA. And then I guess that's when she started working there."

"A perfect match," Bob said.

"Well, guess what? She told me that they have a new thing."

"What? A two for one deal?"

"No, even better. There's a room with especially trained animals who can read minds and speak English, like the article said."

"Oh right. And do they spit nickels too?"

"Oh, you never believe anything. You're such a skeptic."

"I hardly think your believing there's such a thing as an animal with ESP that can also speak English isn't laughable at best."

"Oh yeah? Well, why don't we adopt one and see if it's really true?"

"Ok," Bob shrugged. "But it can't be a cat."

"I know, I know. How about a dog?"

"They're too much work."

"A bird?"

"Well, sure. A bird. If it pisses me off, I can just let it out of its cage and watch it fly away."

"Stop."

The next day, Bob and Ginny went to the SPCA, where they were basically ignored by the two harried and officious-looking women behind a window at the front desk. There was a big cage right as they walked in the door, with about eight kittens crawling around, playing and making sweet kitten noises.

"Awww," Ginny said, watching the kittens.

"We can't get a cat. I told you. I'm allergic to them."

"Okay, okay."

Ginny tried to get the attention of one of the women. "Excuse me? Where is the room with the ESP animals?"

The woman rolled her eyes as the other one pointed to down the hall with a pencil from behind her ear.

Bob and Ginny walked down the hall, not sure if they should just go into the special room or not. There was a big sign on the door. "ESP: Enter at your own risk."

Bob laughed as he opened the door. As they walked in, they saw four cats, two dogs, two parakeets, and one snake all just hanging around and not in cages.

Weird.

"No, it's not weird, you nimrod," chirped the green parakeet.

Bob shot Ginny a look. She looked embarrassed.

"I didn't say that out loud. I'm sure of it."

"No, but the fucking bird did! I love this bird! Let's take this one home!"

"Not without the love of my life, Petunia, here," the green bird chirped.

Ginny looked at the green bird and back at Bob. "Did that bird just talk?"

"I think it did. I love that bird!"

Ginny looked over at Bob. "So, should we adopt the pair?"

"Yeah, why the fuck not?"

"Language. Language," chirped the blue parakeet.

"Oh my God," said Bob. "This is too much!"

"Listen, pal. You two better give us apples, oranges, watermelon, bananas, and vegetables like carrots, squash, pumpkins and nuts… like walnuts, almonds, pecans, millet and sunflower seeds."

Bob looked over at Ginny. "That's quite a list!"

"Well, we can stop by Safeway and get everything on the way home. You can stay in the car with the birds while I go in and say hi to Rachel. She'll be thrilled."

They walked up to the window with the two women and told them they wanted to adopt both parakeets. The eye-roller rolled her eyes once more.

"Good luck. Oh, the last people who had them, donated two cages. They're in the corner. Feel free to take them."

"That's great!" Ginny clapped her hands as Bob took the cages into the ESP room.

The woman with the pencil behind her ear told Ginny, "Today, the birds are on special. Only $20 each." Ginny paid the fee and signed some paperwork. Within minutes, Bob came out with the two birds in one cage. He held the empty one in his other hand.

"They wanted to be together," she said sheepishly.

The eye-roller raised an eyebrow. "Just wait," she muttered.

"I wonder why she is so negative," Ginny commented as they left the building.

"I don't know. Maybe she was an abused parakeet in her past life."

"Stop." Ginny giggled. Bob put the empty cage in the trunk and the cage with the two birds in the back seat before getting behind the wheel.

"I hope you don't drive like an idiot," the green parakeet chirped.

Bob looked over at Ginny.

"I didn't say that," she said.

"But apparently you thought it."

"Well, you do drive a bit dangerously."

"This is getting weirder."

They stopped at the supermarket. Ginny came back to the car with two big bags. Petunia, the blue parakeet, chirped, "What did you do, buy the whole fucking store?"

Ginny looked from the cage to Bob, not sure which one of them she should respond to. She finally landed on Bob.

"I just got them what they asked for."

"Don't be so sensitive," chirped the green bird.

"Jesus!"

"I love these birds!" Bob said. Ginny suddenly wasn't so sure.

They arrived at their apartment. "Where shall we put them?" Bob asked Ginny.

"Oh, I don't know."

Both birds chirped at once. "We like to be near a window." Bob and Ginny obeyed.

As Ginny was in the kitchen putting all the food away, the green parakeet confided to Bob, "Now, we're in for it, your wife just thought."

Bob looked askance at the bird. "Shut up."

"What's a matter, Bob? Can't take the truth?"

"I said, shut up. "

"Okay, okay. Just feed me and I'll shut up."

"Honey," Bob called out to Ginny, "Can you bring a platter of food for our birds?"

Ginny slammed the cupboard door with the platters. The blue parakeet chirped, "No, I don't want a silver spoon. We can't use spoons, remember?"

Ginny came into the living room with the platter and placed it in front of the open cage, looking perturbed. "Honey, I don't think this is going to work out."

Bob looked over at the parakeets as they devoured the food.

"Maybe they'll be better tomorrow?" he whispered. "After all, this is new for them."

"And, for us," Ginny added.

"Well, let's just give them a second chance. If they're obnoxious tomorrow, we'll take them back."

"Do you think they'll sleep?"

"I read that you're supposed to cover the cage and they'll go to sleep."

Ginny grabbed an old tablecloth and threw it over the cage. The birds went quiet. She and Bob sighed with relief. Bob said, "Do you think they can read our thoughts when their cage is covered up?"

"God, I hope not."

The next morning at 11 a.m., Bob and Ginny carried the two bird cages with the parakeets in them back to the SPCA. As they walked in, the eye-roller woman smirked.

"Unnerving, wasn't it?" They nodded.

"Want to donate the cages?" They nodded again.

Buzzy

Ethan sat at the dining room table, folded his hands together on his lap, and looked downwards. He was an only child whose nanny had to constantly reassure him that his parents loved him dearly, that they were just very busy, and that they only wanted the best for him. He knew that as of next Sunday, he would be going to boarding school, and most likely wouldn't see either his parents or his nanny for a long time. Not seeing his parents, he was used to. Not being with his beloved nanny was another story. He loved everything about her: her pale skin, her crisp white blouses, her chubby hands with their chapped skin and broken nails, the way she smelled of soap and sweat. Where would she go? He didn't dare ask. And where would Buzzy go, her beloved Siberian cat?

After the nanny read him a story and tucked him in at night, he heard her footsteps going downstairs into the kitchen to get Buzzy some milk that she lovingly poured into a saucer. Buzzy slept with her in her bed. On many occasions, Ethan had crept along the hallway towards the light coming from her room. Her door was sometimes ajar, and he would see her sitting in the green chair under the lamp, reading a book, with Buzzy on her lap. Ethan would watch her stroke Buzzy over and over.

The night before he had to leave for boarding school, Ethan begged his nanny to read him the book about the genie. He loved that book. She had probably read it to him a hundred times. Ethan imagined finding a lamp, rubbing it and getting three wishes. Although there was an illustration in the book, Ethan pictured the cabinet in the dining room. Behind the glass, there were teacups from his grandmother in Austria and his other grandmother in England. Also, there was a tiny golden lamp. Was it a toy? What was it doing there? He wasn't allowed to touch anything in the cabinet. He knew that, and he was never naughty. But Ethan thought, *Nanny is in her room now, reading with Buzzy on her lap. Lucky Buzzy.* He thought that maybe on his last night before going away to boarding school if he did something really naughty, maybe he wouldn't have to go, and maybe Nanny would be made to stay as well.

He wasn't exactly sure what he could do that was so naughty, but his mind wandered towards the China cabinet. *Yes, the China cabinet and that tiny golden lamp.*

Ethan crept as quietly as he could downstairs. He was afraid that if he opened the door to the cabinet too roughly, it would make a noise, or even tip over, and everything would fall to the floor and break. That was very naughty indeed. But when he reached over and grabbed the handle, it opened easily. He wasn't sure whether to be relieved or upset.

Ethan looked at the teacups, so delicate, so fancy. And then he looked at the curious, tiny golden lamp. What was it doing in there? It wasn't China. Soon, Ethan's six-year-old hands had enveloped the lamp. It felt warm. Very warm. In fact, the more he held it, the warmer it became.

He ran upstairs with it to his bedroom. Sitting up in his bed with the lamp on his lap, he pretended it was Buzzy, and that he was his nanny. He rubbed the lamp slowly. It seemed like every time he rubbed it, the lamp glowed and flickered. Ethan was mesmerized. And then he heard it say, "Ethan. Ethan. Ethan." Ethan's eyes grew wide. He took his hands off the lamp, as it was getting very hot.

"Don't be afraid, Ethan. I'm going to grant you a wish."

"A wish? Just one?" Ethan managed to blurt out. The story had three wishes coming from a genie that was trapped inside a lamp. "Are you inside of there?" Ethan softly asked. The lamp flickered twice, very brightly.

"You want me to let you out?" The lamp flickered again. "And, if I let you out, you will give me a wish?" The lamp flickered twice again.

Ethan looked around the room. He didn't hear any sounds coming from the hallway. Sometimes his nanny walked down the hallway and checked on him to make sure he was asleep. No. No sounds. Ethan pried open the top of the lamp. Nothing happened. He didn't see smoke. He didn't hear anything either. Suddenly he just wanted his nanny to be there, to hug him, to rub his back like she rubbed Buzzy's fur.

And then he felt funny. His legs and arms felt puffy. He put his hands up to his face; it was furry. He looked down at this body. It was furry and white with grey patches. Putting his hands up to his face, he felt whiskers. He had whiskers! *Am I? Am I?*

Ethan jumped off the bed and found himself crawling on all fours to his nanny's bedroom. The door was ajar. With what he now knew was a paw, he opened the door wider, brushed his face and body against the doorway (that felt so good!), and walked up to his nanny, who was sitting in her chair, reading one of her books. Where was Buzzy? He wasn't on her lap.

His nanny turned her head towards him and said in that soft, sweet voice she used when she talked to Buzzy, "Oh, there you are! I wondered where you'd gone off to!" His nanny patted her lap and looked at him lovingly, encouraging Ethan to hop up. Oh, yes. He hopped right up. How easy it was! He curled up on his nanny's lap. And then, she picked up her book again with her right hand. With her left, his dream came true. She petted him over and over, cooing to him, "Sweet, sweet Buzzy. Sweet, sweet Buzzy. I hope they let me take you with me tomorrow. I can't bear to be without you."

When Ethan awoke the next morning, he was in his bed. Did he dream that he had become Buzzy last night? It couldn't have been a dream. At breakfast, his nanny came over to him with tears in her eyes. She gave him a long hug and handed him his satchel.

"Promise me you'll remember me."

Ethan just looked down at the floor. He couldn't imagine not remembering her.

Reginald drove him to the boarding school. His parents were traveling somewhere. Nanny had packed everything for him. The boarding school was about three hours away, somewhere in the countryside. It was a stately stone building, covered in ivy. Ethan wondered if it was cold inside.

A rather stern looking woman in a grey woolen dress greeted Ethan and took the suitcase and satchel from Reginald.

"Good luck, son," was all he heard from Reginald. Ethan watched him walk briskly back to the car.

After sitting down to dinner at one of the three long, dark wooden tables, Ethan was shown to his room. None of the other children had arrived yet. *Had Reginald taken him there early?* He looked at the food: mashed peas, a baked potato, a chicken fried steak and a dinner roll. There was also green Jello with pineapples in it. On the top of the Jello, there was a dollop of whipped cream. He picked at the food, barely taking a bite.

His room was up on the second floor and down a long, cold hallway. It had wood paneling on the walls, three desks, three cots, and a closet. He stared out the window onto the maple and elm trees surrounding the property. Then, shrugging his little shoulders, he opened his suitcase, taking out five pair of trousers, five shirts, five pairs of socks, two sweaters, his winter jacket and *what was this?* He felt it before he saw it. But he knew exactly what it was. The lamp. The lamp! How did it get there? He didn't put it there. Did his nanny put it there?

Ethan put the lamp carefully under his pillow. *I know I can't ask you again. It would be too much, I'm sure. But just in case, if you ever feel trapped inside there, I'll take you out. And then, if I'm really lucky, you can help me turn into a cat again. It doesn't have to be Buzzy. It can be any old cat, really. And if I'm unhappy here, I can wander out and look for milk in a saucer in the dining room, maybe. Or maybe there will be a grownup there who wants a cat on her lap. Oh, Nanny, you put it there, didn't you? You wanted to be sure I'd remember you. I'm purring now, Nanny. Can you hear me?*

Bowl of Soul

Sheila and her BFF Chelsea were sitting in a coffee shop on Central Avenue. This was not unusual. They generally met there every Monday afternoon at 3:00 p.m., while both of their kids were in an art class. That afforded them two glorious hours where they could just share the latest, whether it be gossip in the neighborhood or stuff with their kids, their families, whatever. They didn't have to answer questions, stop fights, prepare meals, do laundry. They could just be. And they had figured out weeks before that, for who knows what reason, The Klatch—that's what the coffee shop was called— had fewer people at that time, on that day of the week.

Sheila loved The Klatch, because it had red velvet curtains like a stage, masks from all over the world on the walls, and soft, cushy chairs in muted colors. They also made the best chai tea in town. Chelsea loved it there too, because they let you take your shoes off when you came in. She had had foot problems for years. The two articles of clothing she was happiest to remove were her shoes and her bra.

Sheila sat with her cup of steaming chai in her hands, head bent over, taking in the delicious aroma. "Yeah, so my neighbor, you know, that man with the biceps? I swear, he just struts around shirtless, lifting weights and staring out his front window, as if he's on display."

"Would you do him?"

"If he'd fix my toilet." They both got a big yuk out of that.

I can fix your toilet.

Sheila jumped. "Did you hear that?" Sheila whispered to Chelsea.

"Hear what?"

"You didn't hear that?"

"Hear what?"

"Well, if you didn't hear it, forget it."

I can fix your toilet.

Sheila looked over at Chelsea. "You didn't hear it?"

"Hear what?"

"Don't laugh. I just heard a voice say, 'I can fix your toilet.'"

Chelsea snorted, almost shooting chai out her nose.

"You're fucking losing it, Sheila."

Sheila sighed and fidgeted with her napkin. "I swear I heard someone or something say 'I can fix your toilet.'"

Chelsea made her index finger go round and round her right ear and sang the familiar four-note TV theme, "Do-do-do-do. Do-do-do-do."

Do-do-do-do. Do-do-do-do.

Chelsea jumped. "Wait! Did you hear that?"

"Hear what?"

"Someone or something is mocking me," she said. "They, or it, went 'Do-do-do-do," just like I did." Sheila raised her eyebrow and curled her lip in amusement.

Chelsea, unnerved, said, "Maybe there's something in the chai?" They both looked into their almost empty cups and sniffed the remaining liquid.

"I have to go to the bathroom,' Chelsea announced. She stood up, leaving her shoes under the table.

"Well, don't take forever. This place is beginning to creep me out."

Sheila loved Chelsea's new shoes. They were Allbirds. She had heard about Allbirds from other friends. She wondered if she and Chelsea wore the same size. And if they did, she figured Chelsea wouldn't mind if she just tried them on. Best of all, they were bright orange; daring and wondrous. She reached down, starting to pick up the shoes, when she heard, *Get your hands off me!*

Sheila stopped cold, withdrew her hands, sat back up and folded them primly onto her lap.

That's better, she heard. Sheila looked down at the shoes, and then sheepishly at the barista and another couple who were at a nearby table. Had they heard the shoes talk? Neither the barista nor the couple seemed to be aware of anything out of the ordinary. Sheila shook her head. *I must be going out of my mind!*

Chelsea made her way back to the table. She looked ashen.

Sheila looked up at her. "What's wrong?"

"This place is spooked. Maybe it's just me."

"Did something happen in the bathroom?"

Chelsea shook her head. "You'll think I'm nuts. *I* think I'm nuts. I think I'm losing it."

"Do tell."

Chelsea leaned in towards her bestie. "Well, you know the beaded Huichol Indian masks in the bathroom?"

"Yeah. They're my favorite!"

"Well, one of the masks, don't laugh, I'm not kidding, talked to me."

Sheila didn't laugh. She knew better.

"What did it say?"

"It said, *Lávate las manos.*"

Now Sheila did laugh. "It told you to wash your hands?"

Chelsea frowned. "I told you not to laugh."

"Yeah, well. Now, you don't laugh." Chelsea nodded.

"I wanted to try on your new orange Allbirds…"

"And…?"

Sheila bit her lower lip. "The fucking shoes told me not to touch them!"

It was now Chelsea's turn to laugh out loud. "Shhhh!" Sheila hissed, looking around and blushing.

Chelsea looked at her watch. "Well, it's 4:55 p.m. How about we just get the hell out of here?"

Sheila, looking relieved, grabbed her purse, quickly stood up, and bolted towards the door, with Chelsea following quickly behind, having picked up and donned her orange Allbirds.

The following Monday at 3:00 p.m., they were both seated at the same table. "I don't think I want the chai this time," Sheila announced.

"I was going to say the same thing," Chelsea echoed.

"How about we try the Bowl of Soul?"

"Looks delicious."

The Balinese mask on the wall next to their table moved its eyes from right to left, opened and closed its mouth, and said in a raspy, ancient voice, *The Bowl of Soul is highly recommended.*

Sheila and Chelsea looked at one another, grabbed their purses, and fled.

Sample Server

Matilda Fairweather closed the door to her apartment. She was breathing heavily. She then pulled the shades and dimmed the lights. She took two wine glasses from the kitchen cupboard and walked over to her liquor cabinet, pulling out a bottle of sherry. She poured a healthy amount into each glass.

Before sitting down on her sofa, she looked at her reflection in the mirror above her piano. She winked and unbuttoned her top two buttons. Into the mirror, Matilda said, "I hope you don't find this too forward of me. I mean, you do like sherry, don't you?" Without waiting for an answer, Matilda patted the seat cushion next to where she had plopped down. "Sit here. I won't bite. I promise."

Earlier that day, Matilda was handing out samples at Costco. The pay was minimum wage, and she was grateful for that. She wished she didn't need to wear that ugly hairnet, but that was one of the rules. Also, the sample servers had breaks every four hours for 20 minutes and an hour for lunch. Matilda watched as the families walked by, the seniors, the teenagers, the athletes from the nearby college, the secretaries from various businesses sent to purchase treats for events, and the women proudly holding onto the arms of their men.

Today she had been giving out samples of yogurt. At least she didn't have to heat that up. It was always a bit of a hassle when she had to heat up items. Anything that had meat or cheese in it usually emitted an aroma that brought clumps of people waiting rather impatiently for the food to be ready. Of course, there were very sweet people who thanked her, but most often they just grabbed the sample, scarfed it down, grabbed another, and then tossed the napkin or paper cup it came in into the nearby receptacle and went on their way without even a hello, goodbye or thank you. Occasionally someone would scrutinize the label on the food and question her about the ingredients. "Is this really gluten-free? How many grams of sugar are in this? How can you be sure?" She was told to never argue with a customer. She would just furrow her brows and adjust her glasses which were always falling down her nose. When the couples would come by, Matilda would scrutinize what the woman was wearing. Was her blouse too tight? Did she have a boob job? Then she would look to see if she or the man she was hanging onto had a wedding ring on. Invariably this wasn't the case. The married couples usually looked a bit forlorn. It was usually the husband who walked up and grabbed whatever it was with the wife somewhat nearby, or at least within earshot. And the poor women with young children. Oh God. "Can I have three of those?" Matilda would see two screaming kids who would probably have preferred to run around the entire store ten times than to have to be walking with their mothers. Matilda would nod yes with the sweetest smile she could muster. She was told never to deny a customer seconds or even thirds.

Her legs got very tired from standing for so long. She found herself rocking back and forth from one leg to the other. Once a woman said to her, "Oh, you look like you just had a baby." Matilda was taken aback before the woman explained, "I mean, when you have a baby, you get used to rocking them to quiet them." That made Matilda sad. Lots of incidents made her sad during the day. The couples hanging onto each other, the teenagers zipping around with their perfect bodies, the toddlers whose mothers shoved samples into their mouths to shut them up, the seniors who could barely walk or were in motorized wheelchairs and came every day just to eat the samples. But what made Matilda the absolute saddest was that no one bothered to talk to her or at least for very long. Weren't they the least bit curious? Didn't they want to know if her parents were still alive? They weren't. Didn't they want to know if she had siblings? She didn't. Did she have a boyfriend? No. What did she do for fun? Fun? Why did she have to work such a lousy job? Did she ever go to school? Of course, she did. College? No. Why not? Did they want to know that her father left the family when Matilda was three, that her mother had been in and out of mental hospitals for most of Matilda's life? Did they wonder if Matilda's mother had died of an overdose? No, they didn't want to know anything. Of course, they didn't.

But Dudley did. Yes, Dudley did. Matilda remembered Dudley

from high school. He sat in front of her. He, like her, had no real friends, but Matilda liked him. She liked his curly black hair. She liked his blue pants that he always wore. She liked how his face turned so red when the teacher called on him and how he stuttered to get the answer out. She very much wanted to answer for him, but she knew that would have humiliated him further.

She made up her mind to ask him to visit her. She imagined him coming to her table to get a sample of the Skinny Pop popcorn and her slipping him her address and phone number. She smiled to herself as she imagined watching him quickly put the piece of paper into his pocket and nodding gratefully.

Matilda leaned over to Dudley on the couch. "Mmmm. You smell so good! Is that Brut?" She had seen that name on the shelves at Costco. "And I'm going to help myself to another glass of wine. May I get you another as well? Matilda jumped up from the couch and sashayed to the kitchen to pour herself another glass. On the way back, she unbuttoned another button on her blouse. As she sat down, she reached up and twirled her hair as she said, "I think it's getting a bit warm in here, don't you?" And then she spilled her wine on her blouse. Blushing, she said, "Oh my! Look what I've done! So clumsy! I hope you'll forgive me." She held onto an end table and lurched into her bedroom. Falling onto her bed, fully clothed, she whispered, "Oh Dudley. Dudley. So sweet of you to come and visit me. I've been waiting for years."

Plaque Anxiety

Marcella had heard it all her life. While in labor with Marcella, her only child, her mother had felt the need to brush her teeth every hour. This was imprinted on Marcella's memory throughout the 18 years before she entered Dental Hygiene school and graduated top in her class.

Marcella admired her mother, and she too brushed her teeth after and even before every meal. She was never without her toothbrush. It calmed her down. She was an anxious child, but this habit kept her from losing it entirely.

All the girls in her class were jealous when Marcella got hired by the dentist most admired in the community. They called Dr. McClure "Dentist to the Stars." Word got out that not only was he handsome, but he gave lavish gifts to his employees every month.

On Marcella's first day, there were balloons and flowers for her and a raffle which she entered and won. To her consternation, it was a ticket to a cage diving expedition. She had never spent much time in the ocean, let alone gone diving. As she envisioned hammerhead sharks floating by, she couldn't help but wonder if their giant teeth had hideous plaque on them. But Marcella knew what to do. If she had a panic attack, she would just brush her teeth to calm down. No one would notice, she surmised.

As she checked in with the instructor on the day of the diving expedition, she was appalled at his demeanor: patronizing, self-congratulatory and paunch bellied. "Well, little lady," he began grinning with a toothpick in his upper right bicuspid. Marcella was quietly disturbed by the discoloration of his teeth. She clutched the toothbrush in her purse as he droned on about the rules. "Don't get near the bars. Always wear your mask." Blah, blah, blah. After changing into her wetsuit, she snuck her toothbrush into the sleeve.

To her great dismay, the other two participants did not show up. Being alone with this tool was going to be as bad as being surrounded by sharks underwater. Why me? crossed her mind more than once.

As they were lowered into the Atlantic Ocean just off the coast near Palmdale, Florida, she watched the annoying gestures of this insufferable human, pointing to his whiteboard and grease pencil, her regulator mask and the bars. She tapped her left wrist with her toothbrush several times, assuring herself of her escape from insanity.

And then, there they were: a school of hammerheads bumping into the bars of the cage. Oh, my God, their teeth. Crusty, filthy. Do they ever brush? With kelp?

Marcella felt her breath quicken as she turned away from the buffoonish instructor next to her, too close to her. Crouching down she pulled down her regulator, held her breath, and whipped out her toothbrush, frantically brushing up, down and sideways. She felt a tap on her shoulder. As she straightened up and turned towards the man, he was agitatedly waving his arms, pointing to her regulator. She ignored him, continuing to brush her teeth. He resorted to pulling out his whiteboard and writing with his grease pencil, "PUT YOUR REGULATOR BACK ON NOW!"

Marcella inched as far away as she could from him, bumping into the bars. This sent the hammerheads into a frenzy. The instructor scribbled yet again on the whiteboard.

"STOP BUMPING INTO THE BARS! DANGEROUS!"

Marcella felt the cage being hoisted up to the surface, the wet-suited oaf ignoring her. She placed her regulator calmly back on her face, grateful to being able to breathe again, and reinserted her toothbrush into the sleeve of her wetsuit. The instructor held out his hand to help her get out of the boat, refusing to look at her. He had taken off the hood of his wetsuit, his lips set in a tight line.

"You, young lady, have broken serious rules. You endangered not only yourself, but me as well. I am going to recommend that you never be allowed on an expedition like this ever again."

Marcella inspected his teeth as he pontificated. She considered giving him her card, but thought better of it, and only nodded. She tried unsuccessfully not to smile.

Peeling off her wetsuit and changing into her street clothes, Marcella breathed a sigh of relief. She whipped out her toothbrush, vigorously trying to erase the last hour of her life from her teeth.

When she came into work the following Monday, the employees all gushed at her. "How was it? Was it thrilling?"

Blinking, Marcella nodded quickly with her best smile. "Oh yes. Quite thrilling. Never had an experience quite like that before. Thanks so much."

3

Days in the Life

creative nonfiction & true stories

Always Right

Now remember, you're never to argue with a customer. They are always right. Always. We can't afford to lose even one customer. They need to feel welcomed, appreciated, and flattered. We want them to feel so good that not only do they buy clothes from us, but they want to come back often.

I was grateful for this job. It was my first one in retail. I'd had another one—rather, another two before this that had turned out badly. The first one was working at the Sears downtown in the basement. They were just changing over to computerized address labels. Six other young women—teenagers, really—and I were given the job of double-checking the addresses on card files against the computerized labels. If they were wrong, we had to pull them out of the pile and put them in another. We were not allowed to talk to each other. We worked from 8 to 5 every Saturday and Sunday.

Our boss, Mr. Sanders, was a short man with a receding hairline. He would pace up and down the three tables at which we were stationed, making sure no one was talking, his hands clasped behind his back, his tiny brown eyes squinting beneath the glasses that didn't quite stay up on the bridge of his hawkish nose. His black shiny shoes squeaked. The combination of sweat, Old Spice cologne, and stale cigarettes emanated from his person as he marched by. None of us dared laugh, but we did on occasion shoot amused glances at each other.

On week two (it was a six-week job), one of the girls burst out laughing when she saw her friend roll her eyes. Mr. Sanders stopped mid-squeak, thrust out his arm, and yelled, "You're fired! Gather up your belongings immediately!" That silenced us for the rest of the time.

My second job lasted only eight hours. This one was in a dingy building, also downtown. It took me three buses to get there. What I had to do was take out a phone book and call each person, promising them that they had won a two-hour beauty session. If they agreed to come to the beauty session, I gave them the address and a time they were to appear. After getting hung up on and sworn at for the first three hours, I began doubting if this was really true. Did they really win a free two-hour beauty session? I felt so bad when an older woman would cackle and say something like, "Honey, at my age, it doesn't really matter anymore. My husband died a year ago. My children never call me. What do I need to look good for? You tell me."

When I asked one of the other workers if this was on the up-and-up, the reply was, "No. Of course not. The minute they get here, they are asked to pay for extra stuff." I looked at the clock then; it was close to eight hours. I wanted to call back the poor women who had agreed to come and tell them not to, but I just scurried out the back door. I never did ask for or get my salary.

And now, there was this job. The Broadway on Wilshire Boulevard. The department store that I and a few of my girlfriends would take a bus to go to and pretend we could afford to buy the latest fashion. We would try on blouses, skirts, and sweaters, imagining we could go home in them. "But Mom, everyone has this kind of blouse," I'd whine. The response was always, "Well, you don't."

I was placed in Jewelry the first day. That wasn't too bad. It was fun looking at all the necklaces, bracelets, and earrings. "That looks so good on you!" I heard myself saying to a customer. That wasn't so hard. Almost everyone really did look pretty good.

Foundations were another story. It was sad watching women squeeze themselves into girdles and bras that didn't quite fit. While I personally wished I had smaller breasts because of all the unwanted attention, I could sense the envy of some of the shoppers. They were looking for Wonder Bras, anything to make them appear bigger.

And then I was placed in Coats. Fellow employees warned me that it was very boring, and that I was supposed to look busy. If no one came by, I was to make sure the coats were all in their appropriate section. It was late in the day when an older woman came by and was looking through the pink cashmere coats. This woman couldn't have been taller than 4'11". She had a nasty sneer on her face. She had taken out four coats and draped them on a nearby chair. The coats were heavy. She put one on and then took that one off. Then, she tried another one on, and another, and another. They all were too long for her and looked ridiculous.

"How does this look?" she demanded in a rasping voice, for the tenth time. I was tired... and I was tired of this woman.

"It looks ridiculous."

The woman stood there, staring up at me.

"What?"

"I said it looks ridiculous. It's much too long for you."

The woman snorted, grabbing a coat. "And what's this?" she said pointing to a dark mark on the side of the coat.

I looked at it, gouging it with my fingernail. "It's just a bug. Get over it."

The woman stepped back, with a coat over her arm, and yelled, "I demand to see your manager! You are a rude young lady. You should be fired immediately!"

Sighing, I took three of the heavy coats that were thrown onto the chair, and waltzed into the dressing room, leaving the woman mid-shrill.

In the dressing room, I looked over at the mink coats that were hanging on a rack. I put one on. It felt luxurious. Wonderful, really. I looked at myself in the mirror and smiled, twirling around.

"Just what do you're doing?" My manager was standing there, arms akimbo.

I noticed her in the mirror, mid-twirl. "I'm dancing in a mink coat to try and forget that obnoxious old woman."

"Don't you remember what I told you? The customer is always right! Always!"

I sighed. "She's a bitch."

"What? What did you say, young lady?"

"I said, she's a bitch."

The manager just stood and stared at me, unable to form words.

"Go ahead. Fire me. That's what you want to do, don't you?"

The manager continued to stand there. Finally, she walked over to the coat rack and put on a mink coat. Smiling, she twirled around. "How do I look?"

I couldn't believe what I was seeing. The manager suddenly looked truly beautiful to me.

"You look very classy."

We two mink-coated women looked at each other smiling broadly.

"She *is* a bitch," my manager said. "You're absolutely right."

Hair and Chocolate

Upstairs and to the left of the banister is my parents' bedroom. Beneath my daddy's starched white cellophane-wrapped work shirts is a jumbo size Hershey Bar with almonds. There are 12 squares. When I double-check that my parents are downstairs, I creep quietly up the stairs, open their bedroom door and the top drawer of the dresser. Looking over my shoulder, I carefully remove one of the squares. I put the wrapper back just as it was and place the bar beneath the exact shirt where I found it. I hope that either of my parents will think the other took that square, as I sneak it into my pocket before going downstairs, where tonight, my sisters and I will be allowed to watch the color TV. It is 1957 and ours is one of the first color sets. It has rabbit ears on top to make sure the picture comes in as best as it can. We can only watch a show once in a while, with their permission.

After I see Elvis gyrating from the waist up on Ed Sullivan, a commercial comes on that is only vaguely interesting to me. The commercial for Suave Hair Conditioner grabs my attention way more. I stare longingly as a woman with straight, shiny hair smiles and moves her head side to side. Her hair moves. It moves!

I get 25 cents a week as allowance. I save up for six months to buy Suave conditioner. I sit in the backseat of our '57 blue Plymouth Plaza and hand my mother the money before we go to the store. I have no idea if I have enough or not. Afterwards, I hold the paper bag with my treasure inside close to me, on my lap. My heart is beating fast. This is the day my life will change.

As soon as my mother parks the car, I open the door, run into the house, up the stairs and into the bathroom, clutching my bottle of Suave conditioner. Smiling, I strip the clothes off my 11-year-old body and jump into the shower. I unscrew the cap, pour some conditioner into my hand, and rub it into my Brillo-pad hair. It smells so good. My hair in the shower, even with Suave conditioner, feels much the same—unruly and obstinate—but I'm optimistic. I try an initial movement of my head. My hair remains tight and unwilling. I wait for it to dry, telling myself, It will change. Of course, it will.

It doesn't. I am devastated.

Four years later, we are living in Los Angeles instead of Maplewood, New Jersey. I have only one friend, Tania. I don't know how to dress like other girls in Geistex sweaters, or how to wear Estée Lauder perfume, and my hair is still frizzy. In a month it will be time for the prom. I beg my mother to let me get my hair straightened. It costs $25, a lot of money. After much begging, she relents.

The chemicals in the hair salon smell foul. I don't care. When the stylist starts to comb out my newly straight hair, I can't believe how happy I am. I look at myself in the mirror. I am stunned. It's straight! Straight. It moves when I turn my head. Oh my God, I'm so happy. I turn my head side to side so many times, I almost get dizzy.

I enter the gymnasium for the prom, feeling like a princess. I move my head side to side, as my hair moves and brushes against my shoulders. I watch all the girls with their beautiful dresses, pretty hair, and dressy shoes. I see all the guys in their uncomfortable suits, ties, and polished black shoes. No one acknowledges me. I'm used to this, but my best friend Tania walks right past me. I purposefully walk and stand beside her, close. She turns quickly and turns back, not recognizing me at all.

"Tania."

She turns again and stares at my face. The slow recognition dawns on her. "Helene?"

"Yes, it's me. My mom let me straighten my hair!"

For the next few years, I pay to have my hair straightened every month and pray it doesn't get foggy outside, or it will frizz up.

During the last year of university, besides trying to be an actress, I am an artist model. I tell a teacher, Jean Barlow, the secret, that I really have curly hair. Her eyes get wide as she makes me promise to wear it naturally the next time I pose for her class. That idea terrifies me, but I agree; I'm used to being directed. I let my hair dry naturally. I don't iron it. I don't set it on beer cans. My father hates it. I go to the class. They love it.

I have metamorphized into being myself. I am not in a role. I don't have to memorize lines. I am not pretending to be someone else. I am me.

The French Poem

Howard, the "A" student was just thrown out of class for cheating. Howard! School valedictorian! Hard to believe. And now, Madame Clifton is making us memorize this Paul Verlaine poem.

Il pleure dans mon coeur
comme il pleut sur la ville.
Quelle est cette langueur
qui pénêtre mon coeur?

When she reads it out loud, she weeps. Her tears drip down into her ample cleavage, much to the delight of the boys in the front row.

Looking out the window, it's not raining now, of course. *Il ne pleut pas.* It hardly ever rains here. Kind of hard to relate. But then again, maybe I'm missing something. Madame Clifton is reaching over to her desk for a tissue. She wipes her eyes and then her cleavage. I'm surprised she didn't ask for volunteers. I'm sure Ricky would have volunteered.

I suppose I could be sad. My boyfriend, Zachary Zelig Zuboffsky, one of the boys in student government, thinks it's fun to give me French tests on dates. What is wrong with him? While his buddy Philip is heavy petting with Cecilia behind his parents' couch on the floor, Zach is quizzing me in the subjunctive. It's supposed to be a mood. Yeah, well, I'm in a mood.

I'm not sure if I still want to go out with Zachary. I mean, it's really my mother who has a crush on him, not me. He's tall, blond, and Jewish, her dream come true. He'll probably end up being a doctor or lawyer too. Maybe I'll suggest he quiz her in French instead.

He hasn't even figured out how to French kiss! I'll bet Frank Stomers has. Oh my God. His juicy lips! And he's in my drama class. When he sits next to me, I can smell his cologne. I can feel my heart beating (*mon coeur*) very fast. And our teacher, Mr. Gordon, just told us we're doing The Crucible! Oh, how I want to be Abigail, and have

Frank cast as John Proctor! I'd get to kiss him. Kiss him! On stage! In front of my parents and the whole world! And there would be nothing they could do about it! I could kiss the only Catholic boy in the school. The one who is kind of a delinquent. We'd be rehearsing a lot. At least a month. That's at least 20 kisses. *O, mon coeur!* Then maybe it would be Zachary and my mother who would feel the *langueur*.

Tomorrow, we have to stand up one by one in the front of Madame Clifton's class and recite the poem. I wonder if they'll let Howard back into the class. I wish Frank were in my class, but alas, he's not taking any college prep classes. I'm supposed to meet Zachary at the library after school so he can quiz me. Oh joy.

So, it's the next day, and Howard isn't here. Interesting. Everyone is talking about it. And Madame Clifton is really dressed up. She's wearing a very tight Pepto Bismol-colored skirt and jacket with a white lacy transparent blouse underneath. She has on matching pink heels with open toes. We can see her dark red toenail polish under her silk stockings. Oh, and let me not forget the bright purple flower on the right side of her French twist. I think's a dahlia.

Of course, she's leaning over while sitting on her stool, exposing her girls, while she asks for volunteers to recite the poem. Ricky is slinking way down into his chair, Johnny too. I'm going to volunteer to get it over with.

Then, I'm up there, starting to recite the poem, but I look to the back of the classroom where there's a window in the door.

Il pleut dans mon coeur…

Frank is walking by the window. My heart just stops. What is he doing here? Why is he walking down the hall? He's coming back to look into the classroom. He's smiling right at me! Oh my God!

I can't remember the rest of the poem. I'm stunned.

"Mademoiselle? Mademoiselle?" Madame Clifton's voice vaguely penetrate my consciousness.

I can feel my face turning red. Everyone's turning around to look at the door, but luckily, Frank has already disappeared.

"I'm sorry. I'm so sorry. I just can't remember what comes next."

"*Asseyez—vous, Mademoiselle,*" Madame Clifton says. I sit down at my desk. She asks for another volunteer. No one raises their hand. Pacing back and forth, her heels clicking, she stops in front of Ricky's desk. He slinks further into his seat, to no avail. She taps him on the shoulder with a blood-red fingernail, smiling sweetly, and motions for him to go up to the front of the room and recite the poem.

Ricky unwraps himself from the desk and slowly walks to the front. It's painful to watch him just try to talk. Even though I have just humiliated myself, it doesn't make it any easier to see him stammer and stutter while Madame Clifton looks over at him, encouragingly. Now she's repeating the words with him in unison, like he's a baby: *Il pleure dans mon coeur comme il pleut sur la ville....* I suppose the *langueur* in Ricky's *coeur* doesn't impress Madame mammaries.

We're all relieved when the bell rings. As I walk out of class and turn the corner, Frank Somers is there waiting for me! Now we're walking side by side to Mr. Gordon's classroom. I feel as if I'm in a dream.

Mr. Gordon announces the cast of The Crucible. "Frank? I'd like you to play John Proctor." There's a murmur in the classroom. Oh please. Oh please. He's announcing all the other characters, one by one. So far, I haven't been cast. Oh please. Oh please.

In his characteristic manner, Mr. Gordon takes his glasses off, wipes them with a cloth, and puts them back on. He's looking straight at me.

"And, Helene, you will be playing Abigail. You will need to be okay with kissing John Proctor." More murmurs. I'm staring down at my desk, trying to wipe the grin off my face.

"Miss Simkin? Are you agreeable?"

"Oh, yes." I whisper. "Oh, yes."

After school, Frank is waiting for me outside. "Can I walk you home?" I nod happily as he grabs my hand. His hand is warm and full of promises.

After dinner, Zachary calls me up at home and asks me how I did on my French test. I tell him that I blew it.

There's a pause on the other end of the phone. Then he says, "I guess we'll have to study some more then."

"Um, no. I think I can study on my own. And there's something else I need to tell you."

"What is it?"

"I got a really big part in the school play, and I'll be rehearsing a lot."

"Is that more important than getting good grades?"

"Oh, yes," I tell him, "I think so. Very much so."

"I don't understand you, Helene."

"Yeah. I know. Um…I think it's over, Zach. I mean, between us."

"Yeah. I agree. Well…*bonne chance!*"

"*Au revoir!*" I say. I hang up the phone and twirl around. No, there is absolutely no *langueur* whatsoever penetrating *mon coeur*. But there is longing. I am longing for a real French kiss.

The next day, after class, I get one. Well, actually, about ten.

Lights Up. Go!

Where does the magic begin? When does the suspension of belief simmer? Is it during the dress rehearsal, or when they call the actors to their places? Or when the actors are putting on their makeup and staring at themselves in the mirror. Perhaps mouthing their lines might be when the spark begins to smolder? Or as the actors hear the warning from the backstage manager that "house is open"—meaning the audience is arriving and they need to be very, very quiet so as not to ruin the magic that the audience has come to see?

And then, there are actors who are "getting into character," repeating their lines over and over, folding into themselves, while others are shamelessly flirting with whoever is willing, stifling giggles at their own naughtiness. Of course, the magic can't happen without the stage crew, the lighting designer and crew, the set designer, the person in charge of music, all the technicians who make this delicate ballet come to life and make it look seamless before the audience. And the mishaps are often remembered more than the perfect performances.

Several of those mishaps come to my mind. One occurred during a performance of *The Crucible* in high school, to the kid playing Giles Corey—who falls to his knees, yells, "more weight," and dies. Because he had to fall to his knees so often, he needed padding to protect them. His mother thought that Kotex sanitary napkins would work just fine. But during one of our three performances, the safety pin securing the Kotex pad under his costume for his left knee came undone—unbeknownst to him—and fell out indelicately onto the stage, just as he was doing his final death scene. Yes, the audience tittered. The parents were trying to be polite; some were more successful than others. Mine weren't.

On opening night of that play, a Hollywood makeup artist went backstage to the boys' side and put a fake nose on the boy playing Giles. The girls, who hadn't seen it happen, didn't know about this addition to his face. Onstage, the boys were trying to warn

us by screwing up their noses at us. We thought they were nuts.
What the hell were they doing? And then we saw him. It was an
enormous nose. It didn't fit his face. And when he fell to his knees
and prostrated himself, his fake nose dislodged. He tried desperately
to put it back on as quickly as he could, but he wasn't very adept at
this new task. When the boy stood up, the character of Giles Corey
had two noses: his real nose and the fake one, slightly off to the left.
It took all of my fellow actors' concentration to not laugh out loud.
However, snorts could be heard all across the stage and into the
audience. The boy's big brown eyes were pleading with us not to
ruin his Tony award-winning performance, to no avail. I don't think
he continued his chosen path to becoming a famous actor.

Another unforgettable incident occurred at UCLA when I was a
Theater Arts student. We had to learn everything to do with working
backstage, even if we were not cut out for it. I, for one, had no talent
for working on the sound crew, or the light crew, or the set design
crew.

When we performed the Shakespeare play *The Tempest*, Arthur
Rubenstein's son John composed the music. This was in the late
'60s, so the equipment we used was reel-to-reel tapes, located up
in the sound booth, at the back of the audience and up a flight of
stairs. We could look down and see what was going on onstage,
and, for that matter, who was in the audience. The sound crew for
this show consisted of another young woman and me. That woman
had a Type-A personality, the opposite of mine. My only job was to
start and stop the tapes (one for Act I and one for Act 2) at the right
time. For Act I, there was some tinkle-tinkle-sounding music for the
fairies who pranced onto the stage. For Act 2, there was some heavy
pounding drum music to accompany the half-human, half-monster
Caliban as he lurched around in the forest. When I screwed up, the
Type A woman would haul off and slug me hard on my arm. That
was unpleasant.

On opening night (and at UCLA, being so close to Hollywood,
we knew that famous people might show up), I looked down at
intermission and saw a dear friend of mine whom I hadn't seen in
a while. I looked over at Ms. Slugger and informed her I was only

going to say hi, and I'd be right back. I asked her if she would change the reels to the second act. She just glared at me.

When I sauntered back in the booth at the last minute, the second act was starting. The curtains had just opened. I pushed the button for the Act 2 reel. *Oh God no. Oh, no!* What we heard was: tinkle, tinkle, tinkle. Distinct fairy music. Not Caliban music. Then we heard over the stage manager's speaker in our booth, "Sound? Sound? Sound?" Bam, my arm got slugged, good and hard. *Oh my God! What are we going to do?* "Sound? Sound? Sound?"

Ms. Type A squeaked "What should we do?" We heard, "Oh my God! Oh my God! We have to start over! We have to close the curtains and start over!" At this moment, I went into stupidity overdrive and decided to try and rewind the tapes by hand, instead of pushing the rewind button, as we watched the curtains close. Ms. Type A slugged me yet again and lit up a cigarette while she put the correct tapes on the tape player. My job now, as it always had been, was to turn the tapes on and off at the appropriate time. We watched as Caliban once again lumbered onto the stage to the correct music.

Then we heard the stage manager over the speaker. "Sound? You will meet me immediately after the play is over. Do you understand me?" We could hear him lighting up what was probably his 10th cigarette.

"Yes," we choked out. But did we meet him after the play was over? I sure didn't. I ran as fast as I could to my red 1966 VW bug and drove straight back to my apartment. The boyfriend I had at the time asked me how the play went. I lit up a joint, fell onto the couch, and said, "You don't want to know."

I have many backstage stories of course, but they weren't always about mishaps. Several years ago, I was in a play produced at a local community theater. One of the actors had been having shooting pains in her legs and was unable to get a correct diagnosis before the play's run. She sat in a wheelchair backstage but had to go onstage and do a dance during the play. We were all very worried that she would collapse. Before she had to go onstage and dance, I would lift her up from the wheelchair, wait for her to reassure me that she wouldn't fall over, prop her up, walk her as close to the stage as possible without the audience seeing me, and then let go. I also had to be right in the area she went off stage with the wheelchair ready for her to fall back into. It all went off without a hitch, and thankfully, her condition eventually improved.

I have a trick I made up for actors who are anxious that I'm very proud of. It sounds weird, but it works every time. I tell them we are going to arm wrestle both sides as hard as we can. Oftentimes we do this in the air, not on a table or bench. It just gets rid of the jitters. I have even taught this technique to my students at the community college who have anxiety about speaking in public. At first, they think I'm weird—and I can't argue with that—but then if they try it, they always come back to me and say, "Hey, you know that arm wrestle technique you taught us?" I look at their happy faces and nod. "Works like a charm, doesn't it?"

I love being backstage. Almost more than onstage. I love hearing the audience talking among themselves, knowing (or hoping) that we are going to make them happy that they decided to spend the time with us. Before I step foot onstage, I tell myself over and over again, "Be real. Listen, react, and be real. This is the first time you've ever heard or repeated these lines. Be authentic and project your voice so that the people in the last row can hear you."

And then, I'm on.

What Not to Do

Ginger's book about the afterlife fell out of her hands onto the bed as she dozed off. She found herself musing about the various interpretations of what happens while one is dying and then what happens afterward. One of the books that her friend Felix had given her talked about people who had had near death experiences and what they had reported. According to them, the first stage was euphorically running—or was it floating?—into people whom you knew from your past. Ginger giggled and then anguished about whom she might see. Or how was it? Do you really see them? Do you just feel their presence? Do you smell them? *Oh, don't go there,* she thought, thinking about that guy Henry whose balls smelled like sweat.

Now she turned on her right side because she read somewhere that it's better for digestion and she had eaten a full bowl of popcorn with ghee drizzled on top after having downed a cheeseburger and fries just a couple of hours earlier. She also read that if one eats before sleep, it causes nightmares. *Stop mind-fucking!* she ordered herself.

Eyes closing, she felt her body lifted gently into an open space. Quite pleasant, really. This space had some sort of Tibetan bowl music playing. Nice. Oh, and what do we have here? She saw what looked to be a blue gauzy curtain flutter and a dark-skinned balding man appear. He cleared his throat in a recognizable way. *Oh, wow! It's Louis! Louis Lyttle Lunetta!* He's wearing his infamous billowing royal blue, scarlet red, orange and lilac colored tai chi silk pants with those Chinese shoes that have curly points going up at the toes and his bright yellow sleeveless t-shirt. What is he doing here? *Oh, that's right, he died. Anyway, where is here? Where am I? Did I die too? From popcorn, or was it the cheeseburger and fries? Shit, I have to stop eating fast food.* "Louis! Louis? Hi! Hi!," Ginger called out to him. He just grinned, cleared his throat and darted his large brown eyes left and right. He didn't seem to see her at all. *Weird.*

She had flashbacks of fucking on his waterbed. He was a wild man. Not particularly satisfying, but different. She'd look around at all the African masks on his walls while he grabbed at her. Sighing to herself, she knew that at least it wouldn't last long. There was that.

And then without warning, he disappeared behind the gauzy curtain. Before she could think about what had just happened, Zachary Zelig Zuboff parted the curtain and appeared with a French textbook under his arm. *Oh, no! He's going to quiz me like he always did on our dates in high school.* He just stood there, seemingly oblivious to her presence. *No wonder my mother was in love with him.* He was tall, good-looking, blond and smart. Oh, and he was Jewish. Ginger's mother's dream. *Oh please, oh please, I don't remember my French. Don't quiz me.* He didn't. He just floated back behind the curtain.

Ginger was afraid to stare at the curtain now but found herself doing just that. *Oh shit! It's Frank.* There he was, the Catholic boy that her mother attempted suicide over. He looked exactly the same as he had in high school. Blue eyes, generous lips, black hair, high cheekbones. Ginger felt a twinge in her stomach. She knew now that these—what were they, ghosts?—wouldn't talk to her. And yes, she did have one regret. She wished she had given Frank her virginity instead of that asshole, Jay. Then her mother would have been justified in believing that other mother who told her that her daughter had slept with this Catholic boy, when in fact, she was still pure as the driven snow, as the saying goes. What the hell does that mean, anyway? Driven? She looked at Frank. *Go away! Go away, you right-wing dickwad.* Ginger had looked him up on Facebook several years earlier and found that he was a Trumper. The worst. Maybe it was good that she had never slept with him. Frank turned slowly, dramatically, while drifting back through the curtain.

Who's next? Please don't be Jay. And then there he was. He was holding a Wagner record to his chest. *Of course he was.* And yes, he still looked like Jean-Louis Barrault in that movie *Les Enfants du Paradis.* Ginger frowned. *What a fucking idiot I was. It was romantic though. He did walk about an hour to my house. Worth my virginity? No.* She looked at him. *Go away! Just go away!* And just like that, poof! he slipped behind the curtain, the *Die Walküre* record in his grip.

Oh, God. Who's next? It would have to be Richard. The curtains billowed. There stood Richard in his karate gi, his large yellow eyes looking stoned. And what did he have in his hand? Of course a beer bottle. His other hand? A joint. *Of course. Are you going to puke into a wine glass and not spill a drop while looking like Gene Wilder and talking like Robin Williams? Disappear please.* He did.

Ginger turned to her other side. She jolted awake, covered in sweat. Shaking her head, she tried to erase the nightmare. *I will never eat a lot before I go to sleep again.*

She hoped she could keep this promise.

About the Author

Helene Simkin Jara is an award-winning author. She is also a theatre director, actor and retired instructor.

Her collections of short stories include, *Because I Had To*, *Turn Left at the Gorilla and Go Down the Hall* and *Me! Me! Me!*

Her non-fiction books are *True Doll Stories*, *We Remember*, interviews with men and women about their childhood memories with dolls, and her memoir of being an artist model in the '60's and '70's, *Life on The Stand*, which is also available in audiobook format.

She is an active member of the California Bay Area theatre scene, including Santa Cruz Actors Theatre, and is a frequent collaborator with the podcast, *Coffee Contrails*.

To stay up to date on Helene's latest projects, follow her on Facebook, Instagram and LinkedIn.

Visit Helene on her website: **www.helenesimkinjara.com**.

Special Thanks to...

Duke Houston, Gino Danna, Julia Huff, Meera Collier, Carol Skolnick, Tom Arns, Kathleen Schwab, Kathy Runyon, Josefa Simkin, Sharon Meinhoff, Laverne Baker Leyva, and Joan Levine.